Acclaim for Kathleen Fuller

"This sweet series launch from Fuller (*Sold*  romance between a socially awkward Amish who once humiliated her . . . Fuller's fluid pro the leads are sure to entertain. This winsome

—*Publishers Week*

"Sparks fly between a forthright heroine and a practical joker with a protective streak . . . but they're not the kind of sparks Charity Raber longs for after embarking on a courtship plan. The two can't agree on anything except that they definitely don't belong together. Does God have a different plan? Kathleen Fuller will keep you guessing with her endearing characters, compelling writing, and unexpected plot twists. A heartwarming and humorous read."

—Rachel J. Good, *USA TODAY* bestselling author of the Surprised by Love series, on *The Courtship Plan*

"Kathleen Fuller is a gifted storyteller! Her latest, *The Courtship Plan*, made me laugh through the hilarity of Charity Raber—but also cry as Charity deals with trauma in a believable way. Endearing characters and precious life lessons make this novel another heartfelt winner!"

—Leslie Gould, bestselling author of *Piecing It All Together*

"Return to Birch Creek for another delightful Amish Mail-Order Bride Novel by Kathleen Fuller. *Love in Plain* Sight combines Fuller's engaging style with a strong plot and compelling characters who will steal your heart. Don't miss this 'must read' story that's sure to remain a lifetime favorite."

—Debby Giusti, *USA TODAY* and *Publishers Weekly* bestselling author of *Smugglers in Amish Country*

"Kathleen Fuller's emotional and evocative writing draws readers into her complex stories and keeps them cheering for her endearing characters even after the final page."

—Patricia Davids, *USA TODAY* bestselling author

"Katharine Miller has everything she ever wants, until she realizes what she's gotten. *Love in Plain Sight* is Kathleen Fuller at her best. She shines the spotlight on an unlikely heroine who runs away to find herself . . . and discovers what true love looks like."

—Suzanne Woods Fisher, bestselling author of *Mending Fences*

"Fuller continues her Amish Mail-Order Brides of Birch Creek series (following *A Double Dose of Love*) with the pleasing story of Margaret, the youngest of four sisters who visits Birch Creek, Ohio, to stay with her aunt and uncle to avoid the temptations of *Englischer* life . . . This charming outing, filled as it is with forgiveness, redemption, and new beginnings, will delight Fuller's fans."

—*Publishers Weekly* on *Matched and Married*

"This is a cute story of two sets of twins learning to grow up and be adults on their own terms and finding love along the way. It is another start of a great series."

—*Parkersburg News and Sentinel* on *A Double Dose of Love*

"Fuller (*The Innkeeper's Bride*) launches her Amish Mail-Order Brides series with the sweet story of love blooming between two pairs of twins . . . Faith and forgiveness form the backbone of this story, and the vulnerable sibling relationships are sure to tug at readers' heartstrings. This innocent romance is a treat."

—*Publishers Weekly* on *A Double Dose of Love*

"Fuller cements her reputation [as] a top practitioner of Amish fiction with this moving, perceptive collection."

—*Publishers Weekly* on *Amish Generations*

"Fuller brings us compelling characters who stay in our hearts long after we've read the book. It's always a treat to dive into one of her novels."

—BETH WISEMAN, BESTSELLING AUTHOR OF *HEARTS IN HARMONY*, ON *THE INNKEEPER'S BRIDE*

"A beautiful Amish romance with plenty of twists and turns and a completely satisfying, happy ending. Kathleen Fuller is a gifted storyteller."

—JENNIFER BECKSTRAND, AUTHOR OF *HOME ON HUCKLEBERRY HILL*, ON *THE INNKEEPER'S BRIDE*

"I always enjoy a Kathleen Fuller book, especially her Amish stories. *The Innkeeper's Bride* did not disappoint! From the moment Selah and Levi meet each other to the last scene in the book, this was a story that tugged at my emotions. The story deals with several heavy issues such as mental illness and family conflicts, while still maintaining humor and couples falling in love, both old and new. When Selah finds work at the inn Levi is starting up with his family, they clash on everything but realize they have feelings for each other. My heart hurt for Selah as she held her secrets close and pushed everyone away. But in the end, God's grace and love, along with some misguided Birch Creek matchmakers stirring up mischief, brings them together. Weddings at a beautiful country inn? What's not to love? Readers of Amish fiction will enjoy this winter-time story of redemption and hope set against the backdrop of a beautiful inn that brings people together."

—LENORA WORTH, AUTHOR OF *THEIR AMISH REUNION*

"A warm romance that will tug at the hearts of readers, this is a new favorite."

—*THE PARKERSBURG NEWS AND SENTINEL* ON *THE TEACHER'S BRIDE*

"Fuller's appealing Amish romance deals with some serious issues, including depression, yet it also offers funny and endearing moments."

—*BOOKLIST* ON *THE TEACHER'S BRIDE*

"Kathleen Fuller's *The Teacher's Bride* is a heartwarming story of unexpected romance woven with fun and engaging characters who come to life on every page. Once you open the book, you won't put it down until you've reached the end."

—AMY CLIPSTON, BESTSELLING AUTHOR OF *A SEAT BY THE HEARTH*

"Kathleen Fuller's characters leap off the page with subtle power as she uses both wit and wisdom to entertain! Refreshingly honest and charming, Kathy's writing reflects a master's touch when it comes to intricate plotting and a satisfying and inspirational ending full of good cheer!"

—KELLY LONG, NATIONAL BESTSELLING
AUTHOR, ON *THE TEACHER'S BRIDE*

"Kathleen Fuller is a master storyteller, and fans will absolutely fall in love with Ruby and Christian in *The Teacher's Bride*."

—RUTH REID, BESTSELLING AUTHOR OF *A MIRACLE OF HOPE*

"*The Teacher's Bride* features characters who know what it's like to be different, to not fit in. What they don't know is that's what makes them so loveable. Kathleen Fuller has written a sweet, oftentimes humorous, romance that reminds readers that the perfect match might be right in front of their noses. She handles the difficult topic of depression with a deft touch. Readers of Amish fiction won't want to miss this delightful story."

—KELLY IRVIN, BESTSELLING AUTHOR OF
THE EVERY AMISH SEASON SERIES

"Kathleen Fuller is a talented and gifted author, and she doesn't disappoint in *The Teacher's Bride*. The story will captivate you from the first page to the last with Ruby, Christian, and other engaging characters. You'll laugh, gasp, and wonder what will happen next. You won't want to miss reading this heartwarming Amish story of mishaps, faith, love, forgiveness, and friendship."

—MOLLY JEBBER, SPEAKER AND AWARD-WINNING AUTHOR OF
GRACE'S FORGIVENESS AND A KEEPSAKE POCKET QUILT SERIES

"Enthusiasts of Fuller's sweet Amish romances will savor this new anthology."

—*LIBRARY JOURNAL* ON *AN AMISH FAMILY*

"These four sweet stories are full of hope and promise along with misunderstandings and reconciliation. True love does prevail, but not without prayer, introspection, and humility. A must-read for fans of Amish romance."

—*RT BOOK REVIEWS*, 4 STARS, ON *AN AMISH FAMILY*

"The incredibly engaging Amish Letters series continues with a third story of perseverance and devotion, making it difficult to put down . . . Fuller skillfully knits together the lives within a changing, faithful community that has suffered its share of challenges."

—*RT BOOK REVIEWS*, 4½ STARS, ON *WORDS FROM THE HEART*

"Fuller's inspirational tale portrays complex characters facing real-world problems and finding love where they least expected or wanted it to be."

—*BOOKLIST*, STARRED REVIEW, ON *A RELUCTANT BRIDE*

"Fuller has an amazing capacity for creating damaged characters and giving insights into their brokenness. One of the better voices in the Amish fiction genre."

—*CBA RETAILERS + RESOURCES* ON *A RELUCTANT BRIDE*

"This promising series debut from Fuller is edgier than most Amish novels, dealing with difficult and dark issues and featuring well-drawn characters who are tougher than the usual gentle souls found in this genre. Recommended for Amish fiction fans who might like a different flavor."

—*LIBRARY JOURNAL* ON *A RELUCTANT BRIDE*

"Sadie and Aden's love is both sweet and hard-won, and Aden's patience is touching as he wrestles not only with Sadie's dilemma, but his own abusive past. Birch Creek is weighed down by the Troyer family's dark secrets, and readers will be interested to see how secondary characters' lives unfold as the series continues."

—*RT BOOK REVIEWS*, 4 STARS, ON *A RELUCTANT BRIDE*

"Kathleen Fuller's *A Reluctant Bride* tells the story of two Amish families whose lives have collided through tragedy. Sadie Schrock's stoic resolve will touch and inspire Fuller's fans, as will the story's concluding triumph of redemption."

—SUZANNE WOODS FISHER, BESTSELLING AUTHOR OF *MENDING FENCES*

"Kathleen Fuller's *A Reluctant Bride* is a beautiful story of faith, hope, and second chances. Her characters and descriptions are captivating, bringing the story to life with the turn of every page."

—AMY CLIPSTON, BESTSELLING AUTHOR OF *A SEAT BY THE HEARTH*

"The latest offering in the Middlefield Family series is a sweet love story with perfectly crafted characters. Fuller's Amish novels are written with the utmost respect for their way of living. Readers are given a glimpse of what it is like to live the simple life."

—RT BOOK REVIEWS, 4 STARS, ON *LETTERS TO KATIE*

"Fuller's second Amish series entry is a sweet romance with a strong sense of place that will attract readers of Wanda Brunstetter and Cindy Woodsmall."

—LIBRARY JOURNAL ON *FAITHFUL TO LAURA*

"Well-drawn characters and a homespun feel will make this Amish romance a sure bet for fans of Beverly Lewis and Jerry S. Eicher."

—LIBRARY JOURNAL ON *TREASURING EMMA*

"*Treasuring Emma* is a heartwarming story filled with real-life situations and well-developed characters. I rooted for Emma and Adam until the very last page. Fans of Amish fiction and those seeking an endearing romance will enjoy this love story. Highly recommended."

—BETH WISEMAN, BESTSELLING AUTHOR OF *HEARTS IN HARMONY*

"*Treasuring Emma* is a charming, emotionally layered story of the value of friendship in love and discovering the truth of the heart. A true treasure of a read!"

—KELLY LONG, NATIONAL BESTSELLING AUTHOR

THE PROPOSAL PLOT

Also by Kathleen Fuller

THE AMISH OF MARIGOLD NOVELS
The Courtship Plan
The Proposal Plot

THE AMISH MAIL-ORDER BRIDE NOVELS
A Double Dose of Love
Matched and Married
Love in Plain Sight

THE AMISH BRIDES OF BIRCH CREEK NOVELS
The Teacher's Bride
The Farmer's Bride
The Innkeeper's Bride

THE AMISH LETTERS NOVELS
Written in Love
The Promise of a Letter
Words from the Heart

THE AMISH OF BIRCH CREEK NOVELS
A Reluctant Bride
An Unbroken Heart
A Love Made New

THE MIDDLEFIELD AMISH NOVELS
A Faith of Her Own

THE MIDDLEFIELD FAMILY NOVELS
Treasuring Emma
Faithful to Laura
Letters to Katie

THE HEARTS OF MIDDLEFIELD NOVELS
A Man of His Word
An Honest Love
A Hand to Hold

THE MAPLE FALLS ROMANCE NOVELS
Hooked on You
Much Ado About a Latte
Sold on Love
Two to Tango

STORY COLLECTIONS
An Amish Family
Amish Generations

STORIES
A Miracle for Miriam included in *An Amish Christmas*
A Place of His Own included in *An Amish Gathering*
What the Heart Sees included in *An Amish Love*
A Perfect Match included in *An Amish Wedding*
Flowers for Rachael included in *An Amish Garden*
A Gift for Anne Marie included in *An Amish Second Christmas*
A Heart Full of Love included in *An Amish Cradle*
A Bid for Love included in *An Amish Market*

The PROPOSAL PLOT

An Amish of Marigold Novel

KATHLEEN FULLER

ZONDERVAN®

ZONDERVAN

The Proposal Plot

Copyright © 2024 by Kathleen Fuller

Requests for information should be addressed to:

Zondervan, *3950 Sparks Dr. SE, Grand Rapids, Michigan 49546*

Library of Congress Cataloging-in-Publication Data

Names: Fuller, Kathleen, author.
Title: The proposal plot: an Amish of Marigold novel / Kathleen Fuller.
Description: [Nashville, Tennessee]: Zondervan, 2024. | Series: Amish of marigold
novel; 2 | Summary: "A headstrong young businesswoman. An unlucky-in-love
bachelor. And the chaperoning assignment that keeps pushing them together."—
Provided by publisher.
Identifiers: LCCN 2023048143 (print) | LCCN 2023048144 (ebook) | ISBN
9780840713070 (paperback) | ISBN 9780840713117 (epub) | ISBN
9780840713247
Subjects: LCSH: Amish—Fiction. | BISAC: FICTION / Amish & Mennonite |
FICTION / Small Town & Rural | LCGFT: Romance fiction. | Christian
fiction. | Novels.
Classification: LCC PS3606.U553 P78 2024 (print) | LCC PS3606.U553
(ebook) | DDC 813/.6--dc23/eng/20231016
LC record available at https://lccn.loc.gov/2023048143
LC ebook record available at https://lccn.loc.gov/2023048144

Zondervan titles may be purchased in bulk for educational, business, fundraising,
or sales promotional use. For information, please email SpecialMarkets@
Zondervan.com.

Printed in the United States of America

24 25 26 27 28 LBC 5 4 3 2 1

To James. I love you.

Glossary

ab im kopp: crazy in the head
appeditlich: delicious
bruder(s): brother(s)
daed: dad
danki: thank you
Deitsch: Amish language
dochder: daughter
dumm: dumb
familye: family
frau: wife
geh: go
grossmammi: grandmother
grossvatter: grandfather
gut: good
gute nacht: good night
haus: house
kaffee: coffee
kapp: white hat worn by Amish women
kinn: chin

kinner: children

maed/maedel: young woman/young women

mamm: mom

mann: man

mei: my

nee: no

nix: nothing

Ordnung: written and unwritten rules in an Amish district

schee: pretty/handsome

schwester: sister

seltsam: weird

sohn: son

wie geht's: how's it going

ya: yes

yer: your

Prologue

SIX MONTHS EARLIER

Second time's the charm. Nelson Bontrager stood outside Stoll's Inn and wiped his damp palms over his pant legs. Although the sun had set a short time ago, the June humidity cloaked the air like a thick wool blanket, contributing to his perspiration situation. Maybe he should wait for a cooler evening when he wasn't so sweaty—or so nervous.

But it was now or never. He loved Norene Yoder. Had loved her since he first laid eyes on her when she moved to Birch Creek. After three months of pursuing her, she'd finally agreed to go out with him, and they'd been dating ever since. He didn't spend as much time with her as he'd like, but she was busy. He was too, working on his family's expansive farm. Unlike his five brothers, who also worked in the family business, he wasn't all that enamored with farming. But it was good, steady work that would enable him to provide for his future family. And he wanted Norene to be a part of that.

He grinned, but it faded quickly. Standing out here musing about their relationship and future wasn't getting him any closer to making

1

her his wife. The proposal was just the first step, after all. A simple four-word question: *Will you marry me?*

Nelson gulped, wiped his forehead with the back of his hand, and ignored his increasing jitters as he walked to the back of the inn. He'd never proposed to a woman before, but he'd come close to asking Miriam Miller two years ago. She also moved to Birch Creek in search of a husband. He also thought he loved her and that she loved him. He'd been dead wrong about that. But he wasn't wrong about Norene. Just keyed up about asking her to marry him. That was normal . . . Wasn't it?

A light shone in the window of her rented room on the second floor of the inn. He picked up a few pebbles and tossed three in succession against the window. Their secret code. He knew she'd be home tonight. She didn't work at the diner on Thursdays, and she'd told him those were the nights she wanted to rest and relax by herself. *"They're my jigsaw puzzle nights,"* she'd said. When he told her he liked puzzles too—not true, but he'd say and do anything to spend as much time with her as possible—she said she preferred to do them alone. He could understand that. Growing up with ten brothers and one sister, he understood the value of having alone time, although he'd give it up in a heartbeat to be with her. But he had to respect her wishes.

When she didn't come to the window, he picked up a few more pebbles. Maybe she hadn't heard the ones he already tossed. *Plink. Plink. Plink.* Then he waited. And waited. And frowned. Had she gone to bed already? By her own admission, she was a night owl, and it wasn't even nine o'clock yet.

The back door opened, and a bright light lit up the large patio, startling him. Selah Stoll, who helped her husband, Levi, run the inn, came outside. "Hallo, Nelson," she said, giving him a smile. "I didn't realize anyone was out here."

"Hi." He thrust his hands behind his back and dropped the pebbles. More sweat broke out on his brow. "Nice night, *ya*?"

"That it is." She glanced at the window. "Waiting for someone?"

He didn't bother fabricating an excuse. For the past three years since the mail-order bride advertisement had swept through the national Amish community—thanks to a prank by his younger brother Jesse—Stoll's Inn had been the primary residence for single Amish women arriving in Birch Creek to find a husband, with somewhat mixed results. "I was just getting ready to knock on the door." A little fib, but he didn't want to explain everything.

"Why not the front door?" Selah's smile widened.

Busted. Oh well, he'd forget this little embarrassing moment after Norene accepted his proposal. "Is Norene here?"

Selah's smile faded. "*Nee.*"

"Oh." Maybe she'd stepped out for a few minutes. "Have you seen her lately?"

"Not since this morning."

She'd been gone all day? That didn't make sense.

"You're welcome to wait for her in the lobby," Selah said. Then she frowned a little. "I'm sorry to pry, but are you seeing each other?"

He rubbed the back of his neck, hesitating. "*Ya.*" Although Amish dating was often kept private, Norene had insisted on keeping their relationship a secret from everyone. *"It's more special that way,"* she'd said, right before she kissed him senseless. She had a way of doing that whenever a niggle of doubt or questioning crept in, and by the end of the kiss, everything was right again. And soon she would be his wife, so there was no reason to hide their love anymore.

Selah opened her mouth as if she were going to say something else, then closed it. "*Geh* on in," she said. "There's coffee, tea, and some fresh lemon water if you want. Help yourself to some snacks too. I'm headed home for the night."

"Danki." He moved to walk past her, then saw a flicker of concern in her eyes.

"I hope she doesn't keep you waiting too long."

Me too.

Selah waved to him, then turned around and headed for the house next to the inn where she and Levi lived.

He walked through the back of the inn to the front lobby, which was empty. His brother Ezra worked here as a handyman and occasionally Nelson would help him with a project or three. That's how he'd met Norene. It was also how Ezra had met his future wife, Katharine. When Norene showed up and accepted his proposal, Nelson would be the second Bontrager to find forever love at the Stoll's Inn.

He grabbed some water and gulped it down, then wiped his face with his handkerchief. He shoved it back into his pocket and sat down at one of the breakfast tables. Surely wherever Norene was, she'd be back soon.

A clock sat above a large stone fireplace on the opposite wall of the lobby. *Tick. Tick. Tick.*

Thirty minutes later, the front door opened, and Nelson shot up from his chair. Beulah, one of Norene's friends, walked inside. He dashed over to her.

"Have you seen Norene?" He inwardly cringed at the desperation in his voice, but he couldn't control it. Waiting on her for so long had sent his anxiety into orbit.

Beulah's round face turned pale. "Uh . . ." Her eyes darted to the still open door.

Finally! He hurried outside and saw two shadowy figures near the large tree in the front yard of the inn next to the gravel lot. A tall male, a short female, embracing each other. The niggle turned into a sour knot as they moved hand in hand closer to the house, the light from the parking lot lamppost revealing their faces. Ben Miller and Norene.

His Norene.

Her giggle reached his ears, and he watched in shock as they stopped close to the inn's long front porch, unaware they weren't alone. She stood on tiptoes and kissed Ben . . . senseless.

Nelson's jaw jerked as they broke apart, and Ben walked away while Norene turned to face the inn. His heart pounded and ached in his chest. How could she lie to him about Thursday nights? *How could she kiss another man when she's in love with me?*

Her brows lifted with shock. "Nelson!" She ran up the stairs and pulled him away from the front door. "What are you doing here? It's Thursday."

His tone turned ugly. "The day you always want for yourself? The one when you insist on being alone?"

Her beautiful blue eyes turned to ice. "I thought we had an agreement. Thursday nights are *my* nights."

"To *geh* out with other men?" He moved away from her as if he were seeing her for the first time. "I thought we were in a relationship."

"We are. Just not a serious one." She frowned. "Wait . . . Did you think . . ."

Nelson almost staggered from her words. "I told you I loved you. Of course I thought—"

"I never said it back."

Nelson froze, searching his mind for the memory, because he was absolutely positively sure she'd said she loved him. Instead, he remembered with newfound clarity how she often changed the subject when he brought up their future together, dodged his kisses unless she was the one who initiated them, and faintly laughed at his jokes while rolling her eyes . . . Oh *nee. Nee, nee, nee.* Had he been fooled again? *No . . . I fooled myself.*

"I do like you, Nelson." Her tone was contrite. "But I need to keep my options open. You understand, *ya?*"

Translation: he wasn't good enough. Not for Miriam. Not for her.

"I'm sorry. I didn't mean to hurt your feelings."

His anguish and shame disappeared as something inside his heart turned to stone. "You didn't."

"Oh *gut.*" She smiled. "We can still hang out, you know. I always have fun playing checkers with you."

Checkers. They played on most of their dates, at her insistence. He didn't even like the game. "Do you play checkers with Ben? Oh wait. Thursday is *jigsaw puzzles.*"

Her smile shifted to a foul expression. "You don't have to be so mean, Nelson. I didn't do anything wrong."

Unbelievable. He turned and walked off, resisting the temptation to run away. His palms weren't damp anymore. They were cold . . . like the rest of him. And as he walked home, he realized he'd reacted the same way when Miriam dumped him for someone else. The feelings he'd been so sure of disappeared, leaving an empty space behind. He'd been dumb enough to think Norene had filled it, but he couldn't completely blame her. Not when the scales were off his eyes. He'd let his hope and desire for a wife and family cloud his judgment. Not once, but twice.

There wouldn't be a third time.

One

Dear Diary,

I can't believe it's been nearly a year since we moved from Lancaster to Marigold. And what a year it's been! Dad and I have been working hard to make our grocery store a success after we took it over from the Burkholders, and thankfully our efforts have paid off. Some days there's more business than we can handle! I even mentioned to Dad that we should find out who owns the empty building next door and see if it's for sale so we could expand. He said no. Not a surprise. He doesn't like taking risks, even though it didn't take much to convince him to move to Marigold. I wish he would reconsider expanding, though. I think it would be good for our family and for the growing community.

I also wish he'd do something about Junia. She's not pulling her fair share—no surprise there either—but he won't say anything to her. She keeps complaining about being homesick for Lancaster, but that's not an excuse to shirk her job and chores, and it's driving me ab im kopp. She's not the only one who's missing home. I do too . . . sort of. I miss all the farmland and my friends. But I don't miss the busyness of the tourists or my aunts' and cousins' unwanted advice, especially when they say they're not surprised I'm still single because of my "personality." I'm only twenty-six. There's plenty of time to find a husband, right? Besides, they're being hypocritical. Neither of them is married.

Ella lifted her pen from the page and looked at her last paragraph. She should mark it out in case anyone discovered her diary and read it. She didn't write anything about her aunts and sister that wasn't true, though. *Aenti* Tabitha and *Aenti* Cora had always been critical of her, and for some reason they never could resist throwing a dig or two at her lack of suitors. Junia was a dreamer and a flirt, and unlike Ella, she was obsessed with getting married. In fact, her sister had complained more about the lack of single men in Marigold than her yearning to go back to Lancaster. *She should just go back if she's so unhappy here.*

But Junia didn't actually seem to be unhappy. Just lazy and completely uninterested in helping her and Dad run the grocery store. And their father kept indulging her slothfulness. Anytime Ella pointed out her sister's lacking work ethic, Junia just scoffed. *"You're so bossy, Ella. And* seltsam. *No wonder you're not married yet."* It was the same thing her aunts had always said.

Ella tossed her pencil onto the diary page. She shouldn't let Junia or her aunts get to her. *Aenti* Tabitha and *Aenti* Cora were in Lancaster and couldn't influence her anymore. Instead, she should ask God to bring her sister a husband. Then she and *Daed* could hire someone who would do some work. More than once over the past three months, she'd proposed hiring another employee, but her father had vetoed that suggestion too. *"We're doing just fine,"* he said in his usual slow, measured tone. And they were. But Ella didn't want their business to be "just fine." Not when it could be a huge success.

"Ella!"

She cringed at the sound of Junia's whiny voice coming from downstairs. "What?" she hollered from her room.

The thudding sound of her sister's fast footsteps grew closer. Ella quickly shut her diary and stuck it under the mattress of her twin bed.

Junia burst into the room. "Guess what?"

"You finally cleaned out the storage room at the store?"

Junia frowned, her large, round brown eyes growing wider. "*Nee.* Why would I do that?"

"Because I asked you to?"

"When?"

"Yesterday." Ella stood up, adjusting the ties of her white apron and fighting the urge to roll her eyes. Junia only seemed to forget something when it was related to work. Otherwise, her mind was a steel trap. "It's almost opening time," she said, slipping on her navy blue cardigan. "Hurry up and tell me whatever you have to tell me."

"Why are you always so crabby?" Her sister pouted, something else that drove Ella crazy but always made her father cave. She lifted her chin. "I'm not going to tell you now."

"Fine." Ella shoved her feet into her black tennis shoes and knelt to tie the laces.

Junia squatted beside her. "It looks like someone's moving in next door."

Shortly after they bought the store and arrived in Marigold, they purchased the Burkholders' four-bedroom home across the street from the store. There wasn't another house for at least two blocks or so. "Next door to our house?"

"*Nee.* The building next to the store. I saw two men get out of a taxi a few minutes ago. One of them—he's kind of burly—had a key and opened the door. The other one . . ." Junia let out a dramatic sigh. "He's so *schee.*"

Oh brother. Ella had never sighed over a man, *schee* or otherwise. She also didn't appreciate her sister's "burly" comment. What did it matter what the men looked like anyway?

Then her sister's words sank in. The building had sold? Uh-oh. There went her plan for expansion. She bustled by Junia.

"Where are you going?" Junia trailed after her.

Ella bounded down the stairs, through the kitchen to the mudroom. She picked up the keys off a hook and tossed them to Junia. They hit her sister in the chest and dropped to the floor.

"What'd you do that for?" She bent over and snatched up the keys.

"You're in charge until *Daed* finishes up the chores." Ella cringed. "Don't make me regret this. Fridays are always busy."

She huffed. "I'm not a child, Ella. I know how to run the store."

"Now you can prove it." She opened the door. A cold draft of wind hit her in the face.

"Where are you going?" Junia called out from the doorway.

Ella whirled around. "To meet our new neighbors."

·❧·

Nelson shoved his hands into the pockets of his jacket and looked around the empty room. His brother Jesse, who had moved to Marigold almost a year and a half ago, told him about this place and encouraged him to check it out. But as had been his habit for more than a year now, he wondered if he was doing the right thing.

"Well? What do you think?"

His nephew Malachi appeared next to him. At twenty-four, Nelson was only two years older and considered Malachi more of a brother—and he had plenty of those. He looked around the area again. He'd learned from the Realtor that it used to be a warehouse and was a decade older than the grocery store next door. Pale morning light beamed through dusty windows into an expansive, empty room. The stairs in the back led to a loft, also covered in dust and cobwebs. There wasn't a visible shred of evidence that anything was ever stored here. From what he could gather, the current owner bought it from the original one and had intended to turn it into a small house to rent out but never got around to it.

"Needs work," he said, turning to Malachi. "A lot of work."

Malachi nodded. His straw hat was pushed back from his head—wavy dark-blond hair curled around the bottoms of his ears. "Agreed. But nothing wrong with hard work, *ya*?"

"*Ya*." The uneasiness increased. What did he know about running a butcher shop? About as much as he did when, right after his relationship with Norene imploded, he started apprenticing with an Amish butcher in Fredericktown where his family was originally from and where his oldest brother, Devon, currently lived with his wife, Nettie, and their three children. During that time, he'd not only learned butchery, but he also discovered he enjoyed doing it—even going so far as to experiment with making and seasoning sandwich meat and sausage. His boss, Samuel, was impressed. *"Best smoked turkey I ever had,"* he'd said.

He couldn't take all the credit. Samuel was not only the best butcher in Fredericktown, but he was also an excellent teacher. In a way, he had Norene to thank for his new occupation. He was so eager to get away from her and his broken dreams that two days after he discovered her with Ben Miller, he'd moved in with Devon. But now he was back in Birch Creek. He'd never been fully settled in Fredericktown, and he couldn't run away from the past. He just wasn't sure what his next step would be.

"You gonna make an offer?" Malachi asked.

Nelson blew out a breath. So much had changed in a short time. He never thought he'd leave his family's farm, much less have a new career and consider opening his own shop. But one thing hadn't changed—his need for a fresh start. Moving to Marigold had been good for Jesse. His brother was happily married and worked in a successful buggy shop. Maybe moving here would give Nelson a new lease on life too. He turned to Malachi. "Possibly—"

The door flew open, and a young Amish woman burst into the room. When she spotted Nelson and Malachi, she made a beeline toward them. "Are you the new owners?"

Nelson blinked while Malachi took a step back. Her breath came out in puffs in the cold warehouse, and she put her hands on her hips and stared them down. There was barely enough light for him to see the determination in her dark-blue eyes. Or were they gray? He couldn't tell, and he didn't care. "Why do you want to know?" he said, staring straight back at her.

She didn't flinch. "You're not answering my question."

He grimaced. After the disaster with Norene, he was through letting women push him around, and this woman in front of him was one of the pushiest females he'd ever met. "That's because it's none of your business."

Malachi stepped forward. "Hi. I'm Malachi Chupp. This is my uncle, Nelson Bontrager."

There was a flicker of recognition in her eyes. "Are you related to Jesse?"

Malachi nodded, but Nelson didn't respond. Putting his hand on Nelson's shoulder, he said, "He's interested in buying the building."

"Maybe," Nelson added. He didn't want Malachi to think he'd made his decision.

She turned to him. "For what purpose?"

"For my purpose." He shrugged off Malachi's hand. What was with this woman? And where did she come from? There was a house across the street from the grocery store. She probably lived there, but that didn't give her the right to interrogate him.

She crossed her arms and lifted her chin. "You haven't bought it yet?"

He moved closer to her. Nelson wasn't a small man. He was downright brawny, a stark contrast from his brother Jesse, who was thin and wiry. She was about his chin level, and he felt a little satisfaction peering down at her. "Like I said, it's not any of your business."

She pointed in the direction of the adjacent grocery store. "That's *my* business," she said, her tone holding a challenge. "If you're going to be my neighbor, I need to know about it."

At some point Nelson must have moved again, because now he was only about a foot away from her. Against his will, a thought ran through his head. She would be kind of cute if it weren't for her sharp tone. He immediately dismissed it. Noticing a woman's looks was also verboten to him now. When it came to females, he was done.

"That's a big if, now that I've met you."

"Nelson," Malachi said. "You're being—"

He held up his hand, forcing Malachi to stop talking. He knew what his nephew was going to say. He was being rude. Again, he didn't care. She'd started it, and he was going to end it. Any second now, she would burst into tears and go running off, probably to cry to her husband about the mean man in the warehouse.

Instead, her lips twitched. A spark appeared in her eyes. She moved a few steps to the side and lifted her arm in a sweeping motion toward the door. "Feel free to leave."

"Oh boy," Malachi muttered. "Nelson, we should go . . ."

When he didn't finish his sentence, Nelson turned around. His nephew was literally slack-jawed and staring at the warehouse door. A slender, lithe Amish woman stood there gazing at Malachi. He looked from her to his nephew, who had finally closed his mouth.

"Junia, why are you here?" The sharp-tongued woman hurried over to her. "You're supposed to be opening the store."

"We're not busy. *Daed*'s there anyway." She leaned closer, continuing to stare at his nephew. "Ella . . . Who is he?"

"That's Malachi. And this is"—she rolled her eyes—"Nelson."

She sounded like she was explaining a contagious disease. Ella—nice name. Unfortunately, she was the exact opposite.

Junia went to Malachi. "Hi," she said, smiling, then looking up at him.

"H-h—" Malachi cleared his throat. "Hi."

"Do you live close by?" she asked. "I've never seen you before."

"I live in Birch Creek."

"Oh, I've been meaning to visit Birch Creek. I just haven't had the time. I've been working so hard in our store—"

"Give me a break," Ella muttered.

Junia whirled around and frowned at her, then faced Malachi again, her flirty smile back in place. "Maybe someday you could show me around your town."

He gave her a dumbstruck grin.

Now it was Nelson's turn to roll his eyes. He'd never met anyone more girl crazy than Malachi, and that was saying a lot, considering his own history.

Ella inserted herself between Malachi and Junia, her back to him. "*Geh* back to work," she ordered.

Junia lifted her chin. "You're not *mei* boss." A slow smile spread across her face. "*Daed* is."

Ella fisted her hands at her sides, her lips pressed together. But she didn't say anything, turning on her heel and blowing past Nelson without a single glance.

"Just ignore *mei schwester*," Junia said, her voice dripping more sweetness than a warm peach pie straight from the oven. "She's always a grouch."

"You're *schwesters*?" Malachi marveled.

"*Ya*. But we don't look alike at all, do we?"

Now that Nelson knew they were siblings, he noted a slight resemblance. They both had round faces, and the same dark-brown hair peeked out from underneath their white *kapps*. Otherwise, they were opposites.

"And we have totally different personalities, thank goodness." Junia batted her eyes at Malachi. "Now, where were we?"

"We were leaving." Nelson headed for the door. "Malachi, let's *geh*."

But his nephew remained in place. "You *geh* on," he said, staring at Junia again. "I'll catch up with you later at Jesse's."

Nelson paused, then shook his head. Well, Malachi would have to find out the hard way that women, especially pretty ones like Junia, weren't to be trusted. He'd had to learn his own harsh lesson. And he'd be there to help his nephew pick up the pieces when this girl inevitably crushed his heart.

He walked out of the warehouse, got into his buggy, chirruped to his horse, and headed to Wagler's Buggy Shop where Jesse worked. One thing was for sure—he wasn't buying that property. He'd start his butcher shop somewhere else. Or he'd stick with working on his family's farm in Birch Creek. Either would be preferable to working next door to Junia. And Ella. Especially Ella.

.~ole~.

Wendy Pearson resisted the urge to rub her temples as the couple in front of her continued to bicker. She wasn't a divorce attorney, but the way these two were carrying on, she thought they might need one.

"We're not leaving anything to the dog in our will, Judy," the man said. "We're only in our sixties. He won't be around when we kick the bucket."

Judy sucked in a breath and stroked the Chihuahua in her lap. "He's only five, Harold. He'll probably live longer than you."

"That's what you're hoping for, isn't it?"

"You said it, not me."

They turned away from each other in their chairs, Judy cuddling the dog. Wendy internally counted to ten. At least they stopped arguing long enough for her to get a few words in. "Mr. and Mrs. Warren, we've been at this for nearly an hour. Maybe you should go home and have some further discussion about the beneficiaries of your estate."

"I already told you. I want Claude to inherit everything." Judy cradled him closer. "You deserve it, don't you, Mr. Claudy Claude?"

"See what I have to deal with?" Harold pointed at her with his thumb. "She's nuts."

Wendy suspected he was right, but it wasn't her job or place to judge. "Mr. Warren, it's not unheard of for pets to be beneficiaries. Your wife obviously loves Claude—"

The dog bared his teeth at her. Wendy pulled back. She usually liked dogs. Her mother had one—Monroe—and he was a great pet and companion. But this little monster . . . Yikes. She needed to get the couple back on track before they spent another hour arguing in her office. "However—"

"We do have six kids to consider," Harold said.

Wendy stilled. "You have children?"

"Yep. Four boys, two girls. One son-in-law—used to have two, but he's the 'ex' now." Harold made air quotes. "Three of our sons are married, and one is still 'finding himself.'" More air quotes. "We also have thirteen grandchildren. But Claude trumps them all."

"Here." Judy thrust her phone at Wendy. "This is from last week, when I took Claude to see Santa."

Wendy glanced at the photo of a man in a sagging Santa suit holding Claude, who was decked out in an elf costume. This woman was certifiable. *No judging, remember?* She glanced at the clock on the wall of her office. Almost four thirty. They wouldn't figure this out today. "Considering this new development, we should schedule another meeting for next week, if you're both agreeable." She opened her laptop and pulled up her calendar. "I'm free on Tuesday at three. Does that work for you?"

"Yes," Harold said, pulling his coat off the back of his chair.

"Claude has a playdate, remember?" Judy looked at her phone. "Can we make it four?"

"Sure." Wendy tapped on the keyboard. She added the date and a note: **Bring dog treats.** That always worked for Monroe. She stood up and held out her hand to the Warrens.

Harold was already standing. Looking eager to go, he shook her hand while Claude bared his teeth at him. Harold looked at Wendy and twirled his finger near his temple.

She almost laughed but managed to stifle it as the Warrens left her office. When they were gone, she plopped back down in her seat and pinched her nose. Three months ago, she decided to open a small law office in Barton, about thirty minutes from Marigold, where she lived with her mother and Monroe. She had taken a nine-month sabbatical from her high-stress job as a corporate lawyer at a firm in Manhattan, ultimately quitting that position with zero regrets. But she couldn't imagine doing anything else, and when she learned there was an office space available to rent, she jumped at the chance to have her own firm, ready to go back to the career she'd dedicated her life to—to the exclusion of all else.

The trouble was . . . she was starting to hate being a lawyer. Well, she didn't exactly hate it, but now that she was back at work, she didn't want to be here.

Pushing away from her desk, she glanced around the office. Her intention had been to grow her practice, perhaps bringing on one or two attorneys and eventually getting a larger office space. She didn't know any other way to work. Her entire career had been spent climbing the ladder to the top. Or in her case, almost to the top. She'd been passed on for partner many times over the years, which was one of the reasons why she quit. Now that she was her own boss, things would be different. She would only take on the cases she wanted, only work the hours she chose, and make a name for herself in small-town Ohio. So far that hadn't happened.

Instead of being concerned, she felt relief.

She got up, put on her coat, and shut off the light, then locked the door. Part of her grandiose plans had been to hire an admin as soon as possible. She'd have to be able to pay a decent salary, but that hadn't materialized yet. How could it when she dreaded every single moment she was here? So much so that she'd cut her workweek down to three days, barely making enough to cover the rent. Good thing she still had plenty of savings from selling her apartment in New York City. Still, that money wouldn't last forever.

Cold wind hit her as she got into her mother's silver sedan. Wendy had sold her Mercedes on a whim a little more than two months ago and had taken over the sedan since Mom couldn't drive anymore. Again, zero regrets.

Once she left the Barton city limits, she fully relaxed, something that was happening more and more regularly. When she first took her sabbatical, she was sure she'd miss the hustle and bustle and sophistication of what she'd always considered the greatest city in America—NYC. Surprisingly, she hadn't had a moment of homesickness since she left.

She called her mother on her cell. The call went to voicemail, and Wendy automatically tried her again. Sometimes it took two or three times for her mother to answer, mostly because she forgot where she put her cell since she wasn't one for chatting on the phone. Maybe it was time to get a landline.

"Hi, honey," Mom said when she finally answered. "Are you on your way home?"

"Yes. Did you need anything while I'm out?"

"No. Oh wait. Some of those sweet rolls from Yoders' would be good. Ella's an excellent baker. "

"And you're a diabetic. But nice try." She smiled. "How about some sugar-free pudding as a compromise? I'll make some when we get home."

"We're out."

"That's okay. Yoders' has some."

"You don't have to go to the trouble," Mom said, disappointment lacing her tone.

"But it was okay to go to trouble for sweet rolls?"

"Sweet rolls are always worth the trouble."

Wendy laughed. "I'll get the pudding. There are a few other things I need to pick up too." Some vegetables for salad and a bag of those delicious croutons Ella made fresh every week. She used to avoid carbs of any kind, but there was something about home-baked bread that she couldn't resist. "What did Charity make for supper tonight?"

"A quiche of some sort. She's been looking through her French cookbooks again."

Salad would be the perfect accompaniment. "Sounds delicious. See you in a bit."

"Bye. Love you."

"Love you too." She smiled. For years she'd been too busy to call her mother, and when she did, she was too distracted to pay full attention, sometimes even neglecting to tell Mom she loved her. She'd always been worried about her, though, ever since her parents moved to Marigold. Her father died shortly afterward, and then Mom had a stroke. Thankfully she recovered, and they had hired Charity Raber—now Bontrager since her marriage to Jesse—to be her live-in companion. Charity and Jesse lived next door, and six days a week she either came over to cook supper for her and Mom or brought a prepared meal from her house. Wendy had wanted to put an end to that, but her mother enjoyed Charity's food and her visits. Wendy did too. *But I really do need to learn how to cook something other than salad and sugar-free pudding.* She'd always ordered takeout when she lived in New York.

After a battle with some unexpected traffic, she arrived at E&J's Grocery five minutes before closing time. She rushed out of her car and into the store. The owner, Barnabas Yoder, was sweeping the floor near a display of Christmas candy. Hard to believe the holiday was only three weeks away. "Hi, Barnabas," she said, grabbing a shopping basket. "I just need to pick up some lettuce, carrots, and croutons. Oh, and sugar-free pudding. I won't be but a minute. Traffic was awful on the way over."

Barnabas smiled. "Take your time," he said in his low, patient voice. "I'm in no hurry."

"Thank you." She went to the baked goods aisle. She liked shopping here, not only because it was convenient, but because it wasn't hectic. There were times when they had a lot of customers, but even then there wasn't the stressful energy she felt when she was shopping in Barton.

She knew the store layout well, so it didn't take long for her to gather her groceries and go to the counter to check out. Barnabas met her there and began calculating her bill using an adding machine. He didn't have a beard like most of the Amish men she'd met in Marigold. She did know he was a widower but had no idea when his wife passed away. Wendy visited the store quite regularly, sometimes when she was on one of her long walks and she didn't bring Monroe, so she knew him and his two daughters, Ella and Junia, better than any of the other Amish in Marigold. It was pretty obvious who the store was named after. The only other people she knew in town were Charity, Jesse, Jesse's boss, Micah, and his wife, Priscilla, and their daughter, Emma. But that didn't mean she knew any of them on a personal level.

"Ten fifty." He tore off the receipt tape and handed it to her. She put it in her wallet with her other receipts. Later she would go through them and make notes in her ledger. She might have growing doubts about being a lawyer, but she wasn't about to give up her meticulous recordkeeping. As Barnabas bagged her groceries in a calm and methodical manner, she let out a sigh, tension falling from her shoulders.

"Everything okay?" he asked, glancing up at her.

She started to say yes, but when she met his eyes, she stayed silent. Even though she enjoyed the slow pace of Marigold life, often she was still living like a rushed city dweller. Had she ever taken the time to look at this man—really look at him? He had clear, bright eyes, and they were an unusual grayish-blue color. He didn't have on a hat today, and his dark-brown hair was streaked with gray. She wasn't sure how old he was, but his daughters had to be in their twenties, and between the grays in his hair and the creases around his eyes and forehead, she guessed he was in his forties—the same as her. Most of all, he had a stoic steadiness about him. She'd never seen him upset or heard him raise his voice or seem rushed. She found that quite appealing.

She blinked, realizing he was expecting an answer. "Just glad to be off work," she said. "Sorry I'm keeping you at yours."

"Like I said, I'm not in any hurry." He set the bag of croutons on top of the vegetables. "Ella got a late start on supper, and Junia . . . well . . ." He shrugged, slightly smiling. "She's off somewhere, like she usually is." He handed her the bag. "Tell Shirley I said hello."

"I will." She took the bag from him and started to walk away. Then she turned. "How old are you, Barnabas?"

Surprise crossed his face, and she wanted to kick herself for asking. She could have found a more appropriate way to discover his age, and she normally didn't go around asking men, or anyone else, how many years they'd been on planet Earth. "Sorry, I don't know what got into me, asking you that. You don't have to answer." When he didn't say anything, she turned to leave, her face heating like charcoal briquettes under a grill.

"Forty-six," he said as she touched the door handle.

She looked over her shoulder. "Same age as me."

His eyes widened. "Never would have guessed that. You look like you're in your thirties."

Wendy laughed and faced him. "Makeup and hair dye help."

He paused for a long moment. "I think you'd look just fine without all that fancy stuff."

She smiled at his unexpected compliment. "Thanks, Barnabas."

He nodded and straightened up the paper bags at the end of the counter.

She turned and went out the door, still soaking in his kind words. She was a plain woman, and compared to her contemporaries, she wore very little makeup and a simple blunt haircut that she hadn't changed in over twenty years. Her former boyfriend, a cretin of a man, had never complimented her looks. From what she'd been able to glean about the Amish since moving here, they weren't ones for flattery.

Wendy glanced at the door and smiled. There was something about Barnabas. About all the Amish, really. Then she got into her car and went back home for some French quiche made by an Amish woman. *I love living in Marigold.*

Two

I never pegged you for a chicken."

Nelson side-eyed Jesse as Charity set a delicious-looking quiche—was that ham he smelled?—next to a skinny loaf of fresh bread in the middle of the table. Brook, their one-year-old terrier mix, sat underneath the table at Jesse's feet, patiently waiting for any crumbs to escape from the table. Malachi was still a no-show, even though he'd been gone the entire day since Nelson left the warehouse. Nelson had returned to the buggy shop and spent the rest of the morning and afternoon helping Jesse and Micah, mostly sweeping and tidying up since he didn't know anything about buggy building. His brother didn't either when he first took the job with Micah, but now he was not only exceptionally skilled at making buggies, but he also machined the brakes. Nelson was impressed. His pesky younger brother had finally grown up.

Charity sat down and put her hand on Jesse's. "You can continue complimenting your *bruder* after we pray."

Nelson smirked and bent his head in silent prayer. After they finished, Charity started to dish out the quiche. "I'm not a chicken," he said as she plopped a big slice on Jesse's plate and handed it to him.

"Then you'll have *nee* problem buying the warehouse and starting your business," Jesse said, setting down his food. "Looks *appeditlich*, Charity. Julia Child?"

"I decided to try someone different. Jacques what's-his-face. The librarian told me how to pronounce his name, but I forgot." She handed Nelson his slice, one that was bigger than Jesse's.

"I'm not even sure I want to open a butcher shop." His mouth watered at the steaming quiche. Charity sure could cook. Malachi didn't know what he was missing. Where was he, anyway?

"You've been talking about it ever since you came back from Devon's," Jesse said. "Now you have an opportunity. You need to seize it."

"Are you talking about the building next to Yoders'?" Charity looked at Nelson. Her cheeks were covered in freckles, like the rest of her, and her carrot-colored hair was tucked underneath her *kapp*. Although she and Jesse had been married for over a year, Nelson still marveled that they'd gotten together in the first place. Jesse had been adamant about not getting married, and because of a foolish prank he'd pulled years ago that had long-lasting repercussions, he'd almost lost Charity. But here his brother was, the man all the Bontragers thought would be the last one to tie the knot, living his happily ever after.

"*Ya*. It's for sale." Nelson grabbed a small slice of bread. A baguette, Charity had called it. He slathered it with fresh butter and took a bite. Whatever it was called, it was delicious.

"You want to buy it?" she asked.

"Maybe. I don't know. Probably not."

"As long as you're sure." Jesse grinned and ducked his hand under the table.

"Stop feeding Brook," Charity said. "She's going to get fat like Monroe."

"Then she'll be fat and happy." But he brought back his hand and kept it on the table, looking at Nelson. "What's keeping you from buying the warehouse?"

Nelson glanced at Charity, who was focused on cutting her slice of quiche. He wasn't keen on having this discussion in front of her. Not because he didn't trust her. He definitely did. But it wasn't easy to admit to himself that he was uncertain about his future, much less say it in front of his younger brother and his wife. "I want to be sure I'm making the right decision," he finally said, landing on the truth without admitting all of it.

"That's wise," Charity said. "*Nix* wrong with taking your time."

"Unless the building sells out from under you," Jesse pointed out. He forked a bite of quiche. "You don't want to miss out on a prime opportunity."

He frowned. Since when did his little brother start giving him advice? Good advice at that?

Jesse glanced at the door. "Where did you say Malachi was?"

"I don't know." He polished off the last bite of his quiche. Charity slid the round baking dish with the remainder toward him. "Last time I saw him he was with Junia. I think that's her name." He took another helping.

"Junia Yoder?" Charity exchanged a quizzical look with Jesse.

"*Ya.* Why?"

"She's, um . . ." She cringed a little.

"She's what?"

"Different," Jesse supplied.

"Not that it's a bad thing," Charity quickly added. "Lord knows I'm different."

"And I love that about you." Jesse grinned, a smitten look in his eyes.

Bleh. It was one thing for Jesse to get married when no one, including Jesse himself, expected him to. It was quite another when it turned out he wasn't shy about showing his feelings for Charity. Not that they were publicly affectionate with each other. That wasn't the Amish way. But when he spouted off a sticky-sweet compliment like that, Nelson thought it was too much.

Charity's cheeks turned rosy underneath her freckles as she gazed back at him, just as moony-eyed.

Nelson shoveled half the quiche slice in his mouth. Anything to distract himself from the newlywed puppy love in front of him. He glanced at Brook, who had moved out from under the table and was lying next to the woodstove. The pup closed her eyes. Even she'd had enough.

One more bite and he would leave Jesse and his wife to . . . whatever. He had to find Malachi anyway. They needed to head back to Birch Creek soon.

The door suddenly flew open. Nelson spun around as Ella Yoder bounded inside, much like she'd done at the warehouse earlier. Without preamble she glared at Nelson. "Where's *mei schwester*?"

.❧.

As soon as Ella saw Nelson, Charity, and Jesse's shocked expressions, she wondered if she should have knocked on the door instead of barging into the Bontragers' tiny house unannounced. But time was of the essence. Junia was missing, and Malachi was the last person she was seen with. She hadn't shown up for work all day—incensing, and then worrying Ella. As usual, her father seemed unconcerned. She couldn't understand why he wasn't upset. All he'd said was Junia was a grown woman, and she would be fine.

Not coming back to work without a word of explanation was not fine. Not in Ella's book.

Nelson stood, frowning. "You haven't seen her?"

"If I had, why would I be here?" Especially after their encounter this morning. He was by far the most unpleasant man she'd ever met. All she did was ask him a simple question about his intent to buy the warehouse, and he scowled at her. Of course that had set her off, and while in hindsight maybe she was a little nosy, he didn't have to be rude. Or scowl, like he was doing now. "Where are Junia and Malachi?"

He hesitated. "I don't know. I haven't seen them either."

The dread that had started a few hours ago when Junia didn't return began to grow. The Bontragers' little dog came up to her. Sniffed her ankles. Sat on her haunches and stared up at Ella, her tail wagging against the floor. She was a cute puppy, but Ella couldn't pay attention to her right now.

"We'll *geh* look for them," Jesse said as he got up from the table.

Charity went to her. "I'll make us some *kaffee*. Or tea, if you'd like."

Ella shook her head. "I'd like to know where *mei schwester* is."

"I'm sure she's fine." Nelson shoved his straw hat on his head and walked to the front door where his boots were. He pushed his feet inside. "Malachi wouldn't let anything happen to her."

"They probably just lost track of time," Charity said with a weak smile.

"Doing what?" Ella put her hands on her hips.

Nelson and Jesse exchanged a look. Charity focused on the wooden floorboards. Brook wagged her tail faster.

"They just met each other!" But Ella wouldn't be surprised if Junia and Malachi had "lost track of time." She didn't want to think about what that might mean, but she hadn't missed the adoring looks they were giving each other before they left the warehouse following Nelson's departure.

Nelson finished putting on his boots and coat while Charity opened the drawer of the end table by the love seat across the room and pulled out two flashlights. She handed one to Jesse, then crossed the small room and gave the other one to Nelson. He opened the door. Ella dashed past him and walked outside, turning on her flashlight. Jesse and Charity lived right next door to the buggy shop, and they shared a parking lot.

"What are you doing?" Nelson asked.

"Going with you." She pointed her light back on him and he shielded his eyes. Oops. She lowered her flashlight slightly.

"*Nee*. Jesse and I can find them."

Behind Nelson, Jesse and Charity came out of the house, closing the door behind them. "We can split up," Jesse said.

"I'll *geh* with Charity," Ella said, moving to stand beside her.

Jesse moved closer to his wife. "Charity and I will go west. You two head east."

Nelson blew out a breath. "Is it really necessary to pair up—"

But they were already walking away.

"Stop wasting time and let's *geh*." Ella motioned for him to follow her.

He turned on his flashlight and caught up with her.

She aimed her light at the field on the left. Nothing but grass and a few trees, the branches swaying in the faint evening breeze. She grimaced. Her feet hurt, she was cold, and she still needed to clean up the kitchen, because of course Junia wouldn't do it unless Ella made her, and tonight she was too tired and angry to get into a fight with her.

Of all the things Junia had done—or more accurately, hadn't done—disappearing with a complete stranger was the most inconsiderate. Not to mention foolish. "I can't believe she did that," she muttered.

"What?" Nelson matched her stride, which was easy to do, considering his legs were so much longer than hers.

She marched on, ignoring his question.

"Women," he grumbled.

"Excuse me?" She shined her light on him.

He guarded his eyes again. "Will you stop doing that?"

"Sorry." She aimed the light straight ahead.

"Wow," he said. "I didn't know you had it in you."

"Had what?"

"An apology."

She clenched her back molars together. "Listen, I wouldn't be out here in the cold, wasting my time, if it wasn't for your nephew's irresponsible behavior."

"My nephew? What about your irresponsible *schwester*?"

It was one thing for Ella to insult her own sister, but she wouldn't abide someone else getting their digs in. "How do I know Malachi didn't lure her away?"

"Because he wouldn't." He halted. "This is a waste of time."

"Finding Junia is not a waste of time—"

"I meant arguing is a waste of time."

"Oh." She had to admit he was right.

"Does she have somewhere special she likes to *geh*?" he asked. "A place where she can be alone?"

Ella lifted her flashlight a little, enough to illuminate his face but not blind him. "Why would she need a place to be alone?"

He smirked. "I can think of at least one reason."

She pursed her lips together. "You're really something . . . Wait."

She remembered an old abandoned barn that was less than a quarter mile from their house and tucked back behind bushes and brush. She was surprised she'd even thought about it since she'd discovered it on a walk a few weeks after she and her family had moved here. She was mad at Junia again and had stormed out of the house, taking a walk to let her anger cool. Did her sister know about the barn? And if she did, it wasn't exactly a place she'd expect Junia to go to. Too dirty and dilapidated. But it wasn't far from where she and Nelson were now, and it was worth investigating. She strode past him, cutting across the road in the opposite direction.

"Where are you going?" Once again, he quickly caught up to her.

She kept her light pointed to the field on the right. So far all she saw was grass. The barn was around here, right?

"Ella—"

"There it is." She saw the shadow from a large area of scrub and headed into the field.

Nelson shone his light in the same direction, and they both headed for the bushes. As they neared, the leaning form of the rickety barn came into view. "You think she's here? When it's so cold out?"

It did seem ridiculous now that they were standing close to the barn. The structure was so old and deteriorated, only a few boards held it together. As they both flashed their lights and did a quick search, it was clear Junia and Malachi weren't there. Good, because it looked like a slight breeze could topple it over.

She started to shiver. In her haste to find her sister, she'd grabbed her thin peacoat instead of her winter coat.

"Any other ideas?" He sounded surprisingly less irritated than he was a few minutes ago.

"*Nee.*" She stuck her cold hand in her pocket and tried to keep still. "I-I have *n-nee* idea where they'd be."

He moved a step closer to her. "Let's get you home," he said.

She shook her head. "I have to find J-Junia."

"If she's with Malachi, she's okay. Trust me. My nephew is a *gut* man. He gets a little *ab im kopp* when it comes to *maed*, but he wouldn't do anything untoward. You have *mei* word on that. I'm sure wherever they are, they just lost track of time."

Ella paused, then nodded. There was something about his calm tone that settled her worry. "Junia tends to have her head in the clouds, so I can see that happening." Although their flashlights were pointed away, she could see Nelson's shadowed face break into a half smile. "All right. I'll wait for her at home. *Danki* for your help." She turned and briskly walked toward the road. When she reached the asphalt, he was already by her side.

"Jesse's house is in that direction." She pointed to the right. "Just turn left at the end of the street."

"I know."

"You've been to Marigold before?"

"Just to *mei bruder*'s. But I've got a *gut* sense of direction." He directed his flashlight in the opposite path. "Your *haus* is that way, *ya*?"

"*Ya*."

"Then let's *geh*." He started to walk, but when she didn't join him, he stopped and turned around. "What?"

"You don't have to walk me home." She preferred he didn't. She was already embarrassed that she'd panicked over Junia, and now that she was thinking more clearly, she'd also insulted Malachi by making assumptions about him, on top of getting Jesse and Charity involved. She was also a little confused about Nelson's gentlemanly behavior. He'd been the exact opposite earlier that day.

"*Nee* self-respecting *mann* would let you walk home in the dark."

"I have a flashlight."

He lifted his. "We'll have double the light." He half-smiled again.

She sighed. Arguing would make her look more foolish, so she nodded and fell into step beside him, prepared for the small talk she would have to engage in. Her house wasn't far, but it wasn't that close either. Plenty of time for banal conversation, something she intensely disliked. If she was going to talk to someone, she wanted the dialogue to be meaningful. Besides, she had enough shallow conversations with Junia, who could chatter nonstop about basically nothing.

Nelson started to whistle.

Ella looked up at him. He was staring straight ahead, his flashlight raised enough to illuminate the road in front of them. His other hand was in his pocket, and tiny puffs of his breath hung in the air as he continued to whistle the pleasant, unfamiliar melody. "What song is that?" she asked, shivering again.

He turned to her. "Song?"

"The one you were whistling?"

He shrugged. "*Nee* idea. Sometimes a tune will come to me. Most of the time I don't realize I'm whistling, so I never remember what I just whistled. It's a habit I developed as a *kinn*. Some of my brothers do it too. Just don't be around Jesse when he starts."

"Why?"

"He couldn't carry a tune if he had a bucket."

"Ah." She shivered again. It seemed like the temperature had dropped even more since she left the house. Then she felt the heavy weight of Nelson's coat on her shoulders. She stopped walking and touched the lapel. "What are you doing?"

"You're clearly cold, so I gave you *mei* coat." He continued to walk.

She hurried to catch up, eyeing his short-sleeved shirt. "But now you're going to be cold."

"*Nee.* I run hot. I usually put on a coat out of habit more than anything. I end up taking it off sooner than later."

She didn't quite believe him, but he also didn't seem to be bothered by the dipping degrees. They were almost to her house, so it didn't matter anyway. But as they continued to walk and he started whistling again, she stopped shivering. His coat engulfed her and was toasty warm. She pulled it closer as they rounded the corner of her street. In the distance she could see the bright streetlamp that shone on the grocery store parking lot. Other than their flashlights, it was the only light around.

Despite the cold and being upset with Junia, not to mention being chagrined that she likely had overreacted—again—she kind of, sort of enjoyed the last stretch of her walk home. Nelson's whistling was a nice accompaniment and much better than striving for a casual conversation. But she was curious about something. "Have you decided to buy the warehouse?"

The whistling stopped, followed by a heavy pause. "*Nee.* I haven't."

Relief washed over her. She still had time to convince her father to purchase it, and she would make sure to stress that there was already another person interested in it. Hopefully that would light a fire under her dad's typical reticence.

"The Realtor couldn't give me much history about it," Nelson said. "Do you know anything?"

He had no idea he'd just given her a chance to influence his decision not to buy the building if she were willing to fudge the facts. But she wasn't, not even for a prime business opportunity. She couldn't live with herself if she did. "*Nee.*" *Other than it's a perfect place to expand my store.*

"Oh. Well, the thought occurred to me that you might, considering you're so interested in whether I'm going to buy the property."

He shrugged and shifted his flashlight to the other hand. "I haven't settled it in *mei* mind about the butcher shop anyway."

"Butcher shop?" Her left brow lifted. "You're a butcher?"

"*Ya*. I was considering opening *mei* own shop in Birch Creek, but we already have a family-owned deli that opened a year and a half ago. I don't want to take any business away from them." He blew out a breath. "I should probably stick to farming."

"You're a farmer too?"

He nodded. "All *mei* life. Thought I would be one too, until recently."

"What made you change your mind?"

Nelson didn't look at her. "Life."

His tone warned her against delving deeper, so she kept quiet. But her mind was whirring. Having a butcher shop next door could be advantageous. They sold a few meats and cheeses at the grocery store, but not the specialized cuts that people had to go to Barton to purchase. Probably Birch Creek too, now that she knew they had a deli. Customers who went to Nelson's shop would then stop by hers for the rest of their supplies. It would be even better than expanding because she wouldn't have to spend the money to purchase the building. "I think you should buy it."

"Why?"

His quick question caught her off guard. "Because . . ." She couldn't just blurt out that her reasoning was self-serving. That might turn him off completely. "We could use a butcher shop here. Marigold is a growing community, and you would have plenty of customers."

"That's *gut* and all, but I have another problem. I don't know anything about running a business."

Ella grinned. "I can help you with that."

Three

Nelson hadn't expected to spend his evening searching for his wayward nephew—who was going to get a stern talking-to as soon as he showed up—and revealing to Ella his plans for the warehouse, much less admitting that he didn't have a clue what he was doing. But the biggest surprise was her offer to help him. For a split second he couldn't fathom why she wanted to, but then he remembered her family owned the grocery store next door and understanding started to dawn. She wasn't doing this out of kindness or for his benefit but with her own motives. He might not know much about business, but it was plain as day that their customer base would overlap. While it made sense that his *possible* butcher shop would be advantageous to her business, it also raised his guard.

"When I, um, *we* decided to move here from Lancaster and open the store," Ella said, her tone tinged with excitement, "I bought at least twenty books about running a business. I keep them in my—in my *daed*'s office. They were very helpful while we were learning the ropes."

He didn't respond. He was open to assistance, and he had plenty of entrepreneurs in his family who could teach him how to run a business. But even with their help, he still had a lot to learn, and most of that would be on the job. What he didn't need was a woman's help, especially not this one. Being around the female persuasion after he'd sworn them off was the worst thing he could do. Besides, even though he and Ella were being cordial to each other, he'd seen her unpleasant side. *No thanks.*

"Well? What do you think about *mei* proposal?"

He turned to her. *A proposal? What?*

"About working together. We can start as soon as the warehouse sale is final." She grinned. His coat was so big the collar was almost covering her mouth, and the hem hung well past her waist. She kind of looked cute, not that he was open to noticing. "What do you think?" she asked.

He pulled his gaze from her and was relieved to see that they were almost to her house. On instinct, he quickened his steps. The faster he took her home, the sooner he could get away. He quickly outpaced her, and he could hear the patter of her footsteps behind him.

"You can use *mei* catalogs to order your equipment." She was still yammering, although it was breathless yammering. "Can you slow down a little?"

He shortened his strides but didn't turn around.

Now she was alongside him again. "I don't have any specific to butchery, but you'll need some display cases, shelving, cleaning supplies—those sorts of things. Oh, and a cash register. I keep telling *Daed* we need one too, but he refuses. He prefers to add in his head or on his little adding machine, which is basically just a calculator. It would be so much faster if we had a register, though."

He never would have guessed she was so talkative. Or presumptuous. He hadn't agreed to anything, including running a butcher shop to begin with, and definitely not to her proposal, whatever that was. They were a few feet from her front porch. *Almost free!*

"Nelson."

He froze. She had stopped behind him, and the adamant way she said his name made him turn around, even though he didn't want to.

"I'd appreciate a little input from you." She lifted her chin. "We can't be partners if you're not willing to do your share."

He barked with laughter. "Partners? *That* was your proposal?"

"*Ya.*" Her chin tilted higher. "Weren't you listening?"

He'd already fallen for two liars, and he wasn't apt to believe her either. And she wasn't just lying, she was trying to take advantage of him for her own gain. "Sounds more like a plot to sabotage me than a proposal," he said.

"What?" She looked and sounded completely offended. "I would never do that to you, or anyone else."

"How am I supposed to know that? We just met and all of a sudden you want to be partners?" Before she could protest, he said, "Don't bother. I made *mei* decision. I'm not buying the warehouse, or any other place in Marigold."

"But—"

He held up his hand. "You're home now. *Mei* obligation is done." He started to walk away.

"I didn't obligate you to do anything," she called out to him.

Nelson spun around. "You sure were trying to."

Her mouth dropped open. Then closed. Satisfied he'd shut her up for good, he spun on his heel and hurried off. If Malachi wasn't at Jesse's by the time he got there, Nelson was leaving him behind. He'd have to figure out his own way back to Birch Creek. Nelson was more than ready to get away from Ella Yoder and Marigold, and he wasn't coming back.

·◦◦◦·

Ella watched as Nelson rushed off, practically running down her short driveway. An icky sensation filled her stomach. She had handled that badly. Very badly, according to Nelson's angry expression. A bit of anger started to rise within her too, though. How dare he accuse her of plotting against him? Her proposal was extremely sensible. She hadn't suggested a legal partnership, but more of a mutually beneficial business relationship that would help make their stores successful. Now that she thought about it, though, she shouldn't have said they would be partners. Or even brought it up. He had a teeny-weeny point about them barely knowing each other. Why would he trust her based on almost nothing?

She winced. It wasn't the first time she leaped before she thought, and it probably wouldn't be the last. But in this instance, she might have cost Nelson a prime opportunity.

She turned and went into the house, searching her mind for a way to fix what she'd inadvertently broken in record time. As she opened the door, she felt a blast of warm air from the woodstove on the opposite side of the living room. *Daed* was sitting in his usual spot—an old hickory rocker with a well-worn quilted cushion on the seat and a crossword puzzle on his lap. And on the couch across from him was . . . Junia.

Ella's eyes widened. In all the excitement about Nelson's butcher shop, she'd forgotten Junia had disappeared. And now she was here, sitting in front of the cozy fire, bringing a mug of hot chocolate to her lips, her eyebrows lifting in mockery.

"Welcome back, Ella," *Daed* said. He looked her up and down. "New outfit?"

She glanced at Nelson's coat enveloping her. That was something else she'd forgotten. Apparently he had, too, since he stormed off without asking for it back. As she yanked it off, she glared at Junia. "Where have you been?"

"Out." Junia cradled the mug in her hands.

"With Malachi?"

"That's none of your business, Ella."

She wanted to scream. "You were gone all day."

Junia took another nonchalant sip of her drink as their father cleared his throat.

"Didn't you stop to think about your job? Or anyone else that was inconvenienced?"

Daed set the crossword book down on the end table next to him. "Now that everyone's home safe and sound, I'm going to bed."

"But, *Daed*—"

"*Gute nacht.* See you two in the morning."

Ella didn't bother saying anything else to him. He always left the room when she and Junia started arguing.

As soon as he was gone, Junia jumped up from the couch. "Ella, I'm in love!" She clasped her hands together and sighed.

"With Malachi?" Ella shook her head. That was ridiculous, even for Junia.

"*Nee*, with Horace," she cracked, referring to their rooster. "Obviously I'm talking about Malachi. He's perfect."

"You've known him for one day. Not even twenty-four hours."

"But it feels like a lifetime." Junia plopped back on the couch and sighed again. "I'm going to marry that man. You just watch."

Ella bit her tongue before she said something she'd regret. Did Malachi have any idea how lazy Junia was, or that this was the third time she'd declared herself in instant love since she was thirteen? Of course not, but there wasn't any point in saying so. Junia would do whatever she wanted, just like she always did. *I wanted her to find a husband, didn't I?* She just didn't think it would be so fast and with someone she knew so little about.

Junia sat up. "Whose coat is that?"

"Nelson's." She'd have to take it to Jesse's tomorrow so he could give it to him. Or maybe she should run it over to him now. No, it was too late to do that. Since Junia was home, Malachi was surely at Jesse and Charity's by now, and he and Nelson were undoubtedly on their way back to Birch Creek. They would arrive late tonight, thanks to Junia and Malachi's thoughtlessness. "I don't suppose you're going to tell me where you two were all day?"

A slow smile spread over Junia's face. *"Nee."*

"Why not?"

"Because I don't have to."

No, she didn't. Her father certainly wasn't going to make her, and Ella didn't care anymore. She walked over to the gas lamp near *Daed*'s rocker and turned it off. Without another word to her sister, she went upstairs to her room and sat on the edge of the bed, still holding Nelson's coat. Without thinking, she hugged it to her chest and caught the scent of woodsmoke and something indefinable. Nelson.

She popped up from the bed and laid the coat over her hope chest. The cedar chest had belonged to her mother, who passed away from meningitis when Ella was ten and Junia was four. Ever since then, their father, with the help of her aunts, had raised her and Junia. When they moved to Marigold, her father had given her the chest. *"Your* mamm *would have wanted you to have this,"* he'd said, his eyes glassy. Ella treasured the gift. *If only* Mamm *were here now.* Sixteen years had passed since her mother's death, and she still missed her very much. There were even times when she sort of missed *Aenti* Tabitha and *Aenti* Cora, who were less than supportive about their move to Marigold and never supportive of Ella's take-charge attitude.

"A woman should be meek," *Aenti* Tabitha would say.

"And mild," *Aenti* Cora always added. "And of course, sweet and pretty."

"Like Junia." *Aenti* Tabitha always smiled at the mention of Junia's beauty. "It won't be long before she finds a husband."

"You could learn a lot from her, Ella," *Aenti* Cora never failed to mention.

Ella yanked the clips out of her *kapp*. What Tabitha and Cora failed to notice or turned a blind eye to was the fact that Junia wasn't always meek, mild, or sweet. But she was pretty. No one could deny that—not even Ella. And although no one would probably believe it now, there was a time when she got along with her sister, especially after *Mamm* died. For almost two years Junia would leave her bed and climb in with Ella, and they would cry over their grief until they both fell asleep. But as they grew older, they grew apart. Now they rarely talked about *Mamm*.

With a sigh, she unbraided her hair, trying not to think about the sister she was mad at and the aunts who refused to talk to her since she and her family arrived in Marigold. As she brushed through the long strands, her thoughts switched to Nelson again, or more accurately, her guilt. She didn't want her foolishness to be the reason he didn't buy the warehouse. That wasn't right or fair to him. She had to apologize, somehow.

Her brushing slowed as an image of him came to her mind. She could see some family resemblance between Nelson, Jesse, and Malachi, especially their eyes, which were all a startling shade of blue. They had the same sloped nose, although Nelson's had a little bump at the top. She was surprised she'd noticed something so inconsequential. But that was where the similarities ended. All three men had different hair—Malachi's straight and blond, Jesse's dark brown and curly, and Nelson's was lighter brown and wavy. Their builds were different too. Nelson was burly, but she wasn't sure why Junia made it sound like a bad thing. He looked strong, and when they were bickering in her driveway, she'd seen the outline of his biceps underneath his short sleeves. If he wasn't such a jerk, she would have thought he was handsome.

She blinked. What was she doing thinking about his burly biceps? She quickly rebraided her hair and readied for bed. When she turned around, she saw Nelson's coat. She was in the wrong and needed to make things right with him, even if he wasn't going to buy the warehouse. She knelt by the side of her bed and said her nightly prayers, asking for forgiveness for what she'd done to Nelson and for patience for herself, a trait that was always in short supply.

As she slipped under the cold covers and pulled the thick quilt over her, she thought about Junia and Malachi again. Her sister wasn't in love—she was infatuated. It was inconceivable that anyone could fall in love at first sight. That only happened in fairy tales. It certainly didn't happen to her and Nelson. More like aversion at first sight.

She rolled on her side and scoffed. *Me and Nelson.* They couldn't even get through a conversation without fighting, never mind a business partnership. Or any other relationship. Not that it mattered. She had more important things to do than worry about a social life— like running the grocery store. Between her father's complacency and Junia's disinterest, the store's success rested on her shoulders. She just wished the burden wasn't so heavy.

Four

"A re you ever going to speak to me again?"

Nelson continued to ignore Malachi, gripping the horse's reins as he guided his buggy down the road where he lived with his parents and younger brothers, which wasn't far from his sister and brother-in-law's farm. He wasn't sure what time it was, but they had left Marigold shortly after eight o'clock, and it took more than an hour to get back to Birch Creek. But that was during daylight, and Nelson was driving more slowly in the dark. He was beat and still irritated with Ella. But he was furious with Malachi.

"I deserve to be in the doghouse," his nephew said, a sincere apology in his tone. "I lost track of time and I'm sorry. I promise it won't happen again."

He knew Malachi would keep that promise, but Nelson didn't care, because other than visiting Jesse and Charity, his nephew wasn't going to spend much time in Marigold.

"We didn't mean to cause any worry," Malachi said. "But . . ."

Malachi's hanging thought caught Nelson's attention. "But what?"

"I've never felt like this before. Ever."

Nelson glanced at him, but with the winter shield over the buggy and the lack of street lighting, it was impossible to see his expression in the dark interior. There were minimal lights on the outside of the buggy, but Crackerjack knew his way home.

"Have you ever been in love?" Malachi asked.

He stifled a groan. Had Malachi lost his mind? He couldn't be in love. He shouldn't be.

"Because I think I am."

"You're not," Nelson grumbled. "Trust me."

Malachi didn't say anything for a minute, and Nelson thought he'd dropped the subject. *Thank you, God.*

"How do you know?" Malachi asked.

"Because you're not. Okay?" The leather reins dug into his hand. "You just met Julia—"

"Junia." He let out a silly sigh. "Her name is . . . Junia."

"Talk to *yer daed* about this," Nelson snapped. "Jalon will set you straight."

"You don't have to be so touchy. I was just telling you how I feel."

"*Yer* feelings are wrong."

Silence filled the buggy again until they were almost to the Chupps'. "At least *yer* speaking to me now," Malachi said.

"Only if we talk about something else."

After a long pause, Malachi said, "Did you leave your coat at Jesse's?"

I wish. "*Nee.* I let Ella borrow it."

"Oh *really.*"

"Knock it off." Practically since he was born, his nephew was a tease. He'd been a precocious child too. "She got cold while looking for you and Junia."

"Oh. Sorry. If you need to borrow a coat, you can use one of mine."

Despite his grumpiness, Nelson chuckled. "You know it won't fit."

He and Malachi were close to the same height but nowhere near the same when it came to weight.

"Maybe one of *Daed*'s?"

Jalon wasn't as slight as Malachi, but his wouldn't fit either. "I'll be fine," he said, although he wished he at least had a jacket. When he was walking with Ella, he didn't feel the cold as much, but he became chilled sitting in the buggy. Fortunately, he had a couple of pullover sweaters he could use until he got his coat back from Ella. He'd realized right before they left Jesse's that she hadn't given it back, and Charity offered to get it from her. While he was hot natured, he wouldn't survive an Ohio winter without his thick coat, and because of his forgetfulness, he'd have to return to Marigold sooner than later.

"I can pick it up for you on Saturday," Malachi said.

Nice. Now he wouldn't have to go back to Marigold for a good long while, and he wouldn't have to risk another encounter with Ella. Although she did help him out in one way—she validated his decision to avoid women. They brought nothing but heartache, and in Ella's case, one big migraine. "You going to hang out with Jesse?"

"*Nee*. I'm going to Junia's."

"Okay." He did a double take. "Wait—you're seeing her again?"

"*Ya*. We have a date."

Nelson turned into Malachi's driveway and pulled the buggy to a stop. His nephew needed to pump the brakes on his infatuation with this woman. "If Phoebe finds out, she'll think *yer* serious," he said.

"We are. I don't care if *Mamm* knows."

"Didn't you say that about Rachel Stoltzfus a few months ago?"

"This is different." He started to get out of the buggy.

Nelson didn't want to remind Malachi about how Rachel had dumped him, or that he'd spent a month moping over her. But maybe he should. "Malachi—"

"*Junia* is different. See you later." He sprinted to the house.

Nelson recognized that pep in Malachi's step, and he was sure his nephew was repeating the same mistake Nelson had made with Norene. With hindsight, he could see he'd rebounded from Miriam with her. That didn't make the rejection any less acute, but he'd learned his lesson.

He started to go after Malachi, then held back. Would he have listened to anyone when he was in the throes of his supposed love for Norene? Probably not. And with Malachi almost inside and the hour being late, Nelson didn't want to broach the subject with him tonight. But he should, and before Saturday. Malachi might pay attention to the voice of experience.

He turned the buggy around and headed for his house, thinking about the reason for his and Malachi's romantic bad luck. He couldn't exactly put all the blame at Jesse's feet, but it was the advertisement that had brought Rachel, Miriam, and Norene to Birch Creek. The prank ad had worked for some couples. His brothers, twins Zeb and Zeke, along with Owen and Ezra, had all met their wives because of it. But the deception had caused problems for others, not only him and Malachi. While Nelson now knew he couldn't trust a pretty face or his own judgment, apparently Malachi needed more schooling. He didn't want his nephew, or anyone else, to have to deal with the heartache he'd experienced.

A short time later, he was home. He quickly put up Crackerjack and gave him a little extra feed before heading to the house. The gas lamp in the living room was still on, but everyone had gone to bed. His stomach growling, he headed for the kitchen. Thanks to Ella, her sister, and his smitten nephew, he hadn't finished his second helping of quiche.

He opened the gas-powered refrigerator and pulled out a packet of pastrami he made last week, a package of thinly sliced Swiss cheese, and a container of stone-ground mustard. Taking a half loaf of fresh bread from the wooden bread box on the counter, he prepared his double-decker sandwich. He was almost finished when his father came into the kitchen.

"Hey, *sohn*." *Daed* went straight to the cabinet and took out a glass. He turned on the tap. "When did you get home?"

"Just now." He put one more slice of Swiss cheese on the pastrami and topped the sandwich with a third slice of bread.

Daed moved to a drawer and opened it. After a quick search, he found a packet of antacid tablets. He opened it and dropped them into his drink. "Your *mamm* made lasagna tonight."

"You didn't like it?"

"I liked it too much." *Daed* swirled the glass, then drank the mixture all in one gulp. He scowled and set the glass in the sink. "Tastes awful, but it works. So, what did you think about the warehouse? Will it work for the shop?"

Nelson shrugged and took his plate to the table. He sat down and picked up the huge sandwich. "Probably, but I'm not going to buy it."

Daed moved to the table and sat next to him. "Why not?"

"Changed *mei* mind about the butcher shop." He took a bite. Mmm. The pastrami had just the right amount of salt and spice. He'd have to write down the recipe.

"When did you decide that?"

The minute I met Ella. That wasn't completely true, but close enough. "I did some more thinking and decided it wasn't for me. I'm not a businessman."

"Maybe you could be. You'll never know if you don't try."

Nelson set down his food. "Why are you so eager for me to do this?"

"I wouldn't call it eager," his father said. "But I've never seen you more content than when you're experimenting with deli recipes. You're also a skilled butcher. I'm amazed at how quickly you picked it up."

He was too, but he'd attributed that to Samuel's teaching. "I can do butchery on the side and farm full-time. I don't need my own shop."

Daed rubbed his thumb over the side of their extra-large kitchen table. "Do you really want to be a farmer?"

Nelson hesitated. He couldn't lie to his father, or anyone else. He'd been on the receiving end of enough deception. He shook his head.

Daed nodded. "I figured as much. This might surprise you, but I never fell in love with farming."

Whoa. "I'm not surprised. I'm shocked."

He shrugged. "I used to think I was, since we come from generations of farmers. It's in *mei* blood, but even after we moved from Fredericktown and became more successful, I've always just seen it as a job. A good job, and at many times a satisfying one, but ultimately only a job." He looked at Nelson. "I had a similar conversation with Owen a couple years ago when I asked him to take over the farm after I retire."

Nelson nodded, remembering when *Daed* had informed them about the decision. No one in the family disputed the choice.

"He loves farming. He gets up in the morning and he can't wait to *geh* outside and take care of the dairy cows, manage the fields, come up with new and improved ways to increase the yields."

Nelson had seen that same excitement in his older brother. Out of all eleven of the Bontrager sons, except maybe Mose and Mahlon, his younger twin brothers, Owen was the only one passionate about farming.

"I've seen that same spark of excitement in you." *Daed* smiled. "But it's not when you're working the land. I first noticed it when you came back from Devon's and started using your skills here. You should be a butcher, Nelson. That much is plain. It would be a shame if you didn't see it through." He brought his fist up to his mouth. "Ugh. That antacid is taking its sweet time. I'm going back to bed." He stood. "Just think about what I've said before you reject the shop idea completely. Don't be afraid to walk out in faith."

"Hope you feel better," Nelson said as his father started to leave.

"Me too."

When his father was gone, Nelson looked at his sandwich, particularly at the bits of pastrami on the sides. He could remember every single ingredient he used to flavor the meat, the exact amounts, and each step of the process. He'd never been one to pay attention to detail . . . until he started making his own deli meat. He wasn't thrilled with the actual butchering, and he always did it as quickly and humanely as possible. But he hadn't been aware there was a creative side to it until he started experimenting with seasonings and methods. That was when he was in his element.

He continued eating the sandwich, mulling over his father's words. By the time he finished the last bite, he still wasn't totally convinced he needed his own shop, and not just because he was concerned about his ability—and possible lack thereof—to run a business. Ella Yoder was still a consideration. If he purchased the warehouse, she might see it as a sign that he wanted to be partners with her. *Definitely not.* Of course he could tell her that under no circumstances would they ever do anything together, but he sensed she wasn't one to be easily put off and he wasn't sure if he wanted the hassle.

He picked up his plate and put it in the sink, then filled a glass with water and drained it before heading to his bedroom upstairs. He was halfway up the staircase when a thought slammed into him. Why was he letting Ella get to him? Worse, why was he letting her influence his business decisions? *Why am I being so stupid?* Or was it cowardly? Either way, allowing her to sway him because she was annoying—and a woman—was dumb. That he was only realizing it now proved he had to get a grip on his life.

Thoughts continued to fly as he reached the top of the stairs. He was using Ella as an excuse. He was afraid of making another mistake. He'd made plenty of those in the past, although they were all relationship related. He'd been impulsive with both Miriam and Norene, and looking back, even his decision to go to Fredericktown had been spur of the moment and done with little thought. While that had turned out well for him, he easily could have landed on his face again. *I don't want to be a failure.*

There was also another motivation for him to move to Marigold, one he hadn't revealed to anyone and barely acknowledged himself. When he returned from Fredericktown, he thought he was over his heartache. Miriam had moved back to her home district in Michigan to marry her ex-boyfriend, who had followed her to Birch Creek to beg her to come back to him. He didn't have to worry about ever seeing her again.

But Norene was still here with Ben Miller. While he was living at Devon's, he'd heard that she and Ben announced their engagement a month after he'd seen them together. Now they were married, and although he didn't have many dealings with her or Ben during the week, he saw them at church on Sundays, blissfully happy. While he wasn't as miserable as he had been when he found out about her and Ben, the ache hadn't completely disappeared.

There was also the added issue of more single women in Birch Creek than men. When Jesse listed the advertisement, there had been a lot more men, and his ad was still being seen in Amish communities nationwide. The women weren't coming in waves anymore, as word was starting to spread that Birch Creek was no longer bachelor central. But they were still trickling in, and they were all looking for a husband. More than once he'd had to turn an eager *maedel* down. Keenly aware of the blistering sting of rejection, he didn't want to be in the position to hurt any of them or waste their time.

He stood in the dark, unable to take a single step farther. He could play it safe and keep making excuses, being stuck in analysis paralysis while never moving forward, continue working a good job that he found little satisfaction in, and ducking every single woman in Birch Creek while trying to avoid Norene and Ben. Or . . . he could step out in faith, buy the warehouse, start his dream business, remain single, and deal with Ella when necessary.

He went to his room and got on his knees. He hadn't spent enough time praying about his decision. That needed to change.

Lord, what should I do?

Five

Wendy snuggled into her gray down coat and tucked her legs underneath her as she watched the sunrise from her mother's front stoop. There was enough room on the concrete slab for a comfortable outdoor chair, and since she'd moved to Marigold, she'd made it a habit to drink her morning coffee as she took in the dawning light. The pale sky grew lighter as soft color streaked across the clouds. Since she had on her coat and fleece leggings, the cold didn't bother her, and the hot coffee warmed her inside. She soaked in the quiet serenity of her surroundings . . . at least until Monroe barked from inside the living room.

She smiled and opened the door for him. He bounded into the front yard, and she kept her eye on him. He used to run off and visit the Waglers next door, frustrating Mom and Charity to no end. Jesse and Micah had built a fence around the backyard, but Wendy trained Monroe to remain near the house so he could explore the front yard too. It took some doing, but now he stayed close to her, despite moments like now when he looked longingly at the field that separated her mother's house from the Bontragers'. Later this morning, she would take him over there so he could have some Charity and

Jesse time and play with Brook. The young dog was always excited to see Monroe, and the two of them acted like they were best buddies.

She placed her half-full mug on the small round table next to the chair and pulled her phone out of her pocket. Internet was spotty here, and after a month she gave up trying to connect online and used her data plan instead. But the longer she lived in Marigold, the less time she spent on the net, and she had shut down all her social media three weeks ago. Probably a bad idea, since she often used her accounts to network for her business—a necessary part of drumming up clients. She didn't miss social media at all, and the less time she spent scrolling, the more time she had to read, something she used to love when she was a kid but had done very little of over the years outside of reading briefs, case law, and endless emails.

Monroe sniffed the ground as he made his way back to her and parked himself right in front of her chair. On alert and sitting on his haunches, he faced the front yard, his pale-blue eyes taking in the morning activity of birds singing, leaves fluttering, and two gray squirrels chasing each other as they darted up the oak tree on the other side of the yard.

She opened her Bible app and started her daily reading. That was another thing she had neglected in favor of her law career—her faith. It had been years since she attended church, and when she first went with her mother several months ago, it felt weird to be in the service. But like all the other changes that had happened since she left New York, she had settled into a routine of church attendance, Bible reading, and prayer. She'd never been more content.

After reading a chapter in Romans while she finished her coffee, she exited the app and stared at her phone. Why was she reading God's Word from this device when there was a print Bible on the coffee table in the house? She was about to set a reminder on her phone to use the printed version, then stopped and stared at the phone, a little shocked at how dependent she was on technology. She shut off the phone and put it in her pocket, relying on her own memory to use her mother's coffee table Bible tomorrow.

She stood, opened the front door, and motioned for Monroe to follow her inside. After hanging up her coat, she headed for the kitchen, where she found her mother sitting at the table with her coffee and a piece of wheat toast with sugar-free strawberry jam, perusing an old issue of *Reader's Digest*.

Mom looked at her. "Good morning, dear. I just sat down. Have you eaten yet?"

"No, but I was thinking about making—"

"Bacon and eggs, right?" Her penciled-in eyebrows lifted in anticipation. "With biscuits?"

"Oatmeal," she said with a grin. "Sorry to disappoint."

Mom frowned and picked up her toast. "Hope springs eternal. Guess I'll have to ask Charity to come over and make me one of her delicious breakfasts. If I have your permission, of course."

Wendy rolled her eyes as she went to the pantry and pulled out the can of steel-cut oats. Sometimes her mother acted like a rebellious teenager, and right now she was sounding like one. "I encourage you to watch what you eat—"

"You dictate what I eat." Mom raised a finger.

She sighed and went to the stove. "Whatever you say. Just know I dictate because I love you and I want you to be around for a long time."

"Oh, sweetie. I know that. But what good is being around if I can't live a little too?"

She had a point. Wendy measured out the oats in a pan. Unlike her mother, she enjoyed eating healthy food. She glanced over her shoulder. "How about we go to Pancho's for lunch?"

"Really?" Mom broke out into a grin. Pancho's was her favorite restaurant.

She added some water to the oats. "It's Taco Tuesday, isn't it?"

"Yes, but I can't remember the last time we had tacos. Thank you, Wendy. I accept."

Monroe barked his approval.

Wendy smiled and turned on the stove, then refilled her coffee and sat down at the table, glad she had made her mother's day. She had planned to go back to her office later that morning, but she could skip today. There wasn't anything pressing on her calendar, and she wasn't looking forward to spending hours inside organizing her files, something she hadn't done yet. Most of her paperwork was digital, but she did maintain some paper copies of important and certified documents. They were in several boxes in the tiny supply closet by her office. She'd tackle them . . . someday.

"You're quiet this morning." Mom bit into the toast.

Wendy nodded.

"Penny for your thoughts? Or is it a nickel now, due to inflation?"

She chuckled. "For you, it's free of charge." Then she grew serious. Even though she was pondering work, she didn't want to talk about it. "I was thinking about planting a garden this spring."

Mom paused, her toast hovering in midair. "Huh," was all she said as she set the toast on the plate.

"Huh? What does that mean?"

"I'm surprised, that's all. You've never been the outdoorsy type."

The oatmeal on the stove started to bubble, and Wendy got up from her seat. She stirred the pot and turned down the gas flame. "True. But I've seen so many lovely gardens around here. The soil seems well suited for them."

"The Amish do have wonderful gardens."

"And we have all that backyard space. We could section off some of it and grow our own vegetables." She sat back down. "Tomatoes, cucumbers, squash, green beans."

"Peas? I'd love to have some English peas." Mom tapped her chin. "Maybe a pumpkin or two." She smiled. "What a great idea. Unfortunately, I don't have much advice to give. Nor would I be much help. I don't know anything about gardening. Your father had thought about it, though."

"Oh? I didn't know that."

"Yes. Before he died, he'd checked out some gardening books from the library. I don't know if he would have actually planted one, though. That's a lot of work for people our age."

A lump formed in Wendy's throat. Her father had passed away a little over three years ago, four years after he and Mom moved to Marigold. It was their dream retirement plan to live in Amish country, and they did it, much to her chagrin. She hadn't wanted them to leave, and she'd worried about her mother after Dad died. She had good reason to, considering her mother wasn't in great health. But that wasn't the reason her heart ached right now. How much time had she missed out on over the years, always taking her parents for granted? Work had taken precedence, even after her father passed and up until she moved to Marigold. And what did she have to show for all those years of climbing the corporate lawyer ladder? Boxes of paperwork and a broken heart.

"I'm sure Charity can help us out." Mom rose from her chair, her movements stiff from arthritis, and grabbed the handles of her walker. Monroe scooted out of the way as she walked over to the kitchen junk drawer and pulled out a pad and pencil. "Your oatmeal is done."

She'd forgotten all about her breakfast. While her mother made her way back to the table, Wendy finished making her oatmeal—plain with a splash of almond milk—and brought it to the table. For the next hour, she and Mom discussed the garden plans, and by the time they were finished, they had a rudimentary sketch with a list of vegetables to plant and needed supplies.

"This is going to be fun!" Sitting back in her chair, Mom grinned. "I can't wait for spring."

"Let's get through Christmas first." But she was also excited. "Which reminds me—we need to get the decorations up. How about we do that when we get back from lunch?"

"You're not working today?"

"I decided to take the day off." She stood and picked up her empty oatmeal bowl and Mom's half-eaten toast. When she had to urge her mother to finish the meager breakfast, she said she was saving room for Pancho's. Wendy didn't argue.

"Not that I'm complaining," Mom said, wincing a little as she stood, "but you haven't been going to your office much lately. I didn't think you could work from home without stable internet service."

"I can't." She turned on the tap and started to wash the dishes. They had a dishwasher, but she and Mom dirtied so few dishes there wasn't a point in using it. Besides, she found the act of handwashing them meditative. "It's the Christmas season. Things are slow."

"Well, that makes sense. It's just that I'm used to you working all the time. I figured when you got your office in Barton you would be spending most of your time there." She was standing by Wendy now. "Again, I'm not complaining. I love having you here." She patted her on the back of her shoulder and moved away, pushing her silver rollator walker toward the kitchen exit. "I'll get some of the decorations out of the closet."

"Mom—"

"Just the ones I can manage. Don't worry, dear. I won't overdo it. I refuse to be too tired for Pancho's!" She snapped her fingers and Monroe followed her out of the kitchen.

Wendy chuckled. Her mother didn't need to snap to get Monroe to do her bidding. The dog was constantly following her around the house, and his favorite spot—other than taking over the love seat—was at her feet while she was in her recliner. Wendy walked him every day, had trained him to stay in the yard, and was working on stopping his penchant for begging, something that hadn't materialized yet. But ultimately his heart belonged to Mom, and Wendy was grateful for that. Monroe had been an abused stray that showed up just when her mother needed him. *I love that dog.*

She paused, her hands in the sink of soapy water. She wasn't an animal person. Or a garden person. Or even a watch-the-sunrise person. She'd also never had time for Taco Tuesdays or to put up Christmas decorations, other than a silver wreath on her apartment door in NYC, and that usually stayed up until April or May. One year it stayed up all twelve months.

But now she was even thinking about adding more decorations to her mother's sparse scheme. Not store-bought ones, though. She had her eye on the pine tree in her front yard that stayed green year-round. Small cones had fallen on the ground around the base, and she thought about decorating with cranberries too, for a spot of color. Mom didn't have a large tree, only a small tabletop one that sat on the coffee table in the living room. Maybe she could craft a few tiny, handmade ornaments. She'd always wanted to learn a handicraft, and sewing appealed to her. As usual, there had never been enough time.

No, that wasn't true. She'd made time for what was important to her—work. Not her relationship with her parents or maintaining friendships or even dating, although she finally had her first real romantic relationship right before she took her sabbatical. That had ended in disaster, and she wasn't going to go through that again. She'd never planned to get married anyway. At least that part of her thinking hadn't changed.

She finished washing and drying the dishes, and after she put them away, she joined her mother and took out the rest of the Christmas decorations. A few of them were heirlooms, and she listened as her mother told oft-repeated stories about the past.

She paid attention and savored every word.

·∾༒ఛ·

Ella followed the hostess as they threaded through the crowd in Pancho's and made their way to a two-seater table. As she sat down facing the front door, the hostess placed a menu in front of her. "Happy Taco Tuesday," she said with a smile. "Your waitress will be with you soon."

She'd forgotten about the weekly holiday until she walked into the restaurant and saw the standing placard sign with *Taco Tuesday* written on it in neon letters. She placed three plastic shopping bags on the floor next to her chair and shrugged off her coat.

A waitress wearing a white shirt with vibrant-colored embroidery on it and her black hair in a bun set a basket of chips and salsa on the table. "What would you like to drink?" she asked with a slight Hispanic accent.

"Iced tea, and I'm actually ready to order. Three crunchy beef tacos, please. Oh, and a bowl of the spiciest salsa you have."

She nodded and walked away. Ella glanced around the restaurant. There were a few Amish here, but no one she knew. They were probably all from Birch Creek. She did recognize two women a few tables away, and she waved to them. Shirley Pearson and her daughter, Wendy, were loyal customers at her store, especially Wendy, who came in at least once a week or more. Ella noticed Shirley had a plateful of soft tacos. She didn't realize the woman had that big of an appetite.

A teenage boy appeared with the salsa and tea. He set them in front of her and quickly walked away. Her stomach growled. Normally she didn't leave the store during work hours, but they needed a few items they didn't have at the store, and Ella wanted to get some fabric to make a new dress. Junia said she would help *Daed* with the customers, which made Ella suspicious. But when her sister asked her to pick up some navy blue yarn at Walmart, it made sense.

"I'm going to make Malachi a scarf," she said. "I'll need two skeins."

"Fine." She was still irritated with Junia about Saturday, and of course her sister wouldn't work without getting something out of it—in this case yarn. She had to admit Junia was an exceptional knitter, something Ella didn't have the patience for. She preferred to sew, although lately she hadn't had much time to sew for fun. A half-pieced quilt was in a box under her bed, waiting for her to come back to.

Whenever she did go to Barton, Ella made sure to stop at Pancho's. She preferred chimichangas, but with tacos being half priced today, she couldn't resist. She had just dipped a chip into the salsa when she saw a familiar man walk inside the restaurant. Her mouth dropped open. Nelson Bontrager.

The hostess greeted him, and Ella saw him lift his index finger. Table for one. She quickly crammed the chip in her mouth and looked around the restaurant again. There was only one empty seat. At her table. After their encounter on Saturday, she was sure he wouldn't want to sit with her. But she owed him an apology—and his coat. If she'd known he was going to be here, she would have brought it with her. After the hostess said something to him, probably about the wait time, he shook his head and started to leave.

She jumped up from her seat and hurried to him. "He's with me," she said to the hostess, then grabbed Nelson around the elbow.

"Oh," the hostess said. "I didn't realize you were waiting for someone."

Confused, Nelson frowned. "I'm not with her—"

"C'mon," Ella said, tugging on his arm. She lowered her voice. "I'll share *mei* chips and salsa with you."

His eyes widened, but he let her lead him to her table. "There," she said, pointing to the chair.

"I see it." He sat down, his frown deepening.

He was wearing a navy blue pullover, and for some reason she noticed how well it fit him, especially around the arms. Why was she paying any attention to that? So what if he looked good in a sweater?

"What are you up to?" he asked, his brows forming a strong V over his blue eyes.

Bright-blue eyes, she noticed. Years ago, when she and her father and Junia had gone on a rare vacation to Sarasota, she marveled at the color of the ocean. That's what Nelson's eyes reminded her of. Ocean blue. Good grief, what was wrong with her? First his sweater, now his eyes?

The waitress appeared with extra silverware, and Ella gained her bearings as the woman took his drink order. "Eight tacos," he said. "Two burritos, an order of refried beans, and . . ." He glanced at the full chip basket. "More chips."

The waitress nodded and walked away. Ella was impressed she didn't have to write down the order.

"Now will you tell me what all this is about?" He sounded a little irritated, but that didn't stop him from grabbing a few chips and shoveling them into his mouth.

"If it weren't for me, you wouldn't be eating those."

He kept his gaze on her, continuing to chew. When he was done, he said, "I would have survived."

She couldn't stop her half grin at his snarky comment.

He pulled the salsa bowl closer to him and dipped a chip, then took a bite and swallowed. Suddenly the rest of the chip dropped from his hand. His eyes widened. His mouth dropped open.

"What?"

"Hot!" He grabbed her tea and gulped it down. "That's not helping!" He sat back in the chair, tears squeezing out of his eyes.

Was there something wrong with the salsa? She took a chip and dipped one corner into the black bowl, then tasted it. Perfect. Just the right amount of heat, and a good tomato-to-pepper ratio. She dug the rest of the chip into the salsa and polished it off.

Nelson wiped his red eyes with his napkin. "You're *ab im kopp*, you know that?" When he finished, he shoved the bowl toward her. "That stuff is deadly."

Their food appeared, and as the two waitresses set the dishes in front of them, Ella said, "He'd like a glass of milk."

"Ella, I don't need any—"

She turned to him as the waitresses walked away. "You'll thank me."

"I seriously doubt that."

Ella ignored his barb and closed her eyes in silent prayer. When she opened them, Nelson was still praying. The busboy set the glass of milk on the table.

Nelson opened his eyes and picked up the milk. He drank half of it in one gulp.

"Better, right? I should have warned you about the salsa. Junia and *Daed* always order mild."

He set down the glass, gave her a curt nod, and dug into the tacos.

At least he acknowledged her help. Now it was time for her to apologize. "Nelson, I'm sorry."

"About the salsa?" He'd already polished off two tacos with record speed. "Lesson learned."

"*Nee.* About our last conversation. I shouldn't have assumed you wanted my help with your business. And I promise I wasn't planning or plotting to undermine you. I just thought—"

"You made it clear what you were thinking." He grabbed a third taco. "Apology accepted. Let's just eat lunch, *ya?*"

"I don't want to be the reason you don't buy the warehouse," she said.

"You're not. I already bought it. Just signed the paperwork at the bank down the street."

Her spirits sank a bit. While she was sincere about not wanting to stand in his way, her dreams of expanding the store disappeared just like that. *Poof.* It didn't mean they couldn't add on to the store. Eventually. Maybe. But it would have been so much easier to buy the warehouse. "Uh, congratulations."

"*Danki.*"

As he plowed through two more tacos and moved on to the burritos, while also taking bites of the beans, two things occurred to her. One: Nelson was a hearty eater. Not a sloppy one, though. The tacos seemed small in his huge hands, as if he were eating mini ones instead of regular size. And two: they were now going to be neighbors, businesswise. "Where are you going to live?"

He was pressing the side of his fork into the last third of burrito number one. "In a house."

"Whose house?"

"Mine. At some point, anyway. I'll bunk in at Jesse's for the time being."

That made sense. She bit into her second taco. Delicious. "When will you renovate the warehouse? Have you decided what equipment you need? How will you change the footprint of the building?"

He gaped at her. "What's with all the questions?"

"I'm just curious."

"I haven't thought that far ahead."

She was surprised. "You still don't have a plan?"

Nelson set down his fork. "Ella, don't you ever mind your own business?" He lifted his hand and motioned for a nearby waitress. She quickly came over. "Check, please—"

"You didn't finish your lunch," Ella pointed out.

"And a to-go box." He turned to Ella as the waitress disappeared. "Look, since our businesses will be next to each other, I need to make a few things clear. This is *mei* business. Not yours. Which means you don't have the right to ask me questions."

"But I'm trying to help."

"I'll have plenty of help from *mei familye*, who are very successful businesspeople."

"They are?"

"*Ya.* My two oldest twin brothers own a horse farm. They also rehabilitate abused horses. My oldest brother owns his own roofing business in Fredericktown. My brother Owen will be running our family farm when *mei daed* retires, and my brother-in-law, Jalon— Malachi's father—also owns a farm."

"Wow." Ella sat back. Maybe she should be asking the Bontragers for business advice. "Do any of them own a butcher shop?"

"*Nee*," he said, a little doubt creeping into his sea-blue eyes. "But I'll figure it out."

His gaze locked with hers, and the strangest thing happened. She should be irritated by his bluntness. But she wasn't. She liked the fact that he was straightforward and sure of himself. He was right, he didn't need her help. He was a capable—and if his physique was any indication—strong man who was making her stomach flutter. Or was it the spicy salsa? She didn't know, and as she continued to gaze into his incredible eyes, she didn't care.

The waitress appeared with the check and a to-go box, drawing Ella out of her daze.

He pulled his wallet out of his back pocket. "How much is hers?" he said, nodding at Ella.

The waitress took the check out of her apron and handed it to him.

Ella tried to stop him, but she couldn't speak a word. Not with her mouth as dry as cotton. When did that happen? She could only watch as he opened the wallet and handed the waitress a few bills. "Keep the change."

"Gracias," she said, taking the money. "You two have a nice day."

Nelson nodded as he quickly scooped the rest of his food into the box and closed the lid. She noticed his hands again. Like the rest of him, they looked sturdy, and there was a scar on the top of the knuckle on his right third finger. Then she blinked. She had to get back to reality. This was Nelson Bontrager. He didn't like her, and she definitely didn't like him.

"Thank you for lunch," she said curtly, yanking on her coat. It would serve her well to ignore his good looks and focus on his grouchy personality. She reached for her bags and purse on the floor. "I'll get your coat back to you ASAP."

"Malachi can pick it up this Saturday when he sees Junia."

She froze, then sat up straight. "What?"

"He and Junia have a date." Nelson finished off the milk.

Ella started to fume. "On Saturday?"

"Ya."

"But we're hosting church on Sunday. We need to spend all day Saturday cleaning." Junia hadn't mentioned anything about Malachi, other than knitting him a scarf. She took the napkin from her lap and tossed it on the table. "She's going to leave me to clean everything by myself. Again." Nelson forgotten, she grabbed her stuff and stood. "Not this time," she said and marched out of the restaurant.

Her taxi wasn't due to arrive for another twenty minutes, but Ella didn't care. She stormed down the sidewalk, needing to blow off steam. Junia would have to cancel her date, and Ella didn't care how much of a fuss her sister raised—and she would raise a fuss. She was tired of Junia dodging work and getting away with it. "Not anymore," Ella grumbled, ignoring the couple she passed by and their quizzical look at her talking to herself. "It ends now."

Six

Dumbfounded, Nelson watched Ella stomp out of Pancho's, his tongue still tingling from the fiery salsa he'd choked on earlier. That was the hottest stuff he'd ever tasted, and he was grateful for the milk, so there was one point in her favor. But she was the pushiest, nosiest, and oddest woman he'd ever met, and that included Charity, who had at one time taken that prize. But his sister-in-law had changed for the better, and so had his brother Jesse, who had always been annoying in his own way.

But Ella? She was on a whole other level.

He grabbed his to-go box and stood. The restaurant was getting crowded again with the second wave of lunch seekers taking advantage of discounted tacos. When he dodged a little girl darting by him, he almost tripped over a wheeled walker. "Sorry," he said to the elderly lady and her female dining companion. Then he paused. He recognized the older woman. Shirley, that was her name. Charity used to work for her.

"That's all right, Nelson." Shirley smiled and shifted her walker a little closer to her table. "Did you enjoy your lunch?"

"The tacos are always good here." His company today? Not so

68

much. Then he checked himself. That wasn't a fair assessment. Other than her unwarranted inquisitiveness, burning his mouth on her crazy-hot salsa, and the weird way she left after he mentioned Malachi and Junia's date, eating tacos with Ella wasn't all that bad. And there was that strange moment when he couldn't stop looking into her eyes. The two times he'd been with her before, he couldn't decide if they were dark blue or smoky gray. In the brighter light of Pancho's, he realized they were definitely gray, round, and with thick eyelashes that enhanced the smoky color. When she wasn't speaking, Ella Yoder was pretty.

If he weren't in a public place, he would have face-palmed himself. Here he was again, noticing a pretty woman. His only saving grace was her off-putting personality. But he couldn't even say that about her when she made sure he had tacos for lunch and milk for his burned tongue.

Shirley pointed at the soft tacos on her plate. "They sure are. Everything here is." She gestured to the dark-haired woman across the table. "Have you met my daughter, Wendy?"

"I don't think so." He held out his hand. "Nelson Bontrager. Nice to meet you."

Wendy shook it with a firm grip. "Are you related to Jesse?"

"They're brothers." Shirley scooped up a spoonful of Mexican rice.

"Ah." She smiled. "Nice to meet you too."

"I didn't realize you knew Ella Yoder," Shirley said.

He caught the slight quizzical lift of her thin eyebrow. Oh brother. Apparently everyone in Marigold was a nosy Nellie. "I don't. Not really anyway." He debated for a second whether to tell the women about his butcher shop but changed his mind. They'd find out soon enough. "I'd better get going. Have a good day," he said, moving away from the table.

"You too," Shirley said.

Nelson shot out of the restaurant and blew out a breath when he reached the curb. Truth be told, while he was annoyed with Ella's audacity, he was grateful he'd been able to eat lunch at all. If he'd had to wait too long to be seated at Pancho's, he would have had to make his ride wait on him, and he wouldn't have done that. As it was, his ride would be here soon. He glanced around and right away a white van pulled in front of him. It wasn't his taxi, but he recognized the driver. He waved to Max, who pushed a button on his door. The window rolled down.

"Hey, Nelson," Max said. "How are things?"

"Good." At least so far, if he didn't think too much about Ella's outburst and the paperwork he'd just signed at the bank. Fortunately, he'd been able to buy the property outright with most of his savings and only had to take out a small loan for renovating the warehouse. He planned to pay off the loan as soon as possible. He didn't like being in anyone's debt, or in this case, being indebted to an institution. "Everything all right with you?"

"Right as rain and too blessed to complain." The gray-haired man grinned. "Just here to pick up a young lady." He glanced around. "Don't see her, though. She said she was having lunch at Pancho's. Ella Yoder is her name. You wouldn't happen to know her, would you?"

It seemed he couldn't escape her. "I know who she is."

Max checked his watch. "Hope she shows up soon. I've got a family I need to pick up in less than an hour."

Nelson looked around the busy street. Ella was nowhere in sight. Not very considerate of her, but she was hopping mad when she left Pancho's and that was partially his fault. How was he supposed to know she didn't know about Malachi and Junia's date? Or that she would be so upset by it?

A horn honked behind Max's van, and Nelson saw a red sedan

pointing to the space Max was halfway parked in. "Guess I'd better make another spin around the block. Would you mind checking to see if she's still inside?"

"She's not," he said. "I saw her leave."

The driver slammed on the horn again. Max put his van in Drive. "Guess I'll see you later."

"Wait." Nelson gestured for the driver behind Max to hold on a minute. He moved closer to the van. "I'll see if I can find her. She can catch a ride home with me. Jackson won't mind."

"You sure?"

"Positive."

"Thanks, that helps out a lot." Max waved to him and closed the window, then pulled out of the parking space. The red sedan whipped inside.

Nelson walked away, dug into his pants pocket, and pulled out a flip phone, one he used for business, emergencies, and when he needed to contact a driver. Texting on the phone was cumbersome, but their bishop, Freemont Yoder, had forbade their community from using smartphones. *"Nothing gut comes from those things,"* he'd said one Sunday morning a little more than a year ago. *"If you've got them, get rid of them. If you don't, stay away from them."*

Unwieldly texting aside, Nelson agreed with the rule. With a smartphone, it was too tempting to jump on the internet, and once you crossed that line, temptations abounded.

Something came up. Do you mind picking me up later, in half an hour? And can you take someone else home? I'll pay extra.

After a minute Jackson responded.

Sure, no problem. Where do you want me to pick you up?

The park. It's less crowded there.

See you there.

He put his phone back in his pocket. He and his family had known Jackson Talbot for a long time, and the guy was best friends with Levi Stoll, the owner of Stoll's Inn. Now that his ride was sorted out, Nelson started on his search for Ella.

Twenty minutes later, he was still searching. The downtown area of Barton was small, but there were several shops, including a fabric store, an antique store run by Ivy and Noah Schlabach, who lived in Birch Creek, a craft store, a hardware store, and two other small restaurants. She wasn't in any of those, and now he was concerned. He had no idea why. She was an adult and clearly capable of taking care of herself. He probably shouldn't have butted into her business and let Max wait for her. He'd wanted to help Max out, but now he'd caused trouble for himself.

He made his way toward the park at the end of Main Street and farther away from the bustle of traffic and shops. He wasn't about to put out Jackson any more than he already had. Besides, Ella had probably called another ride by now and was back home in Marigold. *Why didn't I leave well enough alone?*

But as he approached the park, which was little more than a set of swings, a slide, and a few wooden benches, he saw a lone figure sitting on one of the bench seats, her white plastic shopping bags next to her. Ella. He hurried his steps, and when he reached her, he asked, "What are you doing here?"

Startled, she looked up at him, her face twisted in a scowl. "Sitting, obviously."

"You were supposed to get a ride from Max."

Her eyes widened. "How did you know that?"

He explained his conversation with the driver. "Jackson's taking you home."

"Who?"

"*Mei* friend. He's picking us up. He'll drop you off before he takes me to *mei haus*."

"And he's okay with that?"

Nelson nodded. "He should be here any minute."

She looked down at her feet, the toes of her black shoes barely touching the ground. "I'll find *mei* own ride."

He frowned. "You're not ready to *geh* home?"

She shrugged.

Against his better judgment and a violation of his vow to stay away from women, he sat down next to her. "Why?"

"Why do you care?"

"I don't."

She blinked, hurt flashing over her features. "Then why are you here?"

He couldn't answer, not right away since he didn't understand exactly why himself. Or why he was sitting next to her, a little bothered that she was bothered. "One, I'm curious. I didn't take you for the kind of person who would keep a taxi waiting."

"Normally I'm not," she mumbled, averting her eyes.

A cardinal landed on a nearby bench. He tilted his tiny red-and-black head at the two of them, as if he were just as confused about the situation as Nelson was. "Two," he said, continuing his explanation, "you were angry when you left Pancho's. And three—"

73

"I wasn't angry. I was . . . perturbed."

"There's a difference?"

"Ya." She turned to him. "I wasn't mad. Not even close."

He moved back a bit. If what he witnessed at Pancho's wasn't anger, he didn't want to be around her when she was angry. "Okay," he said, measuring his words. "You were perturbed. And three—"

"Don't I have a right to be upset?" Ella jumped up from the bench, scaring the cardinal away and knocking off one of her bags. But she didn't seem to notice as she started to pace in front of him. "I'm sick and tired of Junia doing whatever she wants to do, and *nix* that I need her to do."

Nelson glanced over his shoulder, hoping to see Jackson's truck. He wasn't there. *Nuts.*

"And you know the worst part? *Daed* lets her get away with it." Her small hands fisted at her sides, puffs of frosty air accompanying her words. "I have to run the store, clean the house, cook, do the laundry, mend our clothes—"

And Junia was the woman Malachi thought he was in love with? Yeesh. "She doesn't do anything?"

"Well, she does hang the clothes on the line. And most of the time she makes breakfast." She halted and turned on her heel. "She does do some things. But I have to tell her to do them. She's twenty years old. She shouldn't have to be told what to do."

Nelson rubbed the back of his neck. The last thing he wanted was to be privy to their sister feud. The *very* last thing he wanted—or needed—was to point out that maybe Junia would have more gumption if Ella weren't bossing her around so much. He bit his tongue, literally.

"What am I doing?" She waved her hand in his direction. "Why am I telling you all this?"

He looked up at her. He didn't know her or her family, and she shouldn't be snapping at him because she was mad at her sister. But when he saw her wipe her eyes with the heels of her hands, he paused. Once again, he ignored his common sense and motioned for her to sit next to him. At first she shook her head, but when he pointed at the seat, she plopped down.

Nelson picked up the bag off the ground and set it next to the other ones between them. They both sat in silence, staring at the swings in front of them.

.ᴥᴥ.

Ella couldn't look at Nelson. Embarrassment flooded her, from the top of her *kapp* to the toes of her shoes. What on earth had possessed her to spill all that private information to him? He'd already made it clear that he didn't care, and she shouldn't be surprised. She also shouldn't care that he, a practical stranger who definitely didn't like her, didn't care. But for some reason . . . she did.

It didn't make any sense. Neither did her tirade, or him sitting next to her on this bench or arranging a ride for her. In her anger she'd expressed to him what she hadn't been able to say to her *daed* or Junia. Her father wouldn't listen, and her sister . . . didn't care. That seemed to be a trend with the people in her life lately.

After a few more moments of silence, Nelson asked, "Feel better now?"

"*Nee*," she said, knowing he was expecting an answer and unwilling to lie to him. "I don't feel better."

"I reckon that's okay. Seems like you got a lot on your plate."

He was sliding his boot over the crushed gravel underneath the bench, still staring straight ahead. He might not care, but he did seem to understand. A little. "*Danki*," she murmured.

"For what?"

She sighed. "Listening. Arranging my ride home. Buying me lunch."

He nodded. "You did make sure I got *mei* tacos today. Guess that makes us even."

"Guess so."

The sound of a vehicle coming closer made them turn around. A white pickup truck with an extended cab pulled behind them. Nelson stood, then picked up Ella's bags and handed them to her. "That's Jackson."

The mortified part of her wanted to decline the ride. She had a phone, and she could call someone to pick her up. But there was something . . . *soothing* about his presence. She had no idea if that was the right description, but she was experiencing a nice feeling that he had taken matters into his own hands and made sure she had a ride. She was used to fending for herself.

Ella stood and followed him to the truck. He opened the back door for her, and she climbed in. He got into the front and sat next to the English driver.

"Hey, Jackson," Nelson said as he shut the door. "Thanks for doing this."

"No problem." Jackson turned around, giving Ella a quick wave.

She replied with a faint smile. He seemed to be in his late twenties, with short brown hair and a chestnut-colored beard that was almost as long as some of the married Amish men. The only difference was the mustache.

He put the truck in Drive and pulled onto the street. Gray clouds had formed over the past hour or so since she'd eaten lunch, and the overcast sky matched her dull mood. Nelson and Jackson talked while she sank deeper into her coat and closed her eyes, suddenly dog-tired. She couldn't remember the last time she'd had such an outburst, and arguing with Junia didn't count. She also couldn't remember the last time any of her comments, constructive critiques, or complaints had been heard. Her father always left or changed the subject when Ella became upset. Junia either egged her on or laughed at her.

Her aunts' voices echoed in her mind again.

"You're too temperamental," Aenti Cora would say.

"The Lord's servant must not be quarrelsome," Aenti Tabitha pointed out on more than one occasion, quoting from part of 2 Timothy.

Ella didn't think she was quarrelsome, not often anyway. Why was it okay that her sister always got a pass from everyone and Ella received the lectures? *It's not fair.*

Tears squeezed from her eyes. Quickly she passed the back of her hand over her face, thankful Nelson and Jackson were still talking. When she heard Nelson mention the butcher shop, her ears perked.

"You actually did it?" Jackson said, flipping on his turn signal.

"Yep. Signed the papers today."

Jackson grinned. "Congratulations. Can't wait to visit the shop when it opens. Do you have a date?"

"There's still a lot of details to work out."

Ella frowned. She was sure Nelson had to deal with more than just details, considering he'd admitted he didn't even have a plan. She also took note of the doubt in his tone, which hadn't been there when he was talking to her at lunch. *I could help him if he would just let me.* She bit the inside of her lip. He had plenty of help, and he didn't want hers. He couldn't have been any clearer about that.

The men had changed subjects and were discussing Jackson's web design job when something suddenly occurred to Ella. "What was number three?" she blurted in *Deitsch*.

Nelson and Jackson stopped talking, and Nelson looked over his shoulder. "What?"

"Earlier you said number three." She started ticking off on her fingers. "Number one was you were curious why I was, um, perturbed." She didn't need to state number two, that he was right in pointing out she was angry. "What was three?"

He frowned, his thick eyebrows forming what was becoming a familiar confused V above his eyes. Those eyes. She hadn't paid attention to them when she was pitching her fit, but she sure was now. *Sigh.*

Shifting in his seat, he averted his gaze. "I, uh, wanted to make sure you were okay." He quickly faced the front and started talking to Jackson again.

She stilled, trying to absorb his contradictory words. If he didn't care about her or her plight, why did he need to make sure she was all right? It didn't make sense. Neither did the warmth flowing through her. Maybe he wasn't as insensitive as she thought.

"Is this it?" Jackson said, pointing to her house across the street from the store and Nelson's future butcher shop.

"Yes." Ella gathered up her bags as he pulled into her driveway. She reached her purse, but Nelson held up his hand.

"The ride's on me."

"But you paid—" She stopped herself. He'd paid for lunch and now her taxi. She recalled what he'd said when they were on the swings—that they were even now. He might have thought that, but he'd just tipped the scales again. She'd have to do something for him to get them back on even ground. "Okay then, bye," she said, getting out of the truck.

"See ya around." Jackson waved at her again, but Nelson didn't give her another glance.

Humph. What a strange man. He was nice one minute, boorish the next. One thing was for sure, he was unlike anyone she'd ever met before.

She headed inside the house as they drove away, her temper at a low simmer again. After she dropped off the yarn, fabric, and other items at the house, she would head to the store. Hopefully Junia would still be there, but she wouldn't be surprised if she wasn't. The parking lot was empty, and if business was slow, her sister grew bored. That was when she usually took off, supposedly on breaks that would end up lasting more than an hour. Sometimes several. And *Daed* never admonished her for it.

Resentment bubbled up within her as she went upstairs to put the fabric in her room. She placed it on her dresser and saw Nelson's coat on her hope chest. If Ella got her way, Junia wouldn't be seeing Malachi on Saturday. She really needed her help around the house that day. Ella would have to figure out another way to return Nelson's coat to him, and she would do that after she got through the weekend. Right now she needed to focus on how she was going to convince Junia to cancel her date and get her father to back her up. *A tall order, indeed.*

Seven

Later that afternoon, Wendy planned to stop at E&J's grocery store. The trip to Barton with Mom had taken up most of the afternoon, the highlight being Pancho's, of course. After they finished their food—Wendy had opted for a vegetable quesadilla while her mother filled up on her beloved tacos—the two of them went to the craft store and then the fabric store. Both visits had surprised Mom.

"You're interested in sewing?" Mom had asked as they entered the small shop.

"I just want to look and see what's here." There wasn't much to choose from aside from Amish fabrics, and Wendy found herself looking at a sample dress on a dressmaker's form. Marigold wasn't her first encounter with the Amish. Growing up, she and her parents would visit Lancaster, Pennsylvania, at least once a year, although by the time she was a teenager, Wendy had lost interest. *You see one farm and buggy, you've seen them all.* She didn't think that way anymore, and she was fascinated by the sample dress. The Ohio Amish wore a different style of white hat than the Lancaster women did. A *kapp*, Charity and Priscilla, Micah's wife, had called it. She remembered the ones in Lancaster were more heart-shaped than the rounded style Marigold women wore.

What was it like not to worry about what you wore every day? Or having to keep up with the latest hairstyle and makeup trends? She was never a clothes maven, and her style was functionally classic, with minimal jewelry and accessories. She touched the dress, appreciating the sturdy fabric, modest design, and deep-plum color. What would it feel like to wear this?

They ended up not buying any crafts or fabric, but it was fun to browse. After she dropped off Mom for an afternoon nap, she took Monroe for his overdue visit to the Bontragers. While Monroe and Brook played together, she visited with Charity, who was copying down recipes from another French cookbook. They were too complicated for Wendy's simple cooking skills, and as she and Monroe walked back home, she tried to decide what to make for supper. Something light, since lunch had been so heavy. Soup sounded good, but they were out of crackers. Despite her aversion to carbs, she couldn't eat soup without crackers.

Wendy then bundled up and headed for E&J's. Thirty minutes later she arrived. She could have driven there, but she was in the mood for another walk. The parking lot was empty, even though it wasn't near closing time. She went inside, intending to buy crackers and leave. But she couldn't resist picking up one of the shopping baskets just in case she saw something else she wanted.

The store was surprisingly deserted. She always saw at least one Yoder in the store—usually Barnabas. As she walked over to the cracker and cookie aisle, she glanced at the back of the store and saw gardening supplies. She had no idea they sold them here. Then again, she hadn't thought about gardening until recently. After picking up a box of saltines and a container of buttery crackers, she went to the garden section. Sparse, but there was a rack of seed packets and a few tools. Some bins were empty, which made sense because it was winter.

She was studying a packet of cucumber seeds when she heard a door open in the back. Junia Yoder rushed past her, her face pinched and red, followed quickly by Ella, who was clenching her jaw. Unlike Junia, she stopped near Wendy and pasted a smile on her face. "Can I help you with anything?"

"I'm just browsing." She put the seeds back. "But I'm thinking about starting a garden in the spring."

"Great," Ella said flatly. "We'll have more supplies closer to that time." Without waiting for Wendy to reply, she hurried off.

Wendy frowned. Odd. Ella was normally friendly, although a little uptight. Wendy could relate. She'd spent most of her adult life being uptight. She moved to examine the two spades that were hanging from a peg on the wall. She and Mom hadn't thought about getting one of these. She'd have to add it to the list.

When she turned around, she caught a glimpse of the open office door and saw Barnabas at his desk, his head in his hands. She should look away, but for some reason she couldn't. Why was he so despondent?

Without thinking, she moved closer to the door. His shoulders were slumped, as if a heavy weight were pressed upon them. "Barnabas?"

His head popped up and he straightened in the chair. "Hi," he said, his normally placid expression replacing the haggard lines she'd glimpsed. "Can I help you?"

"Are you okay?" She shouldn't be prying, but she couldn't help it. She didn't like seeing this gentle man in distress.

"Sure am."

But the crack in his voice said otherwise and his fading pleasant expression wasn't too convincing either. "Um, okay. Have, uh, a good evening, then." She started to retreat, recognizing she had crossed a line by asking him such a personal question. As she turned around to leave, he cleared his throat.

"I think I need some advice."

She faced him, but he had his head down. Silvery gray strands threaded through his brown, Amish-cut hair. "Of the legal kind?"

"No." He coughed into his fist, still staring at his tidy desk. "Of the . . . female kind."

Wendy nodded. She pulled the office door behind her but made sure it was cracked open in case either of his daughters wanted to come in, and she sat down on the metal folding chair in front of him. Considering the state Ella and Junia were in a few minutes earlier, she suspected he wanted to talk about them. "How can I help?"

He finally lifted his head, and she was struck by the weariness in his eyes. She listened as he told her how his daughters were constantly fighting with each other. "They've always been at odds," he said. "I chalked it up to their temperaments. Junia's a free spirit, creative, and clever. Ella is disciplined, orderly, and loyal. But they have one thing in common—both are as stubborn as the day is long."

She didn't know much about Ella and Junia, but the interactions she'd had with them at the store revealed they both had strong personalities. Junia did seem more flighty than down-to-earth Ella, but they had always been courteous and helpful to her. She also appreciated how well Barnabas knew his daughters.

It should have struck her as odd that Barnabas was asking her for advice. He was an Amish man, a father, and owned a small-town grocery store. She was English, a lawyer, and knew nothing about kids. They couldn't be more dissimilar. But there was something natural about this conversation, despite his distress. He was at his wit's end, and she wanted to help him.

"I reckon their squabbling is my fault." He leaned back in his chair and scrubbed his hand over his face. "After their mother died, it was easier to let my sisters handle them. I should have been more of a disciplinarian. But I'm not one for conflict. Never have been."

That was another difference between them. Wendy never shied away from a good fight, especially in the courtroom. But listening to him take responsibility for his mistakes was refreshing. In her line of work, she was used to people doing the exact opposite. "I take it they had another fight recently?"

"Right here in the office." He sighed, then shook his head. "I'm sorry."

"For what?"

"Bothering you with this. I'm not sure why I'm telling you my problems."

She leaned forward and smiled. "Maybe it's because you need to."

He nodded, giving her a small smile of his own. "Thanks for listening. God willing, I'll figure this out. Or I'll build my own house behind the main one, move in, and leave them to their own devices. That's not a bad idea, come to think of it."

"Would it solve anything?"

"No. But I would have some peace."

Leaning back in the chair, she set the crackers in her lap. "Have you ever thought about conflict mediation?"

"What's that?"

"Having a neutral party help you resolve the dispute."

"Do I need a lawyer for that?"

"No," she said. "Although sometimes we do mediate between clients or corporations. All you need is someone who isn't involved in the conflict. Someone from your church could help, for example. They would listen to all sides of the issue and give their input. Sometimes just airing grievances can clear the air."

Barnabas rested his folded hands on the desktop. "My daughters have a lot of grievances," he admitted. "But I'm not sure I want someone I see all the time knowing our dirty laundry. The Lord says to share our burdens, but . . ."

She waited for him to finish.

He looked at her again. "It's shameful I can't manage my household."

Her heart went out to him. She disagreed that he should feel ashamed, but that wasn't her call. Although she was learning more about Amish ways through Charity and Priscilla, they discussed the rules they followed more than anything personal. She did know they followed biblical hierarchy and considered the man the head of the family while women oversaw hearth and home. She wanted to tell him not to be hard on himself, but she wasn't in the position to do so. She did have another idea, though. "I could be the mediator," she said.

He shook his head. "I couldn't impose on you like that."

"You're not imposing. I'm volunteering. As a corporate lawyer I've had a lot of experience with conflict, Barnabas. And I can promise whatever you and your daughters say, it will be kept confidential. You have my word as an attorney and—" She almost said friend but caught herself. She and Barnabas weren't anywhere close to being friends—they were barely acquaintances—and what she was offering was a business solution to a family problem. From his doubtful expression, she didn't think he'd agree anyway.

"All right," he said, surprising her. "I'll give it some thought. Ella might be open to the idea, but Junia will be a tough sell."

"If you decide you need me, just let me know." She pulled her wallet out of the pocket of her coat and opened the magnetic clasp. She always had business cards on her in a variety of places—her purse, wallet, briefcase, and sometimes she grabbed them out of the key bowl near the front door of her apartment and put them in her pocket when she ran out to do errands in the city. She never knew if she would run into someone who could use her legal services. She pulled out a card and a pen, crossed out her New York City address, and wrote down her mother's, then handed it to Barnabas.

"Thank you." He took the card and laid it on the desk. "And thanks again for listening. You're right—I do feel a little better having talked about this."

She smiled, feeling more satisfied than she had in a long time. A good reminder of why she went to law school in the first place—to help others. That intention had been lost somewhere along her climb to the top.

"Now, what can I help you with?" He stood. "You need anything to go with those crackers?"

"I'm making soup tonight," she said, standing up. "Vegetable. We were out of crackers, though."

He nodded. "Can't have soup without crackers."

She chuckled. "No, you can't. At least, I can't."

Barnabas opened the door for her, and she walked through, seeing the gardening supplies again. "I mentioned to Ella that I might put in a garden in the spring," she said. "It will be my first one. I never had the space or time to have one in New York."

"I put one in every year." He straightened up a lone rake hanging next to the spades. "If you need some help, let me know."

"Will do."

"I can ring up the crackers for you," he said, holding out his hands.

She handed them to him. "Thank you."

They made their way up front. Ella was outside the front door, attacking the entryway with a broom. "Guess she's still fired up," Barnabas muttered as he walked behind the counter.

Wendy glanced at Ella. Those bristles were taking a beating. At least Ella was putting her anger to good use.

Barnabas put the crackers in a bag, holding up his hand when she offered to pay him. "It's on me."

"I couldn't—"

"Please. Allow me."

Something shifted inside her when she saw his smile. Such a kind man. She took the bag from him. "Thank you."

"See you next time."

She smiled back and walked out the door. Hopefully next time would be soon. Very soon.

.⚜.

Ella watched as Wendy left the store carrying her purchases. The parking lot was empty, so she assumed the woman had walked here. She had no idea where she lived, and right now she didn't care. As soon as Wendy was near the road, Ella went inside the store and headed straight for her father, who was pulling forward a box of saltines to fill the empty space on the shelf.

"What were you talking to her about?" Ella demanded.

Daed adjusted the saltines, remaining silent.

"She was in our office, *ya*?"

He nodded, now fiddling with a package of chocolate sandwich cookies.

"*Daed*—"

"Our conversation is none of your business, Ella."

She stopped, surprised by his prickly tone. "She's a lawyer, *ya*? What do you need to talk to a lawyer for?"

He turned to her, his jaw clenched. "Did you hear what I just said?"

"*Ya*, but—"

He turned his back to her and moved away. "Mind the store," he said, his tone gruff.

"Where are you going?"

"For a walk." He left.

Ella leaned against the broom handle in her hand. What was going on? She was still mad at Junia, who had somehow convinced her father that making supper for Malachi was more important than cleaning the house for church service. She still didn't understand how she managed that, but by the end of their discussion in the office, *Daed* had given in. "I'll take care of the store," he said. "That will give you time to clean the house."

"It won't take all day for her to make a meal," Ella pointed out.

"I have to finish Malachi's scarf too." Junia lifted her chin in triumph. "I want to give it to him Saturday night."

"*Daed*," Ella blustered. "She's being ridiculous."

He looked at her, then at Junia, then pointed to the door. "Out."

Junia laughed. "Yeah, Ella. You need to leave—"

"Both of you."

Ella scoffed. "But *Daed*—"

"*Geh*. Now."

Anger had flashed in Junia's eyes. She stormed out of the office and rushed through the baking aisle before flying out the door, Ella on her heels. But when Ella saw Wendy looking at the garden tools, she stopped. They had a customer, and she couldn't just ignore her like Junia did. That wasn't good business practice. After speaking with Wendy, she went up to the front, only to hear the door to the office close a minute or so later. She needed to do something about that squeaky hinge.

When Wendy didn't appear after a few minutes, Ella went back and heard muffled voices through the door. She wanted to eavesdrop, but they had another customer. While Ella waited on him, she thought about Junia and got mad all over again. After he left, she went outside to sweep and work off her frustration.

She glanced at the abused broom. Hmm, she might have to replace it. But the front of the store was clean now.

Ella glanced at the clock. Thirty minutes until close. She doubted Junia and *Daed* would return before five. When another customer walked through the door, she put on her best customer service face and went to work.

Close to five thirty she locked the door and left the shop. A few snowflakes drifted through the crisp, dry air as she walked across the street to the house. The light in the kitchen was already on, so someone was home. She entered the back kitchen door and saw Junia sitting at the table, looking at one of the knitting magazines she received in the mail every month.

"Couldn't you have at least started supper?" Ella snapped.

"*Nee.*" Junia slowly turned the page. "That's *yer* job."

Ooh, she wanted to strangle her. She stilled. When she reached that level of anger, she knew she had to pause, count, and take deep breaths to stop her from saying or doing something she would regret. After counting to ten, she went to the pantry, grabbed a loaf of bread and a jar of peanut butter and parked them in front of Junia.

"What's this?"

"Supper." She rushed out of the kitchen to the living room. The fire in the woodstove needed stoking, and she continued to count as she put pieces of split wood inside it. "Ninety-eight," she said through gritted teeth. "Ninety-nine—"

The front door opened, and her father walked in. Ella closed the grate and stood, ready to question him again about where he'd been all this time. But she clamped her mouth shut. Asking him was pointless, just like getting Junia to do any work was fruitless. Instead, she ignored him and started up the stairs to her bedroom. She'd rather be alone than with either of them right now.

"Ella."

She paused, her foot on the bottom step, tempted to ignore him and leave. But she couldn't be that disrespectful. She loved her father, even though he could be exasperating. She quickly counted to eight and faced him.

"I'm sorry I snapped at you earlier," he said.

The fatigue on his face startled her. She hurried to him. "Are you okay? You were gone a long time."

He moved to sit in his chair. "I'm . . . fine. Just needed some time to think." He lifted his palm as she opened her mouth. "Don't ask," he said, looking straight at her.

She shut her mouth and nodded. "Can I get you anything?"

"*Nee*. I'm not hungry."

"Are you sure? I was just about to make supper." She bit her bottom lip at the lie, but she was more concerned about her father than making a point to Junia.

"*Ya*, I'm sure. I'm just going to sit here for a little bit. You and Junia *geh* ahead and eat."

Now she had to go back to the kitchen and make a meal, since she'd fibbed to her father. Which meant she'd have to face Junia again. Great. This day needed to end already.

Ella went into the kitchen. Junia had shoved the peanut butter and bread to the side, and she looked up from her magazine as if she'd expected all along that Ella would return and fulfill her duty. A satisfied grin flashed on her face before she went back to reading.

Lord, give me strength. As she set about making a quick supper that was more substantial than a peanut butter sandwich, she felt the anger melt into exhaustion. She filled a pot with water to boil noodles and looked at the little red bird figurines on the windowsill, surrounded by pine cones, some greenery, and little bundles of red berries. At least Junia had decorated the house and store for Christmas, something Ella hadn't had the time or the talent to do. She couldn't deny Junia had a gift for making simple decor look wonderful, and Christmas wasn't the only time she put her skills to use. During the spring and summer months, her sister made sure there were fresh flowers in glass vases all around the house, and in the fall she decorated with pumpkins, dried berries, gourds, and brightly colored leaves.

But just because Junia could bedeck a room didn't mean Ella forgave her.

She put the filled pot on the stove as Junia got up from the table. "Let me know when it's time to eat," she said and walked out of the kitchen.

Ella hung her head, some of the tension falling from her shoulders now that Junia was gone. Was this how her life was going to be until her sister married and moved out? *I'm doing all the work and she has all the fun.* She didn't understand why her father kept allowing that. *Why are you allowing it, God?*

Twenty minutes later, she set out the bowl of beef stroganoff on the table next to a plate with a few slices of bread. She'd made sure to make enough for all three of them to eat, and she was glad she did because her father showed up with Junia, looking more relaxed than he had when he was talking to Ella. Her sister almost always had that effect on him, while Ella could only accomplish the opposite.

Ella sat down at the table, not looking at either of them. Instead, she prayed over the meal and started to ask God for another dose of patience. She stopped. Why bother? He never answered that prayer either.

Eight

For the second time in a week, Nelson and Malachi were headed for Marigold. This time Malachi was the one out of sorts, and after an argument twenty minutes ago in front of his house when Nelson had shown up and informed him that he was accompanying him to the Yoders', his nephew had been silent, staring at the small pot of violets in his lap. He'd gotten the flowers from Owen's greenhouse as a gift for Junia.

Nelson wasn't happy about the predicament either. But Phoebe had come over to the farm yesterday morning and pulled Nelson aside. "I'm worried about Malachi," she said. "I've never seen him like this."

"Like what?" He'd been in the middle of milking Bernice, one of their cows. Normally they didn't name their livestock, but she was such a friendly, docile cow that she needed a moniker. Nelson wouldn't have picked Bernice, the name his little brother Elam had come up with. But none of his brothers liked his choice, Clara, so Bernice won. A thin stream of milk splashed into the pail.

"Lovestruck. That's the only way I can put it." She touched Bernice's nose. "He's had girlfriends before. I think. He's never been that open with me about his relationships."

Which wasn't surprising. Dating wasn't talked about much, and almost never with parents. Nelson had kept his dating life a secret from everyone, and he was glad he'd made that decision, considering how badly those relationships had ended.

"But Junia is all he's been able to talk about ever since he's gotten back from Marigold." She moved closer to Nelson, who was finished with Bernice and getting up from the stool. He set the almost full bucket aside and picked up another one. "He barely knows her."

Nelson nodded and walked to the next cow, Bernice's sister. Phoebe was right behind him, carrying the stool. She positioned it on the floor. "I tried talking to him," Nelson said, sitting down. "Told him he was jumping the gun with her. He won't listen."

"He didn't listen to Jalon either." Phoebe knelt beside him. "Please *geh* with him to the Yoders' on Saturday."

He almost fell off the stool. "What?"

"I'd feel better if you kept an eye on him. I don't want the two of them being alone together. Not when his feelings are so . . . intense."

Nelson looked at her, startled at the amount of worry in her eyes.

"I know I'm being overprotective." She glanced down at the straw-strewn barn floor. "But . . ."

He turned to her. "I know." And he understood. He was young when Phoebe became pregnant with Malachi, and while no one spoke of the circumstances, everyone in the family knew that Jalon wasn't his biological father, Malachi included. One wrong decision at an English party had changed Phoebe's life forever, and while Jalon was his true father and Malachi had never wanted to meet the other man, there had been repercussions for her, and by extension, their family. "You want me to be his chaperone."

"*Ya.*" She smiled, but the pleading never left her eyes. "There'll be an elderberry pie waiting for you when you get back."

Phoebe didn't have to sweeten the pot, but he was glad she did. His sister had always loved to cook, and her baking skills were exceptional. "How can I resist that?" he said, grinning back.

While Phoebe was happy Nelson had agreed to escort Malachi on his supper date with Junia, Malachi wasn't. His normally jovial and sometimes wry nephew was in a mood. Nelson hadn't told him about Phoebe's request. He just said that he wanted to pick up his coat from Ella. *Oh boy.* He wasn't looking forward to spending the evening with her. Although he was coming by unannounced, she shouldn't be upset about his unexpected attendance since visiting was a major Amish pastime. But she was so mercurial, he wouldn't put it past her.

"I don't need you watching over me," Malachi said, breaking the uncomfortable silence.

"Who said I was doing that?" He shifted in his seat. Light snow floated down in front of them, softly illuminated by the small lights on his buggy. Inside, a mini heater kept them warm.

"Nobody. But it's obvious. You don't expect me to believe you'd come all this way to get your coat, do you? You could have had Jesse get it for you."

He was right—not that it mattered. "Someone has to keep an eye on you," he said. "You've gone *ab im kopp* over that *maedel*."

"You wouldn't understand."

Nelson scowled at his nephew's condescending tone. He was about to correct him on the matter but kept his mouth shut. He didn't want to talk about his past, especially that part.

Malachi sighed. "I'm not going to do anything *dumm*, if that's what *yer* worried about. I know better."

"*Yer* brain might tell you that, but when feelings start taking over—"

"You think I don't know that?" he snapped.

Nelson gentled his tone. "Malachi, I don't want you to get hurt."

"I won't. Junia is the woman for me. I'm going to marry her, Nelson. There's *nix* you or anyone else can do about that."

"Are you sure *yer* ready to take that step?" He steered the buggy into the Yoders' driveway. "Even for people who have been together for a while, it's a big decision."

He turned to Nelson as the horse came to a halt. "I'm ready for a *familye* of *mei* own. A *frau, kinner,* our own *haus.* I've been saving up to buy that plot down the road from *Mamm* and *Daed.* Thankfully it hasn't sold yet. I can't really explain why I love Junia—"

"Love?"

"I just know in *mei* soul that we're meant to be together."

The front door opened, and a man came outside. Ella and Junia's father, Nelson assumed. He thought he heard Malachi gulp.

"Welcome," the man said as he reached Malachi's side of the buggy. He looked at Nelson. "I'm Barnabas Yoder. You can park over there." He motioned to a barn to the left of the driveway and walked toward it.

Nelson followed him and parked at the front of the structure. After he and Malachi got out of the buggy, he started unhitching Crackerjack.

Malachi went to Barnabas, who was standing inside the barn. "*Gut* to see you again, Barnabas."

"I suppose those are for me."

Nelson looked up to see Barnabas pointing at Malachi's flowerpot. He smirked at his nephew's surprised expression.

"Uh . . . ," Malachi said.

"Just joking." Barnabas glanced at Nelson. "Guess I misunderstood Junia. I didn't realize we had two for supper tonight."

"There was a slight change of plans," Nelson said.

"Slight," Malachi muttered. "Right."

Ignoring his nephew, he held out his hand to Barnabas. "Nelson Bontrager. Malachi's uncle."

"The more the merrier, I say. Ella made plenty, so I hope you both brought your appetites." He turned to Malachi. "*Geh* on inside. Junia's waiting."

He grinned and rushed out of the barn.

"I'll give you a hand," Barnabas said. They made quick work of unhitching the horse and getting her settled in an empty stall. "Snow should be easing up in an hour or so, according to the weather report. At least that's what *mei* last customer told me."

Nelson had heard the same thing from his father before he'd left to pick up Malachi. "Were you busy today?"

"Saturdays are usually pretty steady." Barnabas stepped aside as Nelson closed the stall door. "And it always picks up right before Christmas. Everyone's trying to get their baking and cooking done ahead of time. We've got a few specialty items that we've almost sold out of." He crossed his arms. Like Nelson, he wasn't wearing a coat, although Nelson had put on his light jacket before he left. Barnabas had on a sweater. "Ella mentioned to me this morning that you bought the warehouse. Guess that makes us neighbors."

He nodded, tamping down the slight nudge of anxiety. Next week he would buckle down and figure out what he needed to do to get started on the renovation. He'd been confident when he talked about his new business with Ella at Pancho's, but in the days since then, his self-assurance had gone downhill.

"If you need any help, let me know." They were outside now, and Barnabas glanced at the house. "We shouldn't keep the *maed* waiting."

He sounded about as excited as Nelson felt. That was a little baffling. Was Barnabas as wary about Junia and Malachi's instant relationship as everyone else? *Only one way to find out.*

.·❦·.

Ella set a plate of cheese and crackers on the coffee table in the living room and tried to close her ears to Junia and Malachi, who were literally cooing to each other as they sat on the couch. Supper wasn't quite ready, and this would tide everyone over until the chicken supreme was done. She wasn't sure why the dish was labeled "supreme" since it was basically chicken, creamed soup, cheese, and macaroni. But it was delicious, and most importantly, easy. She needed easy after the long day she'd had.

"These are so *schee*, Malachi." Junia cradled the flowerpot in her hand as if it were made of gold. "How did you know I loved violets?"

Since when? Ella ground her teeth as she placed napkins next to the finger food.

"I've got something for you too." Junia handed him a package wrapped in brown paper and tied with white twine.

"You didn't have to give me anything, Junia." But he eagerly tore into the paper. "Wow," he said, pulling out the perfectly knitted scarf.

"Do you like it?"

Ella couldn't stop herself from glancing at the two of them. Junia was batting her eyelashes and Malachi was petting the scarf. *Barf.*

"*Ya.*" Malachi beamed. "It's the best gift I've ever gotten."

They were dripping with puppy love, and Ella couldn't stand it. How was she supposed to get through the rest of the evening? She was tired enough as it was. By some miracle, Junia had finished Malachi's scarf early, and she'd even pitched in and dusted the living room and stair banister. But she hadn't lifted a finger to help with supper or do the hard household chores like scrubbing the bathroom or mopping the floor.

"Ella," Junia said, her smile sweet and totally fake. "Don't you have to get the casserole out of the oven? It would be awful if it ended up burned."

The chicken supreme had ten more minutes to bake, and Junia knew that. A part of Ella wanted to plop right down and tell Malachi the truth about her sister. Instead, she nodded and went back to the kitchen. *He'll find out on his own.*

She was checking the main dish on the stove when she heard the front door close. She was surprised her father had stayed outside so long, but maybe he had a chore to do in the barn. Mixed vegetables were simmering on the stove—a combination of stewed tomatoes, green peppers, peas, corn, carrots, and potatoes. They were *Daed*'s favorite side dish, and in the summer she added fresh, cubed yellow crookneck squash. She started gathering glasses out of the cabinet when she heard him come into the kitchen. "Supper's not quite ready, *Daed*," she said, setting two glasses on the counter and reaching for two more. "There're some snacks on the coffee table if you want some."

"I just came in to wash *mei* hands."

She stilled. That wasn't her father's voice. But she recognized it. Slowly she turned around and faced Nelson. "What are you doing here?"

"Hello to you too, Ella." He smirked and lifted his hands. "Junia said I could wash them here."

Ella stared at his large hands . . . strong-looking fingers . . . uh-oh. Not his hands again. She blinked, then stepped aside so he could access the sink. "You didn't answer *mei* question."

He turned on the tap. "I missed *yer* charming presence."

Her heart skipped a beat. *He missed me?* Then the full effect of his words—and his cheeky tone—hit her. "Very funny." It was, actually. She enjoyed wry humor.

Nelson shut off the tap and grabbed the towel off the holder nearby. He faced her, a touch of annoyance in his eyes. "I'm . . . chaperoning."

Her brow lifted. "Really? You think Junia and Malachi need a chaperone?" After the stunt they pulled earlier in the week, she had to wonder. "You don't think *Daed* and I are capable of keeping an eye on them?"

"I do." He frowned. "There's a personal reason I'm doing this. Let's leave it at that."

"But—"

"You said you had snacks?"

"Um, *ya*. In the living room."

He nodded and walked out.

Ella looked at the empty doorway. What could possibly be the reason he felt he had to watch Malachi and Junia so closely? Or was it just Malachi? Did she need to be concerned?

She tried to ignore her curiosity as she finished setting the table. The timer went off and she opened the oven. The chicken supreme still needed five more minutes—enough time for her to pull Nelson aside and ask him about Malachi. She set the timer and went back into the living room. Her father was there, talking with Nelson while Junia and Malachi were still in their own little world.

Ella cleared her throat. "Nelson, can I have a word with you?"

He turned to her, his brow lifted in surprise. "Uh, sure." He rose from the chair and walked past the two lovebirds, who still hadn't taken their eyes off each other. He stopped by Ella. "What do you need?"

"Not here," she said. Then she grabbed Nelson's elbow and pulled him to the nearest private space—the bathroom. A sensor light came on as she shut the door and leaned against it. The light was dim, but bright enough that they could clearly see each other.

"What in the world—"

"Should I be worried about Malachi?"

"Absolutely not." He crossed his burly arms, which were particularly noticeable under his short-sleeved shirt. "Should I be worried about Junia?"

She mimicked his stance. "Absolutely . . . not." She didn't have the same confidence in her sister that he did in his nephew.

"You don't sound optimistic."

Ella dropped her arms, at the same time trying not to pay attention to his physique, which was proving difficult for her to do when he looked like he could scoop her up into his arms—

"Malachi thinks he's in love with her," Nelson blurted.

It took a second for Ella to focus on his words. Her unacceptable habit of noticing his good looks had to stop. "And Junia thinks she's in love with Malachi."

His arms went to his sides. "Well, at least they're on the same page."

"It's the wrong page." She sighed. "Junia's never acted this *seltsam* about a man before, if that helps."

"So she's had boyfriends before."

"A . . . couple." Or a few. Honestly, she had no idea. She'd always been too busy to pay attention to Junia's social life other than when it impeded on her own activities. "What about Malachi? Is Junia his first girlfriend?"

"Um . . . *nee.*"

"Then I *do* need to worry about him."

"Not any more than I do about Junia." He paused. "Ella, what are we doing? Why are we standing in your bathroom worried about them like they're our *kinner?*"

Ella stilled, his words making her realize how foolish they were being. Correction—how foolish she was being. She'd dragged him in here because she was worried about Junia. Why, though? *She cares so little for me.* "I'm sorry," she said, too embarrassed to look Nelson in the eye. "I overreacted." Again.

"It's okay," he said.

His sincere tone made her meet his gaze. "*Nee,* it's not. I'm not Junia's keeper. She and Malachi's relationship is their own." She turned to open the door, stopping when she felt his hand on her shoulder.

"It's *gut* that you care."

She let out a flat chuckle. "It's annoying." She came close to admitting that Junia couldn't be bothered to think about Ella's feelings or concerns, much less worry about them. But that would compound an already awkward situation—one she had created. "Supper's ready. Hope you like chicken supreme."

"When it comes to food, I like everything."

Ella turned around and looked at him. His expression was relaxed with a full smile. *He's so good-looking when he isn't grumpy.* She couldn't help but smile back . . . and the tickle in her stomach returned.

Nine

The evening had certainly taken a turn. The last thing Nelson expected was to be locked in a bathroom with Ella Yoder. Well, the door wasn't really locked, and he could have left at any moment. But she'd caught him off guard when she dragged him in here. At first he thought she was going to scold him for . . . something. Not that he'd done anything wrong, but she did have a tendency to be snippy. It was strange Junia had sent him into the kitchen to wash his hands instead of the bathroom, which was closer. She had to know that Ella was in there.

Right now none of that mattered because he couldn't stop looking at Ella. This was the first time he'd seen her genuinely smile and it made his heart skip four beats. Make that five. She was so attractive when she smiled.

But that wasn't the only reason he was mesmerized. Even though she and Junia were at odds, Ella was still looking out for her, to the point of pulling him into the restroom and quizzing him about Malachi. Although he didn't want to think about his exes, he compared her to Miriam and Norene. He couldn't imagine either of them—especially Norene—being concerned about someone she didn't get along with. With the blinders of love ripped off, he clearly saw how self-centered she was. Ella might be bossy and contentious at times, but it was obvious she cared about her sister. And now that he'd seen her smile . . . whoa.

A knock sounded at the door, making them both jump. "Ella?" Barnabas said. "You and Nelson still in there?"

Her knockout smile disappeared, her eyes widening into saucers. "Uh, *ya, Daed.*"

"Planning on coming out anytime soon? We're hungry."

There was subtle teasing in his tone, much like the way he'd poked fun at Malachi and his violets. From the alarm on Ella's face, Nelson suspected she wasn't picking up on it. She threw open the door. "Sorry about that, *Daed.*"

The corner of Barnabas's lip lifted ever so slightly. "Hope I wasn't interrupting anything *important.*"

Nelson almost grinned again. He was starting to like Barnabas.

Ella smoothed back her *kapp*, as if she were pushing back invisible stray strands of hair, but there wasn't a single one out of place. Now that got him thinking about what her hair looked like underneath the covering. Was it wavy? Straight? Thick? How long was it?

He froze, resisting the temptation to smack himself upside the head. What was he doing, thinking about her hair? Or her smile? And why was his heart still hammering? *Oh no.* Dread filled his gut. He wasn't attracted to Ella Yoder. Nope, nope, nope. That couldn't be possible. He'd always been a sucker for a sweet smile, but that was the old Nelson. Besides, this was Ella. Smiles from her were few and far between.

"Guess the cat's got both of *yer* tongues. See you in the kitchen." Barnabas turned and walked away.

Ella leaned against the bathroom doorjamb. "How embarrassing," she muttered.

Agreed. "Why didn't you say anything?"

Her head whipped toward him. "Why didn't you?"

"I'm not the one who put us in this predicament."

She faced him. "I know, but you could have said something anyway." She lifted her chin. "You're the most vexing man I've ever met."

"Vexing? Me?" Without thinking, he stepped closer to her. "You dragged me into the bathroom!"

Junia giggled.

They both turned to see her and Malachi standing there, watching them. "Lover's spat?" Junia said, a huge smile on her face.

To his credit, Malachi wasn't laughing, but he shot a quizzical look at Nelson before turning his attention back to Junia. The kid couldn't keep his eyes off the woman. She smirked and they headed toward the kitchen.

"Lover's spat. Humph." Ella wasn't looking at him.

"As if that were even a possibility." He kept his gaze forward. And just for good measure he said, "The idea is beyond ridiculous."

"Right." But there was less verve in her tone, and more . . . hurt? Nah, that wasn't it. Why would she be hurt? They were both speaking the truth.

Without another word she walked away, and he followed her into the kitchen. Delicious smells filled the room. He'd noticed them before when he was washing his hands, and although the aromas were fainter through the rest of the house, he could still detect them. His stomach growled, but everyone had the good grace to ignore the sound. The cheese and crackers hadn't put a dent in his hunger.

Barnabas was seated at the head of the table, and Junia and Malachi had taken their places on one side, leaving an empty space at the opposite end and two on the side. He didn't feel comfortable sitting at the end. That was always reserved for . . . the wife. And mother. He felt a tinge of sadness. He didn't know how Barnabas's wife and Ella and Junia's mother had passed away. He didn't even know her name. But he was sorry for their loss.

He sat in the chair closest to Barnabas. He wouldn't be surprised if Ella took the chair at the end of the table. She seemed to have taken her mother's place in the kitchen and in her concern for Junia.

Ella buzzed around the kitchen, setting a casserole dish on the table, then rushing to get two large bowls of mashed potatoes and a cooked vegetable mixture. Junia was still sitting next to Malachi. Why wasn't she helping her sister? He glanced at Barnabas, who was eyeing the casserole with great interest. What had Ella called it? Chicken supreme? He didn't seem to notice that one daughter was serving the meal and the other wasn't.

Odd. In his large family, all the women helped serve when they gathered for meals. After Phoebe had married Jalon, and *Mamm* was the only female in their household, he and his brothers helped her in the kitchen and Nelson had learned how to make a perfect pizza dough. Otherwise, it was the female domain. He looked at Junia again. Maybe Ella didn't want her help. He could see her refusing to let Junia do anything.

When all the food was on the table, Ella finally plopped down . . . on the seat next to him. Which told him that the chair at the end of the table was ordinarily empty.

Then, as if she realized what she'd done, she jumped up and sat across from Barnabas.

She didn't want to sit next to him? Fine. He didn't care.

Never mind that tiny prick of indignation in his heart. *Wait, what?* Apparently he was so hungry he was losing his marbles.

Barnabas lowered his head to pray, and everyone followed suit.

After they finished giving thanks, Ella started passing around the dishes of food. Nelson was more than ready to dig in.

"Eat your fill," Barnabas said to everyone. "We've got plenty."

Her father was right. Ella had made a feast. Nelson reached for a roll and broke it open. Steam wafted from inside as he slathered it with butter, then bit in. Light, fluffy, and yeasty. Just how he liked them. When he looked across the table, Junia had finished buttering a roll and handed it to Malachi. He smiled and put it on his plate. When Barnabas handed him the bowl of mashed potatoes, Malachi put a dollop on Junia's dish. Hmm. They sure were comfortable with each other. That was fast—too fast.

He frowned and glanced at Ella, wanting to gauge her reaction to the two of them. But she was leaning back in the chair, her eyes closed. He figured she might still be praying, and then she opened them. She wasn't praying. She was exhausted.

Suddenly she sat up, put a few bites of food on her plate, and began to eat.

During the rest of the meal, everyone engaged in small talk, and Nelson learned a bit about the Yoders—they had moved to Marigold a little more than a year ago from Lancaster; Barnabas used to be a cabinet maker before he became a grocery store owner; and while Ohio was different than Pennsylvania, their small family had settled here without much problem.

"Everyone's been so welcoming," Barnabas said, finishing off the last of the vegetables, which were so delicious, Nelson had consumed two helpings.

"Do you miss Lancaster?" Malachi asked, looking at Junia. When wasn't he looking at her?

"I've been homesick." She leaned closer to him. "I'm feeling much better now."

The one topic they didn't discuss was the woman who used to sit in the chair where Ella was seated. While he was mildly curious, he respected their privacy.

Once everyone had their fill, Barnabas said to Malachi and Nelson, "We can continue our conversation in the living room. I need to stoke the fire in the stove anyway."

"But, *Daed*," Junia said, her voice sticky sweet, "I promised Malachi I'd show him *mei* shell collection from when we went to Sarasota. I can bring it in the living room. Nelson might like to see it too."

Nelson wasn't interested in seashells, no offense to Junia. Naturally, Malachi was eager—whatever Junia wanted, he wanted, it seemed—and Nelson didn't blame him. It would be rude not to look at her collection, and she seemed impatient to show them.

Barnabas glanced at Ella, who had her eyes closed again. He turned to Junia. "You should—"

"I'll meet you in the living room." She jumped up from the chair, gave Malachi a sugary look, and disappeared out of the kitchen.

Malachi stood. "*Danki* for supper, Ella," he said, close behind Junia.

Barnabas pushed away from the table. "I'd better get the fire going." Then he paused. "Do you need some help cleaning up, Ella?"

Not looking at him, she waved him off. "I've got it."

"Join us when *yer* done." He glanced at Nelson and left.

Ella put her elbows on the table and leaned forward, rubbing her temples on both sides. She closed her eyes again.

He started to get up and head to the living room. Ella said she would take care of the mess. But instead of leaving, he started picking up the dirty plates off the table.

She lifted her head. "What are you doing?"

"Helping." He took the plates and set them on the counter near the sink. When he turned around to get the silverware, she was standing.

"I don't need any help," she said, weariness tinging her words. "*Geh* look at Junia's shells."

He almost smirked. Even when she was tired, she was bossy. "She won't notice if I'm there or not." He gathered up the silverware.

"That's true." She sighed. "Normally I would shoo you out of *mei* kitchen, but I doubt you'd listen."

"And you'd be right." The way she talked about the kitchen gave credence to his thought that she would have refused Junia's help if her sister had offered. The woman was protective of her domain. "I'll clear and you can wash."

She nodded and went to the sink. As she filled it with water and soap, he piled dishes next to her. Although she'd made a lot of food, there wasn't a single leftover. Nelson had done his part to make sure there wasn't. There was some lingering food on the serving dishes, so he scraped those in the trash and handed the empty bowls and platter to her. She plunged them into the sink.

Without skipping a beat, he took a dish towel and started drying, preparing himself for her to say no. He was surprised when she didn't, and together they made quick work of the dishes in silence.

Ella pulled the plug and rinsed off the dishrag underneath the tap and squeezed it out. She went to the table and wiped it down. "Did you leave room for dessert?" she asked, shaking the rag over the sink.

"Depends on the dessert." He set the dry, sparkling clean meat platter on the stove.

"I thought you liked everything." She pulled over a pie plate that was tucked in the corner of the counter.

"There is one thing I don't like," he admitted, inching over to see what was under the tinfoil covering. "Chocolate."

She gasped. "You're joking."

"Nope. Dark, milk, white—I don't like any of them." But he was liking the look of this blueberry pie she was unveiling. Yum.

"I love chocolate." She opened the cabinet and took out four small dessert plates. "Any kind anytime." She sighed. "Except tonight. I'm too tired to eat anything. Not even a chocolate chip."

He almost offered to cut the pie and put the pieces on the plates, but his serving skills were less than stellar. Hers were perfect, and she put four equal pieces of juicy pie on the plates. She took two, and he quickly gathered up the other ones. She gave him a quick glance but didn't say anything as he followed her to the living room.

Junia and Malachi were sitting close together and looking at the shells. At first glance, Nelson could see she had a decent-sized collection. As he handed Barnabas his pie, he glanced out the window. The snow had eased up. Soon after dessert, he and Malachi would head home, and Nelson would tell Phoebe she had nothing to worry about—as long as Malachi and Junia stayed underneath the watchful eyes of the Yoders. That was unrealistic, though. His sister would have to deal with her concerns herself. He didn't have the time or inclination to be Malachi's babysitter, and Malachi would resent him for it anyway.

Barnabas was sitting in his chair working in a puzzle book. He might seem a little detached, but it was clear he doted on Junia. But Nelson didn't have much of a read on how he felt about his other daughter.

After everyone had received their piece of pie, Ella went upstairs. Nelson brought his plate to sit down on a chair near Barnabas and took a huge bite of the dessert. Oh wow. This was the best blueberry pie he'd ever tasted. Ella was an amazing cook.

"Appreciate you helping Ella." At Nelson's questioning look he added, "I could hear both of you cleaning up. I'm surprised she let you."

I am too. He looked at the staircase. Had she gone to bed? He wouldn't blame her if she had. Obviously, she'd worked hard to make the meal by herself, since Junia hadn't taken any credit for the food—and she struck Nelson as the type who would.

A minute later, Ella came downstairs carrying Nelson's coat. She walked over to him. "Don't forget this."

He nodded and took it from her. "*Danki.*"

She gave a weary nod and went back upstairs.

Nelson and Barnabas continued to eat their pie slices while Junia and Malachi took their dessert into the kitchen, using the need to make coffee as an excuse. Nelson didn't want to be too overbearing, and Barnabas didn't stop them. What trouble could they get into when they were only a few feet away?

Barnabas fell silent, stroking his beard a few times before saying, "What do you think?"

"About what?" He looked at the empty pie plate, wishing he had another piece. But Ella hadn't returned from upstairs, and he was sure she wasn't coming back down. She was probably fast asleep by now. Besides, he'd eaten more than his fair share of food tonight.

"Those two." With a nod, he gestured in the direction of the kitchen. "They seem real smitten with each other."

"That they do. But I don't have an opinion one way or another." Not exactly true, but in the end, it didn't matter what he thought. "They're both adults."

"That they are." He continued to look straight ahead, and after a long silence he finally said, "When are you thinking about starting on *yer* shop?"

111

"After Christmas. Maybe late January." That would give him plenty of time to figure out what he needed, order the materials, and find a place to live.

Junia and Malachi came back into the living room. Nelson noticed her cheeks were rosy. Maybe leaving them alone wasn't a good idea. Just as they sat down on the couch, he stood. "We need to be heading back, Malachi. The snow's stopped, but it could start up again."

Disappointment crossed his nephew's features. Junia scooted closer to him.

While he considered the Yoders a nice family—even Ella had her moments—he was done chaperoning and ready to get home. "I'll hitch up the buggy," he said. When Barnabas stood and offered to help, Nelson motioned for him to sit back down. "I've got it." He turned to Malachi. "I'll be back in a few minutes."

Malachi glanced at Junia, her mouth pursed into a frown. Or was it a pout?

Nelson put on his coat, slipped into his boots, told Barnabas and Junia goodbye, then walked out of the house. While the snow had stopped, the temperature had dipped several degrees. Good thing Ella had given him his coat. He'd forgotten all about it again.

He paused and looked at the warehouse across the street. His warehouse, soon to be a butcher shop. A part of him still couldn't believe he owned a business. Now that he was here looking at it, a flicker of excitement lit inside him. He had to stop worrying about failing and focus on succeeding.

Tucking deeper into his coat, he walked over to the barn and hitched Crackerjack to the buggy, then drove to the front of the house and waited. And waited. And waited. He shifted in his seat, ready to give his nephew an earful if he had to get out of the buggy and go get him. He was about to do just that when the door opened and Malachi finally came outside, Junia following. He looked back at her twice as he made his way down the steps and to the buggy.

"Good grief," Nelson muttered. Had he acted like this much of a fool when he was in love—correction, *thought* he was in love? Probably. He inwardly winced. Knowing he'd engaged in similar behavior made it that much harder to see Malachi so—how had Phoebe put it? —lovesick. Accurate descriptor.

"See you next week!" Junia called as Malachi hauled himself into the buggy.

They already had another date planned? Great. As Malachi nodded and waved, Nelson pulled out of the driveway.

Conversation ground to a halt between them, and Nelson assumed his nephew was reliving every second of the last three and a half hours. All Nelson was thinking about was Ella's blueberry pie. And her—but only a little. He did hope she'd get a good night's sleep tonight. She looked like she needed it.

"I'm curious," Malachi said when they were a little more than halfway home.

He relaxed against the back of his seat. "About what?"

"You and Ella."

His head whipped toward Malachi. "Huh?"

"Hanging out alone in the bathroom—"

"We weren't hanging out. We were—" He clamped his mouth shut.

Malachi crossed one ankle over his knee and gave Nelson a side-eyed look. "You were what?"

He didn't like Malachi's teasing tone, although he was glad his nephew was returning to form and not openly pining for Junia all the way home. "Talking. About things."

"What things?"

Time to switch gears. "That blueberry pie sure was *gut*."

"Hmm." Malachi chuckled.

"What?" Nelson griped.

"I think Junia's right." He grinned. "You and Ella like each other."

"She's wrong," he grumbled. "As wrong as a person can get."

"Or you're in denial."

Knowing that if he responded, Malachi would continue prying, teasing, or more likely a potent combination of both, Nelson zipped his lips. Let his nephew think what he wanted. Nelson knew the truth. So did Ella. They didn't like each other. In fact, they could barely stand to be in the same room. Well, maybe that was a bit of an over-exaggeration, but the point still stood.

He dropped off Malachi, practically kicking him out of the buggy, not that the guy minded. Nelson could tell he was still floating from his date with Junia.

After his nephew went inside, Nelson blew out a breath. Once he moved to Marigold, he wouldn't be able to avoid the Yoders. After spending some time with them, he had to admit they would be good neighbors, especially Barnabas. But that didn't mean he wanted to hang around Malachi and Junia. Phoebe would have to figure something out because he wasn't going to do any more chaperoning. Not even for the promise of a gooseberry pie.

Ten

"That's a perfect seam. Are you sure you haven't sewn anything before?"

Wendy glanced up at Eunice Miller and smiled. "Not a stitch, other than a few half-hearted attempts to reattach a button."

Eunice sat next to her at the treadle sewing machine. "You're certainly making my job easier." She showed Wendy how to turn the material without lifting the needle. "Now sew the other side."

Wendy set to work as Eunice went back to her worktable where she was putting the finishing touches on a brightly colored Christmas quilt wall hanging for an English customer.

After her initial visit to the fabric shop, Wendy returned two days later and asked where she could take sewing lessons, preferably from the Amish. The proprietor had given her Eunice's phone number, who was one of her part-time employees. A week later, she was in the woman's home learning the basics of sewing on a treadle machine. Wendy had brought some black and navy blue plaid flannel and was working on a simple scarf, which was basically cutting the material into a long, thick strip and sewing the sides together.

She'd expected the project to be easy, but she hadn't anticipated how much she would delight in sitting in a simply decorated living room in front of a large picture window, snow falling softly outside as she let the machine do the work. This was much more fun than listening to the Warrens bicker . . . and bicker and bicker. Their first meeting had once again gone nowhere, and the couple—plus Claude—made yet another appointment with her to discuss the issue again. She knew conflict mediation took more time with some people than others, but she wondered if Harold and Judy would ever find common ground. They seemed to enjoy fighting with each other a little too much.

It didn't take long for her to finish the second seam, and after Eunice showed her how to shift the needle back and forth to secure the stitches, she declared the lesson complete. "Usually my sewing lessons are longer, but you've got the hang of it. I'll only charge you half price."

"I don't mind paying the full amount." Her gaze gravitated to the quilt. "That's beautiful. How long did it take you to make it?"

Eunice walked to the table, Wendy following. "About two months. My oldest daughter helped me cut the pieces. She lives next door with her husband and their three children."

Wendy nodded, inspecting the five red-and-green holly basket motifs on a white background, surrounded by a thin red border and a thicker evergreen one. "Such perfect stitches," she said, marveling at the meticulous quilting.

"Oh, there are plenty of mistakes." Eunice pointed to one of the baskets. "Right here is a long stitch. It makes the line look uneven."

"I can't tell." Wendy turned to her. "Can you show me how you made the design?"

"Sure."

The women sat down at the table, and for the next hour, Wendy not only learned about Amish quilting, but she also used the opportunity to ask Eunice some questions about the Amish faith. "If I'm not being too nosy," Wendy said.

"Not at all." Eunice smiled and took off her reading glasses. "What would you like to know?"

By the end of the hour, Wendy had learned more about the *Ordnung* and the church service—three hours long at a minimum! She was surprised that not all Amish ended up joining the church. Some opted to leave their communities and live in the English world. If they did that before they were baptized, they weren't shunned.

"And if they leave after their baptism?"

Eunice paused. "When you're baptized, you make a vow to God in front of your family and friends to always be a member of the church. We're expected to keep that vow for life. I had a cousin who left after baptism, and we had to shun her."

She'd heard of shunning before and recalled that her mother years ago had read a novel with the word in the title. But she couldn't stop her next question. "Isn't that harsh?"

"Depends on how you look at it." Eunice pinned two layers of cloth together. "We believe that shunning helps bring people back to their faith." She frowned, still staring at the cloth. "But it didn't work for my cousin. There are also communities who don't shun. It just depends on the district and its *Ordnung*."

Wendy let Eunice's words soak in as they continued to work. While it seemed heartless to ostracize a family member, she didn't have enough knowledge of the Amish and their practices to make any kind of judgment on what they did among themselves.

Eunice turned to a less controversial topic. "We don't take pictures or pose for them," she said. "It's a sign of humility and we're following the commandment to not have graven images."

Wendy was beginning to understand how important humility was to the Amish faith. That made her think about Barnabas, who was extremely humble. She could spot that trait in half a second, having spent her career around people who were extremely prideful. She could even look at herself and see all the times over the years when she was driven more by pride than anything else. That was probably why she'd been so angry about being passed over for partner so many times.

Sitting in Eunice's living room, sewing and talking about her faith, made Wendy's life in New York seem so distant, even though it had been less than a year since she'd left the city and her practice. She had so many more questions for her new friend, but she would save that for the next lesson.

"Would you like to join us for church sometime?" Eunice asked as Wendy put on her coat.

She smiled, pleasantly surprised by her offer. "That would be wonderful," Wendy answered without hesitation.

Eunice handed Wendy the sewing bag she'd brought with her. "We do have a few rules for English visitors. Please wear a dress—dark colors are best if you have them. No high heels, and not too much makeup. Oh, and no jewelry."

Wendy nodded.

"Service is next Sunday since this is our off week. I usually attend the Birch Creek church during those weeks, and sometimes my sister's church. They're nice districts too."

She knew a little bit about Birch Creek. Charity's husband, Jesse, was from there, but Wendy had only driven around the community on one of her back-road drives. Like Marigold, it was populated with Amish and English houses, with a gently rolling landscape dotted with gardens and farms.

"Thank you so much, Eunice. I really enjoyed myself today. I'll bring more fabric next week."

"I enjoyed meeting you, Wendy. We'll do a more complicated project during that lesson."

"Hopefully not too complicated."

Eunice laughed. "It won't be."

Wendy said goodbye and walked outside into the frigid winter air. She got into her mother's car and turned it on, then grabbed a long-handled window brush and reached out to brush the snow off the car. She glanced at Eunice's house, noting the missing shutters and white siding that was identical to most of the Amish houses in Marigold.

As she drove home, she thought about everything she'd learned today, aside from sewing. The Amish had a lot of rules, but she could see how those rules kept the community cohesive and thriving. But that wasn't the main reason for the *Ordnung*. Everything, including the rules, was centered around God. *"We're not perfect,"* Eunice had pointed out. *"Not even close. Only one person was perfect on this earth, and that was Jesus. Scripture says to love the Lord God with all our heart, mind, and soul."*

"That's Matthew, right?"

"Yes. Those are Jesus' words, and we do our best to live by them."

Wendy pulled into her driveway and turned off the car. She stared at the steering wheel. She'd grown up in church, but how much of her life had been spent loving God so completely? Very little. The energy and effort she'd put into her faith paled in comparison to her obsession with her job. Another verse came to mind, from Galatians: *"For do I now persuade men, or God?"*

She knew the answer, and it seared her soul.

⋅ৎৡৣৣৡৣ⋅

Ella leaned against the store counter. Less than five minutes ago, the store was chock-full of customers, typical for the week before Christmas. *Daed* was in his office ordering more inventory while Ella helped their clientele. The patrons had hit the baking aisle hard, along with the three Christmas candy displays at the front of the store. She glanced at the clock. Not even lunchtime. At least she could slow down and take a breath before the next wave.

She turned and scowled at Junia, who was seated on a stool and writing in a composition notebook. When her father had been up front checking out customers, Junia had made a half-hearted attempt to assist Ella in straightening and restocking the shelves. But as soon as *Daed* disappeared in the back, she sat down on the stool and started writing, something she'd been doing since Malachi left on Saturday. She'd even spent the afternoon and evening after church jotting in her notebook while Ella cleaned up the house after the service. She didn't bother asking Junia to help. It was easier to do the cleaning herself, even though she was still tired from the day before. She was too exhausted to get into another argument.

But this was different. The store was their livelihood, and Junia was slacking even more than before. "The baking aisle needs some attention," she said, facing her sister.

Junia didn't answer or look up. She continued scribbling in the notebook.

"Did you hear me?" Ella moved closer, her fists on her hips.

"*Ya.*" Junia continued writing.

"Ooh." She began to count, but by the time she got to ten her anger was almost out of control. "Get over there and clean it up before we have more customers."

Slowly, with infuriating calm, Junia looked at her. "But you're *so* much better at doing that than I am, Ella." She returned to her writing with a smile.

True, but not because Ella had any special skill at tidying items on a shelf. There was only one reason she did a better job—she cared about her work and about the store. Junia didn't. The blister of rage inside her popped, and she seized Junia's notebook.

"Hey!" Junia jumped up from her chair. "You can't read that!"

But Ella turned her back and started reading out loud.

Dear Malachi,

I just loved your last letter to me. You're so funny and clever! I love hearing about your adventures on the farm—

"Stop it!" Junia shrieked, reaching around Ella to get the notebook. But Ella spun around and hurried away, flipping to the beginning of the notebook.

Dear Diary,

Hmm. She didn't know her sister kept a diary. Which reminded Ella that she hadn't written in hers for over a week. She'd been too busy. And tired. The date on this entry was before Junia met Malachi.

"*Daed!*" Junia screamed.

Ella scurried around the store, glancing at the pages. She couldn't comprehend more than a word or two as she ran from Junia, and it didn't matter. She was—

Junia jumped on her back.

"Oof!"

"That's mine!" She clawed for the notebook. "Give it back!"

"*Nee!*" Ella tried to throw her off.

But Junia clung to her. They spun forward. Crashed into the candy display. Hit the floor . . . just as the bell above the doorway rang.

Ella looked up. Wendy Pearson stood there, slack-jawed.

"*Maed!*"

Ella scrambled to her feet. Junia did the same, then grabbed the notebook off the floor and held it against her chest. They both looked at their father . . . and Ella wished she hadn't.

Daed's face was redder than a cockscomb, a vein pulsing at his temple as he glowered at them. Uh-oh. She'd never seen him this mad. Not even close.

"I'll come back later," Wendy said as she turned to walk out of the store.

"Don't." *Daed* cleared his throat. "Please don't let my daughters' childish behavior inconvenience you." He ignored them as he went to her. "What can I help you with?"

Wendy glanced at the shards of glass and broken candy canes littered on the floor. "Hot chocolate," she said, still looking bewildered. "I thought I'd get Mom a little treat."

"I'll show you where it is." He turned to Ella and Junia. "Clean this up," he ordered in *Deitsch*. "Now."

Ella went for the broom while Junia picked up the display rack off the floor. In addition to the candy canes scattered around, there were red, green, and silver wrapped chocolate kisses, little packages of red and green gumdrops, discs of peppermint candies, and white taffy with red and green lines running through it. Junia started to pick up the candy.

"Stop!" Ella barked.

Junia continued grabbing the candy, still clutching the notebook.

"There's glass all over the floor. You're going to—"

"Ow!"

"—cut yourself." Ella sighed as Junia clutched her opposite hand. All the candy she'd picked up dropped to the floor. She went to her. "Let me see how bad it is."

"*Nee!* It's your fault I'm hurt!"

The doorbell rang again, and three customers walked inside. Junia slipped out behind them.

Ella warned the women away from the mess with a forced smile. "Just a little accident. We'll get it cleaned up right away."

They nodded. One took a shopping cart while the other two picked up the large plastic baskets stacked next to the carts, and each went her separate way.

As quickly as possible Ella swept up the candy and glass together. The candy was ruined—there was a high chance that glass shards could have entered the wrapping, and she wasn't going to take the chance of someone getting hurt. It was bad enough Junia had. *She deserved it. She wouldn't listen to me when I told her to stop.*

But Ella's guilt drowned out her pettiness. Junia was right this time. It was Ella's fault. She shouldn't have taken the diary, and she shouldn't have kept it away from her. But those facts didn't erase how satisfied she'd felt at Junia's panicked anger. Very satisfied.

And that was a problem.

Eleven

Barnabas fell into his desk chair. "I've got a real problem on my hands."

Wendy sat across from him, still trying to process the scene she'd witnessed. As she approached the glass door, she saw Ella and Junia whirl toward the candy display and tumble to the floor in a spectacular crash. It would have been a little funny if Barnabas didn't look so defeated right now.

"I'm sorry you had to witness that." He shook his head. "They haven't spoken much lately, and I thought they'd taken some time to cool off from their fight last week and let things go. Boy, was I wrong. I had three brothers and two sisters growing up, and we never fought like that." He paused, smirking a little. "Maybe us boys did when we were younger. But not my sisters, and not as adults."

She nodded, unsure of what to say. He was right, though. He did have a big problem. Two of them.

He waved his hand. "Nothing I can do about it right now." He looked at her. "You said you needed to talk to me?"

Wendy nodded again, fiddling with her sewing bag. She did want to pick up hot chocolate for Mom, and for herself. She wasn't one for sweets, but a steaming mug of cocoa on a wintry day had sounded good. It also gave her an excuse to come here. After her talk with Eunice, she'd spent the rest of the afternoon and night thinking about her life. She sensed she was at a crossroads of some sort, but she wasn't sure exactly what path to take, or even why she was so uncertain. By morning she had made one decision—she wanted to give Barnabas a gift. Again, she had no idea why, other than thinking the scarf she'd made at Eunice's would look good on him. She needed to give it to him before she chickened out.

She opened the bag and pulled out the scarf. "Merry Christmas," she said, handing it to him.

His bushy brows lifted as he looked at the scarf. But he didn't move to take it.

Her cheeks heated to the boiling point. She'd never done anything on impulse in her life, and she shouldn't have presumed he would want something from her.

"Sorry." She started to shove the scarf back inside the bag. "I shouldn't have—"

"Wait." He held out his hand.

She paused, and when he waggled his fingers a little, she handed him the scarf.

He took it, the shock still in his eyes as he looked at the plaid. Now she felt silly on top of being embarrassed. The scarf was just a piece of fabric with two seams up the sides. Nothing special about it. "I'm taking sewing lessons, and this was my first project. I have plenty of scarves. So does Mom. The black and navy plaid is masculine, and I don't know any other men to give . . . it . . . to." Did she really just admit that? Cringy. "Anyway, you didn't charge me for the crackers, so . . ." Ugh, this was turning into a disaster. "I'll be going now." She popped up from her chair and turned to rush out of his office before she humiliated herself further.

"Wendy."

She turned, her ears tingling. He had such a calm, soothing voice. Not too deep nor too mellow. Just right.

"Thank you." He wrapped the scarf around his neck. And smiled.

Her heart flipped. His smile was even better than his voice, and she was glad she was able to do something nice for him. She smiled in return. He was a kind, humble man who should have some happiness.

But as with so many things in her life lately, she was surprised. She hadn't expected to feel so elated at seeing his happiness over her small gesture. "You're welcome."

·⁓☙⁓·

That evening, Nelson was in the warehouse—his warehouse now—for the first time, figuring out his temporary living quarters. He'd put in a full day of work at the farm, then loaded up his buggy with a small gas heater and a two-drawer wooden chest, hitched up Crackerjack, and headed here. Although it was dark, he had a large camping lamp along with several other lights—a big flashlight, two small ones, and a battery-operated mini-lamp—spread out on the floor, giving him plenty of illumination to figure out the layout of his new abode. Not that he needed a lot of space—just enough for a twin bed and a place to put his clothing.

His initial thought had been to stay at Jesse's until he was finished renovating the warehouse, but upon further reflection, he realized that wouldn't work out. Spending a night or two with his brother and Charity would be fine, but their house was tiny, and they had only one bedroom, so he'd have to sleep on the couch. There was a lot of room in the warehouse, though, and he could set up temporary accommodations until he came up with more suitable living arrangements.

Tonight he would leave the gas heater and chest here, and on the following trip, bring a wagon with his bed and a few other items. Next week was Christmas, but after celebrating that holiday and Second Christmas with his family, he would move here and start renovating his new place in earnest. The longer he waited to get started on his business, the longer it would take for him to repay the loan.

He'd settled on the back left corner of the vast area and was in the process of marking the space when he heard a rustling noise by the rear exit of the warehouse. He grabbed a flashlight off the floor and went outside, shining a light on the woods several yards away.

"Hey!" Ella lifted her hand to her eyes. "Watch where you're pointing that thing."

He set down the light, although not without smiling at the little bit of inadvertent payback for when she'd blinded him several times on their search for Malachi and Junia two weeks ago. "What are you doing back here?"

"None of your business."

Her tone was as sharp as ever, but he didn't miss the weariness lacing it. "*Yer* on my property, so I have the right to know." He flashed the light at her again, but not in her eyes this time.

"Oh. That's right." Her shoulders slumped and she started walking away.

He moved to go inside and finish up, only to halt when he saw that Ella wasn't headed back to the store, or even her house. And the puny little flashlight she was holding was so dim he doubted she could tell where she was going. What if a raccoon ran out of the woods? Or worse, a group of them?

He shook his head. Nothing would happen unless she provoked them, and she was too smart for that. Still . . . Why was she walking at night by the woods anyway? Shaking his head at his inability to leave her to her own devices, he rushed to catch up with her.

She was tapping the body of the flashlight against her palm. "Stupid thing," she muttered.

"Maybe it needs new batteries."

Ella jumped at the sound of his voice. "Why are you following me?"

"I'm not . . ." But that's exactly what he was doing. "Better question. Why are you walking by the woods?"

"I—" Her flashlight blinked out. She shook it, the batteries rattling inside. "Great." She started to shiver.

"What's with you not wearing a coat?" He started to take his off and give it to her, but she held up her hand.

"Thanks, but *nee*. I need to *geh* home anyway."

She sounded like she was getting her teeth pulled. He shouldn't even be here questioning her. "Okay," he said. "I've got to get back to work."

"You're working? Now?"

"*Ya*. Just getting some things done before Christmas."

"Like what?"

He should have known she'd ply him with questions. At least that kept her from walking into the dark woods without a working flashlight. "Setting up my temporary bedroom."

"You're going to live in there?"

"Yep."

She was still shivering, and even though she'd told him no, he took off his coat and put it on her. She didn't protest. "Why aren't you living with your *bruder*?"

"They have a little house. And they're still newlyweds."

"It doesn't seem right—you not having a real place to live."

"It's fine. I've got a bed—well, I'll have one in a day or two—and a heater, plus a chest for my clothing."

"What about a bathroom?"

"Ordered a Port-o-John yesterday. I'll need it for the business. And to answer *yer* next question, I've got a big watercooler where I can wash up."

"What makes you think I was going to ask that?"

"Weren't you?"

She paused, then frowned. "*Ya*. But you don't have a shower."

"I can shower at Jesse's."

"Are you eating there too?"

"Probably." He hadn't thought that much about food, which was unusual for him. He knew Charity wouldn't mind making extra, but he wouldn't impose for every meal. He could go back to his parents' house too. He also had another resource. "I'll be living next to a grocery store," he said with a grin. "Plenty of food there." A gust of wind kicked up, frigid enough that it even made him shiver.

"Have you eaten yet?" she asked.

"*Nee*, but *mei bruder*'s expecting me."

She slipped off his coat and handed it to him. "Better not keep him waiting." She started to walk away, this time toward the store.

It didn't seem right not to properly end the conversation, so he said, "Night, Ella."

"*Gute nacht.*"

He watched her go. Yep, something was bugging her, all right. Even her inquisition didn't have much enthusiasm, as if she were preoccupied. He shrugged. Like she said, it wasn't his business.

Nelson went back into the warehouse. She was right, he did need a proper place to live. He had a vague idea about what kind of house he would build behind his business, but nothing was firm, other than he would have to clear part of the woods. His property line ran back far enough that there was plenty of room for a decent-sized home. He didn't need anything bigger than what Jesse had, although he said they were planning to add on to their place in the spring. Charity might be expecting, or they just wanted more room. If she was pregnant, that was another reason for him to stay here. She didn't need him underfoot, and he didn't want to be.

He finished up, untied Crackerjack's reins from a tree near the warehouse, and started to climb inside his buggy. He glanced at a faded trail leading from the street to the warehouse entrance. He'd have to create a parking lot and put in a concrete path in front of the building. Doubts started to creep in as he added that to his mental list of things to do. There were so many of them, his head was spinning.

As he guided his horse to the road, he glanced at the Yoders' house. A light was on in the kitchen and one in the living room. The memory of Ella's scrumptious blueberry pie made his stomach growl and, oddly, settled his nerves a little bit. She should consider selling those in the store. He'd buy one . . . or five. He turned on the road and headed to Jesse's.

.ঞ৯৶.

Ella picked at the pork chops and sauerkraut she'd made for supper and glanced at Junia's empty chair for the dozenth time since they'd started eating. She hadn't seen her sister since she fled from the store. She owed her an apology, but try as she might, she wasn't eager to give her one.

After she'd finished cleaning up the candy mess and attending to the steady stream of customers that came in during the rest of the afternoon, she went to the office to apologize to *Daed* and tell him she was taking the cost of the candy out of her next paycheck. Her rueful words were met with a curt nod, and he'd spoken very little to her since she'd come home after she closed the store and went for a short walk before starting supper. Running into Nelson was a surprise, and it didn't sit all that well with her that he was living in a cold, empty warehouse for the foreseeable future. But he was a grown man and that was his decision. A dumb one in her opinion, not that her opinion mattered. To anyone.

Daed took a bite of sauerkraut, but from the look of his almost full plate, he didn't have much more of an appetite than she did. They went through the motions of eating for a few more minutes, and suddenly Junia breezed through the door. She sat down at the table as if she hadn't disappeared for most of the afternoon and was over an hour late for supper. She made a face at the sauerkraut and picked up the platter, taking one of the two pork chops and plopping it on her plate. Her eyes closed.

"Junia," Ella said.

"Shhh." She waved her off. "I'm praying."

Ella fisted her hands under the table and waited for her to finish. Junia seemed to take her time asking God to bless the food, and by the time she was done, Ella decided to keep her mouth shut. What was the point in trying to find out where she'd been or why she was late or if her hand was okay, or even to apologize? Every syllable she'd say would be met with a smirk, a sassy chin tilt, and a knowing look that no matter what, Junia wouldn't be held accountable. Not for being late or for the fight in the store . . . nothing.

"Where have you been?"

The women jerked their gazes to *Daed*. His brow flattened above angry gray eyes, his tone deep and harsh, something Ella hadn't heard from him in, well, forever.

Junia's eyes widened in surprise. "I was out."

"Out where?"

Confusion replaced surprise. "I came back here to take care of my wounded hand." She held up her index finger, the tip covered with a single bandage.

"That didn't take all day."

Ella shrank back in her chair.

Now Junia looked annoyed. "If you must know, I met with Malachi."

"He came over here?"

"*Nee.*" A blush appeared on her cheeks. "We have a special place. Halfway between our homes. It's a far walk from here, so it took a while to get home."

Daed grew quiet. "You met with him alone?"

"*Ya.*" But the confident tilt of her chin dropped.

He didn't say anything for a long moment. Junia glared at Ella. Ella glared back. "Don't look at me like that."

"Like what?" Junia snapped.

"Like it's *mei* fault you ran off with Malachi."

"I didn't run off with him!" Junia let out a dramatic sigh. "He's the only one who understands me."

Ella scoffed. "If he really understood you, he'd run in the opposite direction."

"You take that back!"

"*Nee.* I'm sick and tired of you taking off all the time and leaving me to do everything. You're acting like a spoiled brat."

"Am not." Junia shoved her pork chop away. The edge of the dish clanked against her glass of watered-down tea. She turned to *Daed*.

"See what I mean? She bosses me around and calls me names. She has no idea how hard it is on me—"

"What!" Ella exploded, jumping up from her chair. "Hard on you? You don't do anything but make breakfast, and lately it's been lumpy oatmeal, soggy eggs, and rock-hard biscuits. You don't put an effort into anything. You're lazy—"

"And you're jealous." Junia leapt to her feet. "You're mad that you're ugly and frumpy. *Nee mann* would want a single date with you, much less to marry you."

Ella stilled, every word piercing her heart. Then she loaded her final arrow. "You're a liar," she said quietly.

"Everything I just said is true." She crossed her arms.

She leaned forward. "You're lying to Malachi. Because if he knew the real you—the lazy, selfish, mean woman you really are—he'd never look at you again."

Junia stepped back. "*Daed*, tell her to take that back!" She looked in his direction.

So did Ella. Then she gasped. *Daed* was gone.

Twelve

Wendy was drying the last dish from supper when she heard the doorbell ring. Her mother was in the living room, and while it would take her more than a minute or two to get up out of her chair and answer the door, Wendy let her. Mom was independent to her core, a trait she'd passed down to her daughter. While being self-reliant was a good thing, Wendy was realizing how nice it was to have and give help, something she infrequently had and did when she was living alone in New York City, apart from working for her clients.

She hung the damp towel on the hook near the sink and headed for the living room. They rarely had company in the evening, although Mom's friend Susan sometimes stopped by and stayed for supper and to play cards. Wendy wasn't interested in playing gin and usually took Monroe on a walk during that time. When she entered the room, she was stunned to see the dog was seated at Barnabas's feet.

"We've got company." Mom grinned as Monroe wagged his tail and stared up at him. Then she turned to Wendy, her left eyebrow lifted in a questioning arch.

Barnabas gave him a quick pat on the head. "Sorry for dropping by like this." He turned to Wendy. "Can I talk to you for a minute?"

"Of course."

Mom pushed her walker toward her recliner. "You two go on into the kitchen. Don't mind me. Come here, Monroe."

Monroe obeyed and plopped down next to Mom's recliner. But his gaze never left Barnabas, his tail swishing across the wood floor.

After they entered the kitchen, Wendy said, "Would you like some coffee or tea? Water?"

"Water sounds good." He glanced around the small kitchen, shifting his feet as he stood next to one of the four chairs surrounding the table.

Wendy quickly filled a glass with tap water. She used to insist on bottled or filtered water, but the water in Marigold tasted just as good as what she bought in the store. She walked over to the table, gesturing for him to sit down. His brow furrowed as he sat, his shoulders rounding forward. Not only did he look tense, but she could feel frustration radiating off him. She set the glass in front of him and sat in the opposite chair.

"What brings you by?"

His gaze jumped to hers. "Remember that offer you made the other day?"

"Regarding conflict mediation?"

"Yeah." He pushed the heel of his hand back and forth on the table. "I'd . . . I'd like to take you up on it. If you're still willing."

She listened as he explained what had happened after his daughters' fight and at the supper table. "All they do is argue now. They don't talk to each other. They don't listen to what the other has to say. And they definitely don't listen to me." He sighed. "This is my fault."

"They're adults. They need to own their behavior."

"But they wouldn't be like this if I'd—"

"Barnabas." She reached out to touch his arm, then stopped herself. She didn't go around touching her clients. Or men, for that matter. She put her hands in her lap. "Right now, the goal is for Ella and Junia to be civil to each other. Concentrate on that, not on the past."

He nodded, meeting her gaze again, but her words didn't alleviate the pain she saw there. Her heart ached for him. Again, another surprise, and this one was stronger than all the others combined. Over her years as a lawyer, she'd always been able to distance herself from her clients' issues. Her mother always said she had a gift for compartmentalizing, an advantageous skill in the legal profession. But for some reason she couldn't put Barnabas and his agony in separate boxes.

"I'll try." He took a gulp of the water. "There's one thing you and I need to settle before we start resolving things, though."

Inexplicably, she gripped her hands together. Had her expression or tone revealed too much? Could he tell she was struggling with keeping objectivity when all she wanted to do was comfort him?

"I want the conflict stuff to be biblical. We have to follow God's word, not man's."

That caught her off guard, and it also helped shift her emotionally charged thoughts to more practical ones. "Yes." She stood. "I'll be right back."

She went into the living room to get the Bible from the coffee table. She made a mental note to get her own print copy, discovering that she enjoyed the feel of the book in her hands as opposed to holding her phone. Mom looked up from the large-print book she was reading. Monroe rolled over on his side.

"Everything all right?" Mom asked. The brow lifted again.

Wendy smiled. She could tell her mother was dying of curiosity but had the good grace not to ask questions while Barnabas was still here. But it was guaranteed she'd cross-examine her after he left. "Just need the family Bible," she said. "And yes, everything is fine."

Mom nodded and went back to her book. But Wendy didn't miss the faint smile on her face.

Barnabas's glass was empty when she returned to the kitchen. "Would you like more water?" she asked.

"No. I'm filled up, thanks."

She got a pad and a pen from the junk drawer and sat down. "I think it's wise we start with some verses before we come up with a plan."

"We?"

"I could make a basic resolution plan, but without your input, it won't be as effective as you want. Or need." She opened the cover and turned to the book of 1 Thessalonians. "The key component of resolving conflict is communication. That includes stating facts and feelings, and active listening."

"Good luck getting them to do that," he mumbled.

"With prayer and a biblical perspective, we won't need luck."

For the first time since he'd arrived, his shoulders relaxed. "You're right. We won't. I'm not sure why I even said that."

Poor man. He was so discombobulated over the situation. But that only showed how much he cared about his family. Because he did, she had to be honest with him. "That doesn't mean it will be easy."

"I'm sure it won't be. But I do have some hope . . . now. A few minutes ago, I didn't have any." He smiled. "Thank you, Wendy. Even if this doesn't work out and I gotta come up with something else, I'm grateful for your help."

She smiled back. "Anytime, Barnabas. Anytime."

.❧.

Nelson held up his glass of milk and a small plate above his head as he threaded through the crowd—otherwise known as his family—in his parents' living room to the last empty chair. Several conversations were going on at once, and everyone except for him was talking to someone. He sat down with his milk and a pile of snickerdoodles, ready to feast as his eldest brother, Devon, made a huge batch of popcorn—the third one that night—while his wife, Nettie, corralled their three young girls. Adults, teens, young kids, and toddlers and babies filled the room. And his ears. It was getting loud in here.

But his parents loved it, and Nelson did too, despite the crowded clamor. It was Christmas Eve, and Devon and Nettie were visiting from Fredericktown. His other married siblings—twins Zeke and Zeb, Owen, Ezra, and Jesse—had brought their wives and kids, and his younger brothers Perry, twins Mose and Mahlon, and the youngest, Elam, were scattered around the room. Phoebe and Jalon were here with Malachi and his younger sister, Hannah. Nelson didn't bother to count heads. Ezra's wife, Katharine, was expecting, and possibly Charity, so the number would change soon anyway.

He glanced at Malachi, who was seated at a portable card table playing Dutch Blitz with Perry, Zeb, and Mose. It was toasty warm in the room, but Junia's scarf was wrapped around Malachi's neck. Nelson wondered if he even took it off to bathe. He was sure he slept with it, considering he hadn't seen his nephew without it since Junia had given it to him last week. When Nelson started working on his temporary bedroom in the warehouse, Malachi had come by to "help," invariably ending up at E&J's Grocery or Junia's house less than an hour after he arrived.

At first he was irritated because it would have been nice to have some actual assistance, although it wasn't necessary right now. The real work would start in January, and he was just about done making an acceptable bedroom in the cavernous building. But he didn't like being used as an excuse. Love was making Malachi not only *ab im kopp* but also a little self-absorbed.

One person he hadn't seen much of was Ella. Except for that one evening when she was walking behind the warehouse, she'd been scarce. He did see her at the grocery store the three times he stopped by, but she'd been busy with customers. Even Junia had been working, checking out groceries at the counter. The last time he'd made a purchase, she said in a sticky-sweet voice, *"How's Malachi? Will you tell him I miss him?"*

Blech.

"Are there any snickerdoodles left?" Phoebe appeared next to him and gave his shoulder a small push with her hip.

"Three, to be exact." There were plenty more and she knew it. She'd made four dozen of them. He moved to stand up. "Want a seat?"

She shook her head, crouching next to him, her gaze on Malachi as he dipped his chin into the scarf. "What am I going to do with him?"

"Let him be?" Nelson dipped a cookie into the milk. "That's always an option."

"I have a bad feeling about his relationship with Junia."

"Still worried they'll do something they'll regret?"

"Somewhat. I've been praying for God to help with that. No use borrowing trouble."

"Amen." He shoved the cookie in his mouth.

"But this is moving so fast. It's like he's obsessed with her. I see him writing notes all the time, and he disappears whenever he has a chance. I think they're trading letters. Probably talking on the phone too." She sighed. "Ever since I asked you to chaperone him, he won't talk to me about her."

"Can you blame him?"

Phoebe filched a cookie off his plate. "*Nee*. I guess not."

But Nelson was a little concerned too. Malachi had always been precocious. He was also thoughtful, and he and Phoebe were extremely close. Maybe that's why she was having such a hard time with Malachi pulling away, but that wasn't the case for Nelson. The tension between Ella and Junia in E&J's was palpable. All families had their problems, including theirs, but the fact that the two women couldn't even look at each other was a bad sign. Did Malachi even know how estranged they were? Or was he so caught up with Junia he didn't care—about that or anything else?

She looked at the cookie but didn't take a bite. "He said he was going to help you build the butcher shop."

Sure he is. "You still want me to keep an eye on him, *ya*?"

"Please. It would make me feel better."

He turned to her. Saw the worry in her eyes. And swallowed what he'd planned to say—that she needed to let him live. He wasn't a parent and couldn't fully comprehend why she was so worried, but that didn't mean he should dismiss her misgivings. Then there was that great mystery of life—female intuition. Maybe she was sensing something more troubling than he was noticing. Other than his farm duties, his time had been consumed with plans for the butcher shop. Only his scarce Yoder sister sightings and Malachi showing up supposedly to help, then vanishing within thirty minutes, put that situation on his radar. "Sure," he said. "Whatever you need me to do."

She grinned. "*Danki*. Now you'll get two gooseberry pies."

"You still haven't made me the first one."

"Make that three, then." She stood, touched his shoulder, and polished off the cookie as she went to the card table and stood behind Malachi, watching the game.

Nelson munched on the rest of his snack as he watched his family.

The scents of cinnamon-flavored apple cider and fresh popcorn mingling with the wood fire and pine boughs decorating the expansive living room filled the air. Normally he found them comforting, and he always looked forward to the family getting together and celebrating the Savior's birth. He still did, but this time it was to a lesser extent than usual. Six months ago, he'd planned to share this Christmas with Norene as a married couple, or at least an engaged one. Instead, he was alone with a roomful of people. And although he loved them all, there was a dull ache in his chest.

He shook his head, mentally stopping the heartache before it consumed him. He was over her, and over women—all women.

Yet the yearning in his heart that appeared when he met Miriam, and was even stronger when he was with Norene, had never fully disappeared no matter how much self-talk he engaged in. Malachi wasn't the only one who wanted a family of his own. Now that seemed a distant, if impossible, goal. He'd fallen in love twice. He wasn't sure he could handle opening his heart a third time, even if that meant the alternative was being alone. Somehow he had to figure out how to accept that reality.

His father stood in the middle of the room and whistled, the yearly signal that it was time to read the Christmas story in Luke. Nelson finished his milk as all the kids gathered around on the floor, their parents behind them, and the rest of the men and younger teen boys scattered around the room. Everyone grew quiet as *Daed* started to read:

"'Joseph also went up from Galilee, out of the city of Nazareth, into Judea, to the city of David, which is called Bethlehem, because he was of the house and lineage of David, to be registered with Mary, his betrothed wife, who was with child. So it was, that while they were there, the days were completed for her to be delivered. And she brought forth her firstborn Son, and wrapped Him in swaddling cloths, and laid Him in a manger, because there was no room for them in the inn.'"

Nelson listened to the story with rapt attention, even though he'd heard it every Christmas since he could remember. He glanced around the room, his emotions settling. Regardless of what his future held, he had his family and his faith—and he was grateful.

Thirteen

Ella picked up the vanilla-scented miniature candle crock in the middle of the kitchen table, put it on the counter, and finished arranging the place settings for their Christmas Eve supper. She wasn't in a merry mood, though. In fact, she was downright gloomy. Ever since their catastrophic fight in the store, her relationship with Junia had gone downhill faster than a wooden sled on a mountainside.

It wasn't her fault—not completely anyway. Junia wasn't helping things by sneaking off to meet Malachi every day. At least she was helping in the store more than before, but Ella figured that was to appease *Daed*, who had said very little since he'd left them during their fight in the kitchen last week. He was gone for more than three hours, and Ella had wondered if she and Junia needed to search for him. Fortunately, he came back before she'd acted on her thought. But he didn't say a word. Just went upstairs to his room. He was silent the next morning as well.

She hoped that tonight things would be better, at least between her and *Daed*. She didn't hold up much hope for improvement between her and Junia, but she vowed not to argue with her during the Christmas holiday. This was a time for celebration, not for fighting.

Junia came into the kitchen and frowned. "Why did you move *mei* candle?" She hurried and picked up the crock.

"It's suppertime."

"So?" She set the candle in the middle of the table. "It's not taking up much room."

Ella bit her lip and counted as Junia stepped back and admired the terra-cotta crock. The candle was half gone already due to her insistence it be lit every time she was in the house and extinguished only when they were at the store or at bedtime. Malachi had given it to her as a Christmas present two days ago, and at this rate, the candle would be gone before the end of next week. Ella had pointed that out yesterday, but Junia refused to blow out the flame. *"It reminds me of him,"* she said in a dopey, lovestruck tone.

But Ella wondered if there was another reason Junia made such a fuss about it. She had a boyfriend. Ella didn't, and the candle was a constant reminder of the words her sister had spewed. *"You're mad that you're ugly and frumpy. Nee mann would want a single date with you, much less to marry you."* Junia was pretty, and if things continued down the serious path they were taking, she and Malachi would be married sooner than later. Ella had no one.

That just added to all the times her aunts told her she would have trouble finding a husband. But even they hadn't called her ugly and frumpy.

Was that why no man had paid attention to her back in Lancaster? Or in Marigold? Because she was ugly, frumpy, and bossy? Not that she had time for romance. But was Junia right? *Am I jealous?*

The scent of vanilla brought her out of her thoughts, and Junia and her candle came into view. It took pride of place in the center, where Ella had planned to put the baked turkey that had been cooking all day. It was a small bird, but there would be enough meat and bones to keep them in turkey leftovers for the week. Now she'd have to move the other dishes around to accommodate the large platter, all so Junia would shut up about the stupid candle.

The timer went off on the oven, and Ella went to pull out the turkey and replace it with the rolls that would bake while the meat rested and the juices soaked back into the bird. She smiled at the perfectly baked, golden-skinned turkey. At least the food would be delicious.

She turned to tell Junia to finish setting the table, but her sister was gone, probably off to knit something for Malachi or write him a letter or draw hearts and flowers all over another notebook. She was acting so childish about this relationship, like she was a teenager instead of a twenty-year-old woman.

"Everything smells *appeditlich*," *Daed* said as he entered the room. "I know I've said this more than once today, but you've really outdone yourself, Ella."

Her father's compliment warmed her heart, and she was glad to see that he was more relaxed this evening than he'd been all week. They closed the store yesterday, and it would be closed for the next few days—today was Friday, they would celebrate Christmas tomorrow, and the next day was church service. She was looking forward to the time off to slow down and rest. Maybe she would do a little sewing tomorrow too. She could finally hem that blue dress she'd been meaning to work on for the last few months.

"Is it time to eat yet?" He came up behind her and looked at the turkey.

"In about ten minutes, as soon as the rolls are done." She set the butter and honey on the table, and when she turned around, her father was cutting off a piece of the steaming meat. "*Daed*," she said, putting her hands on her hips. But she was still grinning. "That just came out of the oven."

"*Gut*. It's nice and hot." He put the sliver of meat in his mouth and chewed, happiness clear on his face. "Where's Junia?"

Who knows? She caught the caustic remark before it flew out of her mouth and ruined the evening before it started.

"I'll *geh* find her." But not before he nipped another tidbit of turkey.

Maybe tonight would be enjoyable. They used to have fun during Christmas when they were back in Lancaster. But there were family members to act as a buffer, and in her aunts' cases, manage everything. It wasn't until she and her father and sister moved here that Ella had taken on so much responsibility.

She glanced around the kitchen. Everything was ready but the rolls, and they had seven more minutes left in the oven. She started wiping down the counters when she saw a small stack of mail on the end near the back door. She set down the rag and flipped through the pile. Two cards from her relatives in Lancaster, a gas bill, a large post-card advertising plow services . . . and a letter to Junia from Malachi. Hmm. How had her sister missed this? Usually she pounced on the mailbox right after the postal worker arrived.

Malachi's handwriting was neat and compact, and the envelope felt like it contained a normal letter, not a thick missive like the ones Junia wrote to him. She wrote several a week, and they talked regularly on the phone. Ella couldn't remember the last time she'd used the phone. She'd lost contact with her friends in Lancaster since the move to Marigold. That was mostly her fault—she'd been too busy working at the store and tending to her other chores to take time to write them back. Eventually they'd stopped writing her at all. Same with phone calls, although she was never one to talk on the phone much anyway. And she hadn't put in much effort to make friends here either. The reason was the same—work, work, and more work.

"What are you doing?"

Ella whirled around to see Junia march toward her. She snatched the letter out of her hand. "You were going to open it, weren't you?"

"*Nee*. I was going through the mail . . . Why in the world would I want to read a *dumm* letter from Malachi?"

"Because *yer* nosy." Junia clutched the letter against her chest. "And jealous."

The timer on the oven went off and Ella shoved past her. "For the last time, I'm not jealous. Not of you or your relationship." But she heard the undercurrent of doubt lacing her words.

"I don't believe you."

"Believe what you want." She opened the oven, flinching at the wave of heat hitting her in the face.

"Oh," *Daed* said, entering the kitchen. "There you are—"

"*Daed!*" Junia flew to him. "Tell Ella to leave *mei* mail alone."

Ella yanked out the rolls and plopped the tray on the stove next to the turkey. The baking sheet clattered against the burner grates. One . . . two . . . three . . . four . . .

Daed sat down at the table. "Ella, don't read Junia's mail."

"I didn't!"

"Then why were you holding Malachi's letter?" Still clutching the envelope, Junia went to her chair. "She was going to read it, *Daed*. I just know she was."

Ella threw the rolls into the breadbasket and tossed it on the table in front of her sister, one roll escaping. She wanted to pick it up and aim it at Junia's head. This argument was so ridiculous, and Junia wasn't listening to a word Ella was saying. "I wasn't going to read your mail!"

"You read *mei* notebook." She lifted her chin. "Right in front of me. How can I trust you not to read *mei* letters?"

"That was one time, and I was mad at you."

"You're always mad at me."

"*Stop!*"

Ella jumped at *Daed*'s booming voice. He shoved back his chair and stood, glaring at both her and Junia. Then he turned and went to the stove. He paused, his shoulders drooping. She thought she heard him let out a sigh before picking up the turkey platter and bringing it to the table. He set it next to the candle crock, picked up the wayward roll and placed it back into the basket, then sat back down.

"It's Christmas Eve," he said in a low, weary voice. "Is a few hours of peace too much to ask?"

Contrite, Ella sat in her seat and shut her mouth. They closed their eyes and prayed, and she asked for forgiveness for her behavior. How could they act this way on the night before Jesus' birthday? They should be contemplating his birth, not fighting. *Please, Lord. Help me control* mei *temper.*

After the prayer, she opened her eyes and reached for the turkey, determined to honor her father's wishes.

"You started it," Junia muttered as she picked up a roll.

"Did not," Ella whispered back, unable to control herself. Ugh, she couldn't even last for five seconds before her temper took over.

"Did too."

Ella glanced at *Daed*. If he heard them, he didn't respond. She handed him the turkey, and for the next few minutes they filled their plates and began to eat in blissful silence. Finally, their latest discord was over.

"I'm going to Malachi's tomorrow," Junia said, cutting into a piece of white meat.

Daed's brow raised. "On Christmas?"

"He invited me. He wants me to meet his *familye.*"

"But what about our Christmas?"

"You and Ella can have it without me." She took a sip of tea. "I can pick up *mei* presents later."

Silence. Then one word from *Daed*. "*Nee*."

Junia looked up. "What?"

"You can meet his *familye* another time. We're spending Christmas together."

"But, *Daed*, that's not fair."

He continued to eat, not looking at her.

"I don't want to be stuck here with—"

"With me?" *Daed* said, a note of hurt in his tone.

"With her." She pointed her butter knife at Ella.

Ella's eyes narrowed. She didn't exactly want to spend a whole day with Junia either. Although she'd planned to spend part of tomorrow taking a long nap, either before or after her sewing, so that would cut down on their time together. Still, it hurt to hear her sister say it out loud.

"You'll be spending a lot more time with Ella." *Daed* dabbed at his mouth with the napkin. "At the store and here at home."

"But—"

"I've had enough of the two of you warring with each other. Ella needs help around the house. We both need help at the store. You've been shirking *yer* duties far too long, Junia. And it ends now."

Ella fought to hide her shock. Her father not only noticed Junia's behavior, but he was actually doing something about it. It was a miracle.

"And, Ella," he said, turning to her. "Stop frustrating Junia."

"Me? How?"

"You're bossy," Junia said. "And—"

"Junia," *Daed* warned.

"Okay." Ella didn't want to hear a list of her many faults. "I'll watch *mei* temper."

"*Danki.*" *Daed*'s shoulders finally lowered a bit. "Oh, and two more things—we're closing the store on Tuesday afternoon and meeting Wendy Pearson at her office in Barton."

"Huh?" Junia said, her expression still sour.

"Why?" Ella chimed in. "Isn't she a lawyer?"

Daed nodded.

"Why do we need a lawyer?" Junia asked.

"To help us settle our differences. It's called conflict mediation."

"What?" the sisters exclaimed together.

"It's past time you got along with each other. To act like adults and treat one another with respect."

"But why do we have to do it in front of her?" Junia wailed.

"She's not Amish," Ella added, confused.

"Do you want to take this to the bishop?" *Daed*'s gaze bounced from one to the other.

"*Nee,*" Junia said softly.

"I don't." Ella glanced at her lap.

"Wendy is a neutral party, and it's part of her job to keep things confidential. She's also well versed in Scripture and is taking a biblical approach. But hear me on this—if you two can't work things out with her help, I will get Bishop Fry involved. Understand?"

"*Ya.*" Junia sat back in her chair, her chin dipped.

Ella nodded, more shocked than confused now. "What's the second thing?"

He turned to her. "From this point forward, you will be Junia and Malachi's chaperone."

Junia popped up from her chair. "We don't need a chaperone. We're not doing anything wrong!"

"I didn't say you were. But I also don't like how you're running off with him all the time." The tops of his cheeks above his beard turned red. "The temptation is there."

"*Daed*—"

Ella's stomach dropped. Ugh. Chaperoning Junia and Malachi was the very last thing she wanted to do.

"What if I don't agree?" Junia crossed her arms.

Daed's brows flew up, surprise in his eyes. He didn't answer right away, as if her defiance caught him off guard. Then he turned to her, facing her fully. "If you disobey me, I will send you back to Lancaster to live with Cora and Tabitha."

"You wouldn't."

Daed didn't flinch. "Try me."

Junia didn't move. Or speak. But Ella could see she was mulling it over. Unbelievable. What was there to think about? And how dare she consider challenging *Daed*? After an excruciatingly long standoff, Junia tossed her napkin on her plate and rushed out of the kitchen.

Daed slumped in his chair. Ella could see how much standing his ground had taken out of him. "Are you all right?"

He nodded. "*Ya*. I know *yer* not happy with *mei* decision either, but it had to be done."

"I know." It was clear her sister was out of control. Even though she was an adult, she lived under their father's headship, and she had to respect that. "I'll chaperone them," she mumbled. Just because he was right didn't mean she had to be happy about it, though.

"After today, it might not end up being an issue. She'll do as I say, or she'll face the consequences."

"What if she and Malachi decide to get married right away?"

Daed looked at her wearily. "God give him strength, then. He's gonna need it."

151

If the situation wasn't so upsetting, Ella would have chuckled. She still wondered if Malachi knew the real Junia. She doubted it. While she'd never had any dating experience—work, and apparently her bossy, frumpy, and ugly attributes always got in the way—she'd seen how some of her friends back in Lancaster had acted around the boys they liked, and they never showed their true selves early in a relationship, at least to Ella's knowledge.

She and *Daed* went back to eating supper, although most of it had grown cold by now. When they were nearly finished, Junia reappeared. She sat back down at the table, her expression calm. "I won't disobey." Then she looked at Ella, scowling.

He blew out a long breath. "*Danki*, Junia. Now, with all that out of the way, can we enjoy the rest of tonight and tomorrow?"

"*Ya*," they said in unison but without a single shred of enthusiasm.

Fourteen

Wendy stood in front of her mirror and smoothed down the pleats at the waist of the emerald-green Amish dress she'd bought last week. Barton didn't have any dress shops, and she'd looked for something suitable for Amish church at the thrift store but couldn't find anything. She considered driving to Akron, or even Columbus, to shop at the department stores there. But when she passed by the fabric shop, she went inside and was stunned and pleased they had a dress in her size.

She couldn't remember the last time she'd worn a dress. Even in court she wore pantsuits, and when she had worn a dress or skirt, it was never this plain. No patterns, buttons, or snaps, and the length was longer than the current style. She noticed something else too. It was so comfortable.

The dress had long sleeves for the cold weather, and she purchased a navy blue sweater to wear over it. She didn't go so far as to buy a *kapp*, although she'd considered it. She didn't want to appropriate the Amish culture, just respect it.

Wendy ran a brush through her hair. It was a little past her shoulders now. When she arrived in Marigold, she had the same style she'd worn for years—a short, sleek bob that stopped at her chin and took five minutes to fix in the morning. Now she could put her hair up in a clip, and she did just that, noticing a few threads of gray throughout the dark strands. She'd given up dyeing her hair, and there would be more gray coming. But she didn't mind. She wore no makeup or jewelry, and she'd picked up a pair of dark stockings that went well with the rich green color. She slipped on her sweater, put on her plain black flats, and went into the living room.

Her mother's friend Susan had picked Mom up to take her to church half an hour ago, and she would be back later this afternoon. Wendy let Monroe out for a few minutes. After he scampered around the backyard and did his business, she let him back inside, put on her coat, and headed for Eunice's church in Marigold.

When she reached the Amish house, she experienced a small attack of nerves as she saw all the buggies parked on the lawn. She didn't feel right pulling into the driveway, or even in front of the house. The weather was nice, and she didn't mind the cold temperature. She parked the car farther down the road and made her way to the Beilers' house, the family that was hosting today's service.

Wendy searched for Eunice, who said she would be waiting for her. She'd expected to be more self-conscious, but while a few people gave her second looks, most everyone was heading into the barn, where the service would be held.

She glanced around again and saw Ella walking inside. The Yoders attended this church? Then again, she shouldn't be surprised. She'd been doing more reading about the Amish and how they lived in communities called districts, which were headed by a bishop and consisted of a group of families, and those families were part of one church. According to Charity, Marigold wasn't a large district, but it was growing and had been formed by a few families from Birch Creek, although there were other families, like Eunice's, who had come from different parts of the state and country. The town of Marigold had been in existence for over a hundred years—only the district was fairly new.

Wendy followed Ella inside the spacious barn, and the first thing she noticed was how clean it was, considering it was a barn. The second thing were the benches lined up in two columns. The males were sitting on one side, females on the other. She'd read about that too, but it was interesting to see. It was also warm, and she noticed two large gas-powered heaters on either side of the barn.

Eunice came up to her, a big smile on her round face. "Good morning and welcome. I saved a seat for you right over here." She looked at Wendy's dress. "Did you get that at the shop?" When Wendy nodded, she added, "I think I made that one. It looks familiar."

Wendy didn't know how Eunice could tell, since there were several women wearing the exact same dress.

As they walked to a bench a few rows from the front, she saw Charity and Priscilla sitting together. Charity waved her over, a surprised look on her face.

"I didn't know you were visiting today," she said. "If I had, I would have saved you a seat."

"We can scoot over a bit." Priscilla started to slide on the bench. Emma, Priscilla and Micah's almost one-year-old daughter, sat in her lap, leaning her back against her.

"Thank you, but I'm with Eunice," she said, gesturing to her friend behind her, who was visiting with another woman.

"Okay." Charity smiled. "If you visit again, maybe we can all sit together."

"I'd like that."

Wendy and Eunice made their way to their seats and passed by Ella and Junia, who were sitting three pews back with enough space between them for another person. Neither woman looked happy. Before Barnabas left her house a few days ago, he'd said he was a little hopeful, but he also admitted something else. *"I fear their relationship might be permanently broken,"* he'd said, a catch in his throat.

Wendy considered herself a realist and never gave her clients false hope if she could help it. *"Perhaps. But that doesn't mean we shouldn't try."*

Barnabas had surprised her by ending their meeting with a prayer, something she'd never thought of or bothered to do before while working with her clients. Not that a voiced prayer would be welcome by many of them, but she could have taken the time to pray alone before and after her meetings and when she went to court. And it wasn't because she lacked the time to do so. The thought had never entered her mind.

She and Eunice sat down on the bench, with Wendy taking the end. Eunice introduced her to her daughter and her daughter-in-law, who were sitting on the other side. As she told them hello, she caught sight of a man sitting on the end of the opposite bench. Barnabas.

Although all the men wore the same outfit—black pants, white shirt, black vest, and some had on their black overcoats—he looked especially fit in his church clothes. His rounded Amish haircut was neatly combed, his shirt crisp, his vest nicely fitted. The word *handsome* came to mind as she sat back. *Very handsome.*

The service started, and Eunice whispered to her throughout, preparing her for different parts and explaining a little bit about them. Wendy appreciated the information. She didn't know German, and the monotone singing of the hymns threw her off a bit. But she found herself immersed in the service, and when it was over, a little more than three hours had flown by.

"Now we eat!" Eunice grinned.

Wendy followed her into the house. From her research, she knew that the meal was potluck with only cold dishes because cooking wasn't allowed on Sunday, the day of rest. Everyone would share a meal and then go back home to relax for the remainder of the day. Eunice put her to work, and she was amazed at how welcoming the women were to her. She enjoyed the camaraderie.

Ella and Junia also helped, but other than telling the girls hello, she didn't speak to them. She did a little observing, though, in preparation for their upcoming meeting. Wendy noticed that Ella helped in the kitchen much the same way she'd seen her work in the store, with quick diligence and a take-charge attitude, even with the older ladies. Junia focused on one task with another woman who looked to be around her age. They were immersed in conversation, speaking in *Deitsch* as they smiled and laughed.

But what stood out to her the most was how they avoided each other, staying at opposite sides of the kitchen. She didn't see them interact one single time, and while the Beilers' kitchen was large, with twelve women working, there wasn't much room.

Eunice appeared at her side, holding a platter of sandwich meat and cheese slices. "It's too cold outside, so the tables are set up in the basement. The stairs are off to the left of the kitchen."

They went downstairs to a surprisingly large area with cinder block walls. Many of the men were there, sitting at the tables waiting for the women to serve the meal. Before she'd studied the Amish culture, Wendy would have been offended that the men weren't pitching in to help, but she understood the division of duties between men and women. She didn't get the sense that any of the women resented their tasks. Charity and Priscilla sure didn't. And she noticed that the men helped with the children. Everything was running smoothly—the service, preparing lunch, and now serving the meal. Wendy appreciated the efficiency.

As she placed two jars of chow chow on the food table, she saw Barnabas. This time he was looking at her. Like Charity, he seemed surprised to see her. She smiled at him and was pleased when he smiled back. Then he turned to his friends and resumed their conversation.

Lunch was delicious, and she ate too much. She'd have to walk some extra steps this week, but it was worth it. She helped with the cleanup and thanked Eunice for inviting her. "I'll see you next week for our lesson," she said as she left the house and headed for her car. Only a few buggies were parked in the yard now, and she shoved her hands in her coat pockets as she made her way down the gravel driveway.

"Wendy."

She turned at the sound of Barnabas's voice. A tiny flutter appeared in her stomach as he walked toward her. She still couldn't get over how good-looking he was in his church clothing.

He stopped a few feet in front of her but didn't say anything. He looked to the left. The right. His gaze dropped to the ground.

"Did you need something?" she asked.

"Uh." He finally looked at her. "Um . . ."

His awkwardness was endearing. "You can ask me anything, Barnabas. Is it about our appointment this week? Do you need to reschedule?"

He shook his head. "I was wondering . . . Do you need a ride home?"

His question was so surprising, she almost didn't understand what he was asking. When she realized what he was offering, she couldn't help but smile. How sweet. "I drove," she said, pointing at her parked car. "But thank you. I appreciate the offer."

"No problem." He started backing away. "Um . . ."

"Yes?"

"Good to see you." Then he turned and hurried away.

A thought occurred to her, and she caught up with him. "Barnabas?"

He turned, his cheeks a little red, his right eyebrow rising.

"I would like to ride in a buggy sometime." It was true, but she wasn't sure why she was telling him this. "It looks like fun."

He nodded, a slight smile on his face. "Maybe someday you will."

She watched him leave, the flutter intensifying. Barnabas Yoder had to be the nicest, most considerate man she'd ever met. He wasn't anything like the men she was used to being around. Definitely the opposite of her ex.

Still smiling, she got in her car. Despite the challenge of helping Ella and Junia reconcile their differences, she was eagerly looking forward to their meeting . . . and seeing Barnabas again.

⁂

Although there was less than a week left before January first, and there was still Second Christmas to celebrate, Nelson decided to officially move to Marigold. On Monday he packed up his few belongings and piled them into his buggy. *Mamm* and *Daed* came outside to tell him goodbye.

"I didn't know you were leaving so soon after Christmas," his mother said, her eyes glassy. "I would have packed some things for you. Especially food."

"I'll be living next to the grocery store, remember? Plus there's Charity's cooking to enjoy." He smiled and gave her a hug. "I'm not that far away."

"I know. I know." She blew her nose, her cheeks red from the cold air. The temperature had dropped to below freezing overnight and hadn't risen much after sunrise. The heavy cloud cover had a hand in that. "But I don't know why *yer* in such a hurry."

Daed nodded. "Did something happen to make you want to leave sooner?"

Nelson couldn't answer because he didn't want to admit that, other than praying about buying the warehouse and then purchasing it, he'd been winging everything. Now he was restless and starting to stress out a little. He wasn't a planner, never had been. But at some point, he had to learn how. Hopefully, living in the warehouse would give him some clarity. "I've just got a lot to do," he said, which was the truth. "Ordering the equipment, putting up drywall, picking out paint, clearing trees for *mei haus*—"

"You'll have plenty of help," *Daed* assured. "If you'll just wait until—"

"It's time for me to *geh*," he said. There was no reason for him to put off moving any longer. "That's all I can say."

"All right."

Nelson ignored his father's concern and turned to his mother. She gave him a watery smile. "We understand." She sighed. "It's not like we haven't been through this before." She pulled out a jar from her coat pocket. "Here's a little housewarming gift."

He looked at the handwritten label. Cherry preserves. His favorite. "*Danki, Mamm.*"

"Don't eat it all at once," *Daed* joked.

"Can't guarantee that." He climbed into the buggy and grabbed the reins. "See you soon."

They waved as he pulled out of the driveway. His brothers were at work—the younger ones taking care of the animals, and Owen and Perry working the winter vegetables and the flowers in the large greenhouse. He'd given them quick goodbyes, but his leaving seemed so uneventful. Last year when Jesse moved away, Elam had been down in the dumps for a week. But with so many of his brothers moving out in the last few years, he must have gotten used to it. And it wasn't like Nelson wouldn't see his family soon, so there was no reason to make a big deal out of anything.

But as he drove the buggy farther away from home, excitement was building inside him, counteracting his confusion and nerves. He'd wanted a new start, and now he was getting it. Still, he would miss his family. Especially *Mamm*'s cooking.

He arrived in Marigold and went straight to the warehouse. His timing was good for it had just started to snow. He pulled around to the back and brought Crackerjack to a halt. Unable to help himself, he glanced at E&J's Grocery. The parking lot was empty, which was unsurprising, considering most people were still visiting with family and friends over the past few days. He lifted out a box of miscellaneous items and walked to the back door. He entered the warehouse . . . and froze. Ella Yoder was sitting on the edge of his bed.

"What in the world?"

She jumped up and staggered back. "Nelson, you scared the life out of me!"

"I scared you?" He set the box on the floor with a *thud* and marched over to her. "What are you doing in *mei* shop?"

"I—" A look of uncertainty passed over her face. Then she lifted her chin. "You shouldn't have left the front door unlocked."

He hadn't realized he had. Even so, it wouldn't be anything he had to worry about. No one was going to enter the place without permission. Except for this woman. "So it's my fault *yer* trespassing on *mei* property?"

Her bluster faded. "*Nee.* I'm sorry, Nelson. I needed to get away, just for a few minutes. I was out walking and . . ." She waved her hand. "Never mind. I'll *geh.*"

She started to move past him and exit out the open back door. He should let her leave so he could get back to unloading his buggy and make an official start on his new adventure. "Wait."

Ella turned to him, pain and confusion in her eyes.

Technically she did do him a favor by revealing his carelessness. Maybe he should be concerned about locking his place. Although crime was low in Marigold and Birch Creek, it would be smart to be more security minded. But he was also concerned about her distress. This was the third time he'd seen her this agitated.

He closed the door and guided her away from the cold draft, although it wasn't much warmer in the cavernous, unheated warehouse.

"I thought you wanted me to leave," she said. "What made you change *yer* mind?"

Now that was a loaded question. "I do want you to leave, but not while *yer* upset."

"I'm not upset." But she was looking away as she spoke, and she sighed again. "Okay, maybe a little. Or more than a little."

"I understand the need to have some privacy. Growing up with eleven siblings, it was hard to come by."

"I just have one. She's enough." She scowled.

He should have known this had something with to do with Junia. His brain was telling him to let her go. She could solve her problem on her own. But he couldn't do that, and there was no point in telling himself he should. "Do you want to talk about it?"

Fifteen

Ella couldn't respond to Nelson's unexpected question. First, she was still stunned he hadn't kicked her out of the warehouse. She had no business being here, but after a morning of putting up with Junia's stony silence punctuated with grimaces and heavy, my-life-is-so-terrible sighs, she couldn't stand it anymore. She'd grabbed an apple and gone for a walk, but she didn't get very far. The apple was still in the pocket of her coat, and it was too cold to walk any decent distance. She didn't want to go home—although her father and Junia were at the store, their house wasn't a peaceful place either. It was as if their fighting and now silent treatment had polluted their living space. When she passed by the warehouse, she'd checked the door on instinct. When she found it unlocked, she turned into Goldilocks and went inside, not expecting Nelson to arrive until after the holidays.

And here she was, caught red-handed encroaching on his property—even being so bold as to sit on the edge of his bed. But she was so tired . . . of everything, including always being upset when he was around. *He must think I'm* ab im kopp.

"Or you don't have to," he said, jerking her out of her daze. "It's up to you."

She looked at him, realizing she'd been so deep in her thoughts she hadn't answered his question. She really needed to get back to the store. Today's customers were few and far between, but there was always work to do—shelves to stock and straighten, inventory to check, planning for the spring and summer, sweeping, mopping, wiping the counters . . .

"I've got another box to bring in." He opened the back door again. "You can stay here as long as you need to. I'll work around you."

She shook her head, not wanting to be in his way. "I really am sorry," she said, walking out with him. "I shouldn't have come here."

"It's okay." He went to the buggy and pulled out another box.

Ella followed him and peeked inside. There was one smaller box, and she lifted it out. He raised an eyebrow at her but didn't say anything as they both went back into the warehouse. "Is this all you have?"

"*Ya.* Don't need much for one little space."

She looked around at the single bed, a short, two-drawer dresser, and a wooden crate for a nightstand. "You need more than what's here."

"It's okay, Ella. I won't be living in here permanently."

"*Gut.*" She still didn't like the idea of him staying in this cold building during the winter, even if it was temporary. But he had a heater, a place to lay his head, and hopefully a plan. He'd set his box down on the concrete floor next to the crate. "Where do you want this?" she asked, nodding at the box in her hands.

"On the dresser."

She placed it on top of the piece of furniture, which reached only to her waist. He hadn't asked for her help, but it would only take a few minutes for her to unpack this box and she would go back to the store. She flipped up the cardboard flaps—

"Don't open that—"

—and saw his unmentionables. Her cheeks reddened as she quickly shut the box.

He skidded to a stop beside her and whisked it away. "I'll take care of this."

A sick feeling filled the pit of her stomach. Nothing was going right for her today. Unbidden, her eyes filled.

Sniff.

Great, now she was crying. She quickly wiped her eyes with the back of her hand. She had to get it together before she went back to work. She couldn't let her customers see her upset. Or Junia, although she would probably be thrilled she'd gotten so deep under Ella's skin. And she couldn't let *Daed* see her cry. She and Junia had caused him more than enough problems lately.

"Ella?"

She stilled. Not because Nelson said her name. But the way he said it, with a touch of tenderness. Or she was so desperate for some comfort, she imagined he had. It didn't matter. She'd trespassed, saw his underwear, and now she was crying in front of him. What else could go wrong?

She ran her hand over her eyes again, inhaled a deep breath, and turned around. "I'll be going now. Sorry to bother you."

He motioned for her to sit down on the bed. When she didn't move, he said, "Ella . . . sit."

Quickly she obeyed and perched on the mattress. Earlier she'd been so consumed with her thoughts she hadn't thought twice about using his bed as a chair, but now she was keenly aware of where she was sitting.

He sat next to her, his legs straddling the opposite corner. "I reckon since the chance is high that we'll eventually be family—"

"Wait, what? Oh . . . right." How could she have forgotten Junia and Malachi's love of a lifetime? "Has Malachi been talking about marriage?"

"Not to me. But his *mamm* is pretty sure it's going to happen."

"Junia is too."

"Given that . . ." He rubbed his chin. "If you do need someplace to get away, you can come here."

She turned to him. He was staring straight ahead, his hands on his knees now. He was confusing her again. First he wanted her to leave, then he asked her to stay, and now he was letting her use his warehouse. She wasn't sure what to think, other than he was being uncharacteristically kind. Right now that was exactly what she needed. "*Danki*, Nelson."

"I'll get you a key, since the doors will be locked when I'm not here." He turned to her with a businesslike expression. "But no stopping by after eight o'clock. I need *mei* sleep."

"Got it. And I promise I'll come here only on really cold days. On nice ones I can *geh* to the barn."

"That old one you showed me a few weeks ago when we were looking for Malachi and Junia?"

"*Ya.*"

He frowned. "Is it safe?"

She shrugged. "Safe enough."

He stared straight ahead again, not looking at her. "Just come here."

A little spark of . . . something . . . lit inside her. Not only was he being nice, but he was looking out for her safety. "Are you sure?"

Clearing his throat, he said, "*Ya.*"

His answer made her more confused, but in a good way, and she was acutely aware that her thoughts and feelings weren't making any more sense than he was. Still . . . She sighed. He was thoughtful. And handsome. Because even though she was upset when he arrived, she'd continued to notice his looks. There was no point in berating herself for it.

"I need to get that box," he said, starting to get up from the bed.

"Okay. Oh, by the way—" The momentary spark of joy she'd just felt disappeared. But as Nelson had just mentioned, they might end up being family soon and she wanted him to know what her father had decided to do about Junia and Malachi. "*Daed* wants me to chaperone," she said, this time letting out a real bedraggled sigh.

"Malachi and Junia?" He sat back down. "That doesn't surprise me. They've both lost their senses over each other. Well, that will put Phoebe's mind at ease. *Mei* sincere condolences."

She nodded, then stared straight ahead. "Is it always like that?"

"What?"

"Love." She turned to him. "Does it always make you do crazy things?"

He cleared his throat again. "It can. For some people."

"Well, if I ever fall in love, I won't let that happen to me. Not that I have to worry about that ever happening."

"Why do you say that?"

"I've been told I'm not marriage material."

His brow lifted. "By who?"

"More than one person." Regret flooded her. She'd already said too much—there was no need to go into embarrassing detail.

He looked sincerely baffled. "Why would they say something like that?"

Ella glanced at him, surprised at his reaction and seemingly genuine interest. She averted her gaze, wishing she'd kept her mouth shut. "I know I'm a little bossy," she said.

"That's true."

Her ego pricked. He didn't have to agree so quickly.

"So are a lot of women. Men too."

"I'm also . . . frumpy." She waited for him to respond, anticipating the polite reply. *"No you're not. You're just fine."* Her spirits hit the concrete when he remained silent. There was no reason to hold back now. "I'm ugly too." There. She'd said it out loud. And even then she held some smidgen of hope that he would negate that fact.

But he was staring at his feet. Sliding his left heel back and forth. And not saying a word.

Humiliated, she shot up from the bed. "Time to get back to work."

He jumped up too. "Same here. Lots to do today."

"*Ya*. Lots." She wished she could disappear into the floor. But she'd brought this shame on herself. Saying she was ugly and frumpy could also be construed as fishing for compliments, and that was one of the most prideful things she could do. Not that she meant to, but she would understand if he saw it that way.

"See you later," she said and dashed out of the warehouse.

She hurried back to the store and went inside. She leaned against the back door and closed her eyes. Leave it to her to take a decent moment and turn it into a nightmare . . . for herself. One thing was for sure, she wasn't going back to the warehouse anytime soon, despite Nelson's kind offer. How could she face him again after she'd made a fool of herself? That was becoming a habit every time she was around him.

But there was something important she had to acknowledge. She had misjudged him. He wasn't a jerk like she thought he was when she first met him. He was direct, and now she knew he was honest.

He wasn't going to flatter her with feigned kind words, and she respected him for that . . . even if the truth was unbelievably painful.

.⟶ঞ৶⟵.

After Ella flew out of the warehouse—and that was how fast she moved, like a bird in flight—Nelson wanted to kick himself. Her revelations had caught him so off guard he didn't know what to say. That was his own doing because he'd opened the door by asking her why anyone would tell her she wasn't marriage material. He had a sneaking suspicion Junia had either hinted that Ella wasn't, or outright told her. Either way, it wasn't true.

Then why didn't I tell her that?

He went outside, careful not to slide in the inch of snow that had fallen in the past hour, and got into the buggy, leading Crackerjack to the Yoders' barn. Since Ella hadn't brought it up, Barnabas must not have told her that Nelson was renting stable space from him. She'd find out soon enough. He settled his horse in and walked back over to the warehouse.

He went to the box of his underwear that Ella had peeked in and shoved it all into the top drawer, still bothered about why he hadn't corrected the insults she'd admitted to him. All he had to do was tell her they were wrong. She wasn't as beautiful as Norene or as cute as Miriam. But she wasn't ugly or frumpy. Not even close. Ella Yoder was pretty. He'd thought it before, and he believed it now.

But cute, beautiful women had made him lose his mind in the past, and he wasn't going to let himself go *ab im kopp* over Ella. He'd almost laughed when she asked him if love made people do crazy things. *It sure made me act crazy.*

He shut the drawer and went to unpack the rest of his clothes from the other box, being more careful with his shirts and jeans. He hadn't thought about needing a closet, but that would only be for his church clothes, and he could keep them neatly folded for the time being. Once he was finished unpacking, he looked around the warehouse . . . and stopped, anxiety riddling him again.

He sat down on the edge of the bed and ran his hand through his hair. Not only couldn't he figure out where to begin, but he also couldn't stop thinking about Ella and what she'd said about chaperoning Malachi and Junia. He agreed with Barnabas's decision, but was it right for Ella to have to accompany them? He also remembered his promise to Phoebe about keeping an eye on Malachi. He didn't like the thought of her taking on part of his responsibility, even though she wasn't aware of it.

Nelson stood, shoving Ella and the young lovers out of his mind. He had more important things to do—like coming up with a business plan and implementing it. *I can do this . . . I can do this.*

But he heard a faint echo in his mind. *What if I fail again?*

Sixteen

Dear Diary,

I know it's been weeks since my last entry, and I plan to be more consistent in the future. I'm not sure why, but I do feel better when I've written down my thoughts, even if they're bothersome. And painful. Yesterday I had a seriously painful day, but today, and moving forward, things are going to be different.

After talking with Nelson yesterday and embarrassing myself by saying I was bossy, ugly, and frumpy, like Junia had said, I realized that I could change one out of three of those things. I can't do anything about my looks. I don't even understand how I'm frumpy since I think I look like most Amish women my age. True, I'm not as thin and graceful as Junia, but I don't look like a middle-aged frau either. Not that there's anything wrong with that. And as for being ugly . . . well, not much I can do there either, other than accept it. Looks aren't everything. Besides, God sees the heart, and my heart has been in a dark place lately.

What I can do is try not to be bossy. Or at least let up a little. I'm not sure how since a lot of what I do is automatic, but there must be a way. It would help if Junia didn't have to be told what to do every minute of the day. If she just took some initiative—

Ella paused. She was doing exactly what she had promised herself last night she wouldn't do—continually blame Junia. She crossed out the last line.

Later today we're meeting with Wendy Pearson at her office for conflict mediation. I'm disappointed in myself for being part and parcel of Daed having to get a lawyer to help our family relationships. That had to be embarrassing for him. But I'm glad he didn't go to the bishop. I think that would probably be worse. At least this way no one in our church will know that we're not getting along.

She paused again. Writing things down was really giving her clarity. Were she and her family being secretive? Should *Daed* have gone to the bishop first? He would have had to if Wendy weren't available, or even around. There was that time she was in *Daed*'s office too. She frowned. Was there something going on between the two of them?

Ella shook her head. What a ridiculous thought. Wendy wasn't Amish and *Daed* would never be interested in an English woman, for friendship or romance. He was just doing what he thought was best, and that was for Lawyer Wendy to help them.

I promised myself and God last night that I would listen to what Wendy said and do what needed to be done to get Junia and I back on track. I don't think we'll ever be close because our personalities are too different. But we do need to get along, especially since we'll

be living and working together until she gets married. Which will
probably be sooner rather than later if Nelson's right. We also owe
it to Daed. And Mamm. If she were here, she wouldn't like that we
were fighting either.

Ella closed her diary, a lump in her throat. There wasn't a day
that went by that she didn't think about her mother, even though the
memories of her were distant. She'd forgotten the sound of *Mamm*'s
voice long ago, but she still remembered what she looked like—the
kindness in her eyes, the cuddles she gave at night before tucking her
and Junia in the bed they shared. Ella smiled a little, thinking about
how she and Junia had leaned on each other after *Mamm* passed.
When had everything gone wrong? She'd assumed things became
bad when they moved to Marigold, but now that she thought about
it, she and Junia had been fighting for years before that. Just not as
much, since *Aenti* Cora and *Aenti* Tabitha wouldn't abide the argu-
ments and had grounded them both numerous times during their
teen years.

She was about to put the diary away when she thought of something else.

PS: I really misjudged Nelson. He was so considerate yesterday,
even though I was trespassing. I like seeing this side of him, and
I'm not sure why he is usually irritable around me. Maybe because
I've been cross around him. I want that to change too.

She tucked her diary underneath her mattress and headed downstairs to wait for the taxi that would be arriving soon to take them to
Wendy's office. She'd found out last night that Nelson was renting
stable space from *Daed* and was surprised her father hadn't mentioned

it. At least Nelson was doing the sensible thing and making sure his horse had adequate shelter.

There I go again, thinking about Nelson. It was hard not to now that they were neighbors. But as she tossed and turned last night, reliving the mortifying exchange about her bossy frumpiness, she decided she couldn't, and shouldn't, avoid him. She had to go back to being business minded, and once he got his butcher shop up and running, they could discuss ways to share customer bases. Eventually she would stop noticing his good looks and see him as any other man—and possible business associate. Not a partnership. *Just focus on business.* That was the one successful thing in her life right now.

She walked into the living room. Junia was sitting on the couch, wearing her coat and writing in her notebook—it was undoubtedly another letter to Malachi. Ella looked out the window. No taxi yet. "Where's *Daed*?"

No response.

Ella shook her head. At least with the silent treatment there was less of a chance either of them would say something and start fighting, so she was glad for that. But it seemed immature to her. And infuriating, although she tamped that emotion way down inside. She had to fulfill her promise. Losing her temper was unacceptable.

Daed came into the living room, a nervous expression on his face. He also looked a little different, and Ella realized he'd changed clothes. Odd, since the only difference between his work clothes and his current outfit was a trip through the washing machine and the clothesline. But there wasn't any need for him to have changed. He hadn't gotten his other clothing dirty at all.

A honk sounded outside, and Ella grabbed her coat and slipped into her black tennis shoes. Yesterday's light frosting of snow remained, and it was even colder today.

As they made their way out the door, *Daed* stopped them. "*Danki* for not giving me trouble about this."

Ella and Junia turned around. She could see how important this was to *Daed*.

"I think this is going to help all of us." He opened the door wider. "I pray that it does."

Junia didn't respond. She turned and went to the car.

Ella heard him sigh and she touched his shoulder. "I pray it does too."

She waited for him to put on his coat, but when she saw him wrap a blue-and-black plaid flannel scarf around his neck, she asked, "Is that new?"

He nodded and shoved his feet into his boots.

"Where did you get it?" She leaned forward, taking a closer look at the simple scarf. "It looks handmade."

Daed cleared his throat. "Don't want to be late," he said, rushing past her and out the door.

She shut the door behind them. He was right. They shouldn't be tardy for their first meeting with Wendy. Hopefully it would be the only one.

.⟊⟊⟊.

Wendy glanced at the clock for the third time in the past five minutes. She'd never been this nervous before meeting clients, and she would see Barnabas and his daughters at two o'clock. Maybe some of the anxiety came from her third meeting with Harold, Judy, and Claude. At the end of the hour, she ended up referring them to another lawyer in the Columbus area, explaining that she couldn't help them. She wasn't sure anyone could. Some people loved to live in conflict and chaos, for some bizarre reason. At one point she thrived on the conflict because it brought in clients and money. But now she was weary of it all.

She looked around her office. Other than today, she hadn't been here in two weeks—the longest she'd ever gone without working, other than the nine-month sabbatical she'd taken. She hadn't missed a minute of the commute to Barton, which was nothing compared to getting to her office in Manhattan or dealing with clients. She had a few easy ones, but even helping them hadn't given her the same satisfaction it used to. And she'd decided to stop taking divorce cases and clients who wanted to sue each other. She didn't have that in her anymore.

Wendy heard voices outside the door of her office and took one last look at the conflict management notes on her desk, the scriptures front and center. She said a quick prayer as the door opened and Barnabas, Junia, and Ella entered her office.

As she usually did with her clients, she visually sized them up in a few seconds. Barnabas looked trepidatious, as if he still had doubts that he and his daughters should be here. She also noticed he was wearing the scarf she made. He slipped it off and stuffed it in his pocket. She hid a smile and turned her attention to the women. Ella seemed more determined than hesitant, and from Junia's strained expression, it was clear she didn't want to be here.

Barnabas said she'd have her work cut out for her. *I sure do.*

After they exchanged greetings, she motioned for them to join her at a medium-sized round table in the corner of the room. Sometimes it was better to discuss sensitive issues from a less formal position than behind her desk. She'd typed up the list of scriptures she and Barnabas made and had a copy in front of each chair. She scooped up her materials and sat down between the two women.

"Thank you for agreeing to meet with me," Wendy said. Then she set ground rules for their meeting. No outbursts, no talking over each other, along with other boundaries that were crucial in order to reach their goal. "I'm a big believer in getting down to business, so we're going to start our conflict mediation session reviewing these scriptures."

Junia looked over the list but didn't pick it up. Ella studied hers, and Barnabas did a quick read since he was already familiar with them.

"I know all these," Junia said.

"Do you have them memorized?" Ella asked.

"Of course you do," she mumbled, angling her body away from her sister and crossing her arms. "Perfect Ella."

Wendy gauged Barnabas's and Ella's reaction to Junia's barb. Ella pressed her lips together and focused on the list. Barnabas stared at his lap.

"We should start on a positive note." Wendy picked up the paper. "First Thessalonians 5:11. 'Therefore comfort each other and edify one another, just as you also are doing.' These are good words to keep in mind when conflict arises. Sometimes it can be avoided with a kind word or two."

"What if there's nothing kind to say?" Junia peered at Ella.

Anger flashed across Ella's face, but she immediately hid it.

In the first five minutes of their meeting, Wendy could already see an issue, and it might be the major one. These two sisters were angry. Definitely at each other, and probably at their father too. It would take more than one session to get to the root of the problem, if the Yoders were willing to do the work. For the moment she needed to do some triage. "All right, we'll skip that part for now. Ella, what do you think is the main problem between you and your sister?"

Ella blinked, as if surprised at the forthright question.

"Remember, you can speak honestly here. No judgment."

After a pause she said, "To be honest, my sister is lazy."

Junia's face resembled a big prune. "And you're—"

"It's still Ella's turn to speak." Wendy held up her hand and turned a stern eye on Junia. "You'll get your chance."

Junia opened her mouth, closed it, and sank back into the chair.

"She didn't used to be lazy," Ella said. "There. I found something nice to say."

Barnabas's head fell against his fingers.

Now Wendy could see a second problem. A man as mild and benevolent as Barnabas had two very strong-willed daughters to contend with.

"Okay, Ella. You've defined the problem as you see it. Now, Junia, what do you think the problem is?"

"All she does is nitpick and boss me around. And she always gets her way."

"I always get my way?" Ella exclaimed. "Who doesn't have to do a single thing around the house anymore? Or at the store—"

"I never wanted to work in a store!"

Wendy held up her hands. "Ladies, remember the rules—"

"No one asked me if I wanted to move here or leave Lancaster," Junia cried, ignoring Wendy. "I was just told what to do and expected to agree."

"Junia, why didn't you say anything?" Barnabas asked.

"Because it wouldn't make a difference. And as it turned out, Ella was right. We're a lot better off here than we would have been in Lancaster."

"I would have found a job," Barnabas said. "We didn't have to move."

She turned to her father. "You don't need to be standing on a factory floor eight hours a day. Your knees couldn't have taken it."

Ella's eyes widened. "You actually care about *Daed*'s knees?"

"I care about a lot of things."

"You don't act like you do," Ella mumbled.

For some reason, Wendy felt that she needed to let the argument play out despite the high emotions. If it escalated any further, she'd step in.

"And why should I? I can't do anything right. I never have. I'm either too slow, too messy, or it's not done the way Ella would do it." Her voice cracked as she glared at her sister. "You wanted to be in charge of everything? Fine, you're in charge. Now you're even going to be in charge of my dates with Malachi." She burst into tears, jumped up from the table, and left the room.

Uh-oh. Wendy hadn't anticipated that. She moved to get up. "I can go check on her—"

"No," Ella said, already standing. "I will." She hurried off.

Wendy glanced at Barnabas. He looked defeated. And worried. "I'm sorry," she said. "I should have stepped in and stopped the argument early on. I usually do. Something held me back."

"It's okay." Barnabas sat up straighter, his expression changing to a more positive one. "For the first time, Junia is being forthcoming about how she feels. She hasn't done that for years. She's right about me and Ella not consulting her about moving to Lancaster, at least not until the deal to buy the grocery store was almost done. She did mention a time or two that she was homesick, and so was I. But she admitted she liked Marigold too."

"And what she said about Ella? Was that true too?"

He hesitated, then nodded. "Yes. In the past she's hurled insults at Ella, and those haven't been true. But Ella is a take-charge person. She's good at what she does, and she is picky. I didn't realize Junia felt that she didn't measure up. And I always gave in to her because

I felt guilty for uprooting her from our home." He started to nod. "Wendy, I think this was a good thing. At least I found out how my daughters really feel. I never fully knew until now."

"Had you ever asked them?" Wendy posed the question gently.

"No, and that's on me. I guess I hoped they would figure things out on their own. They're adults. I didn't figure they needed me solving their problems."

Wendy smiled. "They need you, Barnabas. Not in the same way they did when they were kids, but they do." Her throat thickened. "I didn't realize how much I needed my father until he was gone."

"I'm sorry. Losing someone you love is tough."

She blinked away the tears, surprised and a little annoyed they'd appeared at all. Since moving in with Mom, she'd worked through her latent grief over her father's death over three years ago. But there were still times when the thought of him made her weepy.

"I apologize," she said, shuffling her papers. "I don't usually get emotional with my clients. It undermines my credibility." Her wits gathered, she looked at him. "I promise it won't happen again."

"It's okay if it does," he said gently. "As you can see, I'm used to emotional women."

She couldn't help but grin a little at his smile.

He grew serious. "My wife, Evelyn, would cry at the drop of a hat. Sad, happy, angry . . . the tears would appear. Not that she would lose control or anything. She just cried easily. And that was fine with me."

This was the first time he'd brought up his late wife. And although she knew she shouldn't pry, she couldn't help but ask, "What was she like?"

He paused, staring at a still life print of gerbera daisies on the opposite wall. "Imagine Ella's brains and Junia's free spirit. That's who she was—a mix of both, but still her own person. It was love at first sight for me." He chuckled. "It took her a while longer."

"How long?"

"Seven years, give or take. Met her when her family moved to our church district from another one in Lancaster. We were both thirteen, and I knew she was the one for me. So I understand how Junia fell hard for Malachi. I just hope he doesn't hurt her. I guess all parents want to spare their children heartache."

"I suppose so. I can't exactly speak from personal experience. I've never been married. Never had kids. I worked most of my life to be a lawyer." She glanced around the office. This, along with a decent nest egg, was all she had to show for it.

"I hope you don't mind a personal question," Barnabas said.

"We're talking about personal things, so go right ahead."

"Do you have any regrets?"

His question was almost too intrusive, and she was tempted to tell him no and move on to more surface conversation while they waited for his daughters to come back. But that would be a lie. Not that she'd been the most honest person all her life. She'd lied in court—what lawyer hadn't? Over the years she'd lied to her parents more times than she could count, mostly so they wouldn't worry about her or pry into her life. Most of all, she'd lied to herself.

"There was a time when I thought all I needed was my job. I let it consume me so there wasn't room for anything else, even if I wanted there to be. And for a while, it was enough. The money, the accolades, the challenge of making partner, the competitive spirit in the court-room. I wasn't like a lot of women who wanted a husband and family. I wanted to be a career woman. And I reached that goal. But"—she blew out a breath—"I felt empty inside. And it wasn't a new feeling either. I always had. Like there was something missing in my life, but I didn't know what it was."

"Did you figure it out?"

"Yes. But not until I moved here. Living in Marigold is the exact opposite of the way I thought I wanted my life to be. I enjoy the slower pace. The long walks with Monroe have been good for my soul . . . and my waistline. I've reconnected with my faith, something I ignored since the moment I left for college. My relationship with my mother has never been better. Most importantly, I don't miss anything about New York or being a lawyer."

Barnabas didn't reply.

Wendy flinched. She'd said too much, basically spilling her heart and soul to this man who probably just wanted a simple yes or no answer to his question. "Sorry," she said, jumping up from her chair and dashing to the coffee machine. "I'm sure that's more than you wanted to know. Coffee?"

He shifted in his chair. "No, thank you."

She quickly poured herself a cup and sat back down, annoyed that her professionalism kept slipping away. She took a gulp, hid the fact she'd scalded her tongue, and looked at her notes. "While we're waiting for your daughters to return, there are some things we can go over that can help you with conflict at home."

"Uh, sure. What are those?"

Time to stick to the task and keep her personal feelings to herself. Barnabas was a client. Not a friend . . . although, in all honesty, she wished he could be.

Seventeen

"Junia!"

For the second time since her sister had bolted out of Wendy's office, Ella shouted her name, and once again she was being ignored. The building had four floors and Wendy's office was at the top—she'd been too late to reach Junia before she got on the elevator and went downstairs. Ella had no choice but to run down four flights of stairs, something she'd never done before in her life, and hoped she'd never have to do again.

She was breathless when she burst out through the stairwell door, just in time to see Junia dash outside. She chased after her into the back parking lot, thankful they weren't running on the front sidewalk in front of passersby. Somehow Ella managed to pick up speed and followed Junia, finally catching up to her in the neighborhood next to Main Street.

"Leave me alone!" Junia yelled, then doubled over, gasping for air.

Ella staggered toward her, legs and lungs aching. She hadn't run like that since she was a kid. She didn't want to run like that again soon either. Or ever. She glanced at their surroundings. They were standing on the sidewalk of a residential street, and except for two cars that quickly passed by, they seemed to be alone. She moved closer to Junia, also gulping down air. "Why did . . . you run?"

Still bent at the waist, she looked up at Ella, then shook her head. "You wouldn't . . . understand."

"Try me."

Junia stood up and staggered back a step. "*Nee*. I said all I'm going to say."

Ella wasn't sure what to do next. Drag her sister back to Wendy's office? She just might have to if Junia didn't agree to return on her own accord. Her sister wasn't just being obstinate—she was being embarrassingly immature. "Are you coming back or not?"

She paused. Her shoulders drooped. "I made a promise."

"To *Daed*," Ella said with a nod.

"And to Malachi."

"You told him about this?" Ella gasped.

"Of course. We don't keep secrets from each other."

"You don't have to tell him every single thing about your life." Ella shook her head. "Even I know that."

Junia shrugged, her chest still heaving. "It's not like he's going to tell anyone. And I need someone to talk to, since no one else listens to me."

For someone who claimed to have said all she had to say, she sure was talking a lot. "We need to *geh* back. We're wasting *Daed*'s and Wendy's time."

"I'm not walking with you."

Ella's blood started to boil. She didn't have time for Junia's petulance. Or the energy for it since she'd just used up almost every ounce of it chasing after her. She opened her mouth, ready to unleash her fury, when she remembered the promise she'd made to God and herself just this morning. She was going to control her temper. What was one of the scriptures she'd read from the list Wendy had given them? *"He who is slow to wrath has great understanding, but he who is impulsive exalts folly."* Proverbs. Her lungs still burning from her run, she inhaled and started to count, while Junia shoved her hands in her coat and glared at her in silent challenge.

And then it hit her. Her sister was goading her, trying to make her upset. And if Ella hadn't remembered her promise, she would have played right into her sister's hands. Why Junia was so eager to trip Ella's temper was another thing altogether, and Ella didn't particularly care what her sister's motivation was. *Lord, please give me peace.* She closed her eyes and repeated the phrase again.

"What are you doing?" Junia asked.

Ella opened her eyes. "Fulfilling a promise." She turned on her heel and headed back to Wendy's office, ignoring the temptation to look over her shoulder and see if Junia was following. It didn't matter if she was or not. All Ella was responsible for in this moment was her own behavior. Her own reaction. And with God's help, she was choosing not to react.

When she walked back into the office, she saw her father and Wendy talking, several sheets of paper in front of them, a pen in *Daed*'s hand. They both looked up as she moved toward them and sat down in her seat as if she'd just taken a restroom break instead of chasing her sister into the next neighborhood.

"Is everything all right?" *Daed* asked, hope in his eyes.

Ella paused. After years of her father ignoring the situation between her and Junia, he was doing his best to rectify things. She wished she could tell him they'd worked things out. Instead, she shook her head.

His hope disappeared. "Where's Junia?"

"She still needs some time." Ella turned to Wendy. Their session might not have solved their family conflict, but she had found some of it helpful. "Do you have any advice for how to control my temper? I, um, have a problem with that."

"I do have a tip sheet," she said, looking through her papers. "But if you ever find the secret, let me know." She handed her the paper. "Everyone can use help with their anger."

Ella looked at *Daed*. Surprisingly, he didn't seem too upset and went back to writing on the sheet of paper in front of him.

A few minutes later, Junia entered. She sat down at the table without looking at anyone. Ella was reading one of the suggestions called "Taking a Time-Out." She'd been doing that on her own with her walks, and now she had a place to go if she needed one—Nelson's. And despite making a promise that she wouldn't avail herself of his offer, being able to manage her temper was more important than her ego. If she needed a place to go for a time-out, she would go to the warehouse.

She expected Wendy to say something to Junia, but instead she started writing on a yellow legal pad, sitting back in her chair and using her knees as leverage. Ella suspected she was writing down some notes she didn't want them to see. *Daed* also continued writing, and Ella moved on to another paper Wendy had given them. "Ten Steps for Resolving Conflict." Junia was shifting in her chair, but Ella resisted the urge to look at her.

"Our hour is up," Wendy said, setting the legal pad face down on the table. "I've given you some resources and tasks to work on at home. If you want to schedule another meeting in the future, let me know. My door is always open." She turned to Junia. "And if you have any questions, feel free to ask."

Junia glanced away, but Wendy didn't seem offended.

After they left her office, the taxi was already waiting for them in front of the building. The ride home was silent, but Ella didn't mind.

She had a lot to think about. And pray about. Because even if Junia continued her quest to make her angry, she had to figure out a way not to give in to her temper. Right now the best thing to do would be to ignore her altogether. *Daed* probably wouldn't like that, but if he wanted peace, it was how it had to be for the near future.

Then she remembered she would be chaperoning Junia and Malachi, and her newfound resolve would soon be tested. Although, her sister hadn't said anything to her about any upcoming dates or outings. Did Junia dislike the idea of Ella accompanying her and Malachi so much that she'd prefer to have a long-distance relationship with him? *I hope so.*

When they arrived home, Ella was emotionally exhausted. Although she hadn't been happy about losing a day's worth of business, now that she didn't have to go back to work, she wanted to take a nap. Junia must have had the same idea, because as soon as they walked through the door, she ran upstairs to her room.

She turned to *Daed*. "Do you need anything?"

He shook his head, weariness in his eyes. "Just some rest. After today we can all use some of that."

Ella nodded, but she couldn't resist saying, "If you need anything later, let me know."

Daed smiled. "I can fend for myself for one night, Ella. Junia can too." He touched her arm as he walked to the staircase.

She watched him walk upstairs. He seemed tired, but there was also a little lightness in his step as he made his way to his bedroom. Their meeting had to be hard on him too, but like her, maybe he had some hope that things would work out. She was about to follow him when she heard a knock on the door.

"I'll get it," she said. It was probably someone wanting to know why the store was closed.

But when she opened the door, she wasn't looking at a disappointed customer. It was Nelson Bontrager.

·⁂·

Nelson sat in the Yoders' living room across from Ella, who was perched on the couch. A cumbersome silence had stretched between them. When he arrived, they exchanged pleasantries, and she had offered him tea or coffee, which he refused. Then she told him to sit in her father's chair. Now they were both staring at the floor, not saying a word. That was his fault, though. He was the one making things awkward.

Last night and most of the morning he'd wrestled with himself about helping Ella chaperone Malachi and Junia. There were so many reasons he shouldn't—he had a house to build, a warehouse to renovate into a business, and Ella to avoid, although he wasn't as gung ho about evading her as much as he used to be. He realized that his vow to stay away from all women was not only excessive, but it was also impossible. They were officially neighbors now. He was renting stable space from her father, and his nephew and her sister were romantically involved. He didn't need to flee from her or any other woman. It was romance he had to shun, not females.

And since he wasn't romantically interested in Ella Yoder, there was no reason why he couldn't do his part to watch over Malachi and Junia, although it would plunk him right in the middle of romance. *At least it won't be mine.* He'd also told Phoebe he would keep an eye on Malachi, and he never went back on his word.

"Nelson?"

He looked at her, noticing her drooping shoulders. He was surprised the store was closed today, and he'd been so caught up in his own thoughts that he hadn't considered that maybe something was wrong. "Are you okay?"

She straightened a little. "I'm fine."

He didn't quite believe her, but she didn't seem upset right now. More like tired—the way she'd been at supper a few Saturdays ago.

"Was there something you needed?" she asked, tilting her head at him. "Did you want to talk to *Daed*?"

"*Nee*. I want to talk to you."

"Why?"

He couldn't help but smile a little. She was so direct, and he was discovering he liked that about her. Miriam and Norene had been evasive with him—

Wait. He had to stop thinking about them and comparing them to Ella. It wasn't fair to her. "I'll help you chaperone Malachi and Junia." There. Now he was committed. *No turning back now.*

"You don't have to," she said. But her stiff shoulders relaxed a little.

"I do. And before you say that you can handle them yourself—"

"How did you know I was going to say that?"

This time he couldn't hide his chuckle. "Was I right?"

"*Ya*, but—"

"I know you can do the job yourself. But you don't have to. Malachi's *mei* nephew, and I'll take responsibility for him." He shook his head. "He's not going to like it."

"Junia sure doesn't. But it's for their own *gut*."

"Agreed." He rubbed his hand over the arm of Barnabas's comfortable chair. "If you don't mind me asking, why is the store closed?"

She stilled and looked away, making him wish he hadn't been nosy. He'd made it more than clear he didn't like her prying questions, and here he was doing the same thing. He was about to apologize when she said, "We had a family meeting."

"Ah. I know all about those. We had a lot of *familye* meetings while I was growing up."

"Not like this one," she mumbled. Then she sat back against the couch. "We met with a lawyer."

That surprised him. "Wow."

"For conflict mediation." She tugged on one of her *kapp* strings. "Between me and Junia. *Daed* too, but we don't argue with him. He gets the brunt of our fights, unfortunately." She let out a long sigh. "Believe it or not, we used to get along."

"All siblings argue," Nelson said. "I've had some knock-down, drag-out fights with *mei bruders*. I've got this scar on my knuckle from when Jesse and I had it out a few years ago. Zeke's got one on his foot. He and my oldest *bruder*, Devon, used to get into it a lot when they were younger."

She looked at him. "How do you get along now?"

"*Gut*," he said, trying to remember the last time he'd gotten into a huge argument with one of his siblings, and realized it had been with Jesse again when he first moved to Marigold. When Nelson discovered Jesse was the one who put the bride advertisement in the papers as a joke, he'd been furious. But after Jesse apologized and admitted his wrongdoing, they made up. In the end, he and his family members always did.

Ella crossed her arms—not defiantly but in a protective gesture. "Junia said she talked to Malachi about our problems, and I was mad that she did. Now, for some reason I'm telling you about them, even when I know you don't care."

Her words hit him hard because they were *his* words. And when they first met, he didn't care. Inexplicably, now he did. *Because we'll probably be family in the future.* Surely that was the only reason.

She jumped up from the couch. "I said too much. Again."

He stood and went to her. "Does it make you feel better to talk about it?"

After a long pause, she nodded. "Some."

"Then I'm glad you told me. We all need a little help sometimes."

"You don't seem to. When it comes to your business anyway."

She had no idea how lost he was, and he couldn't admit it to her. Although they weren't sniping at each other anymore, he didn't forget how she'd wanted to be partners before he even bought the warehouse because it would benefit her business. He also didn't forget that his initial reaction was to think she was plotting against him. But despite her apologizing for it, he didn't want to give her any ideas that they could collaborate on anything other than chaperoning. Eager to change topics, he asked, "So when do our besotted relatives have their next date?"

"Besotted?" She grinned. "That's a word I've never heard before."

Oh, that smile again. It really did make her look completely different. In a good way. *A very good way.* "I've read a book or two."

"I'm impressed with your vocabulary."

He laughed. "Don't be. That's the only fancy word I know."

"Hmm. You keep surprising me, Nelson Bontrager." Instead of yanking her *kapp* string, she was now twirling it, the action much more natural . . . and, he had to admit, cute. "But to answer your question, I don't know. Junia hasn't said anything about future dates with Malachi."

He frowned a little. "Don't you think that's strange?"

"Very. But then again, I've never been in love, so what do I know?"

She released the string. "Other than when she's fighting with me and getting mad at *Daed*, Junia seems happy. Happier than before she met Malachi."

"He's happy too." Nelson had experienced some happiness with his exes. That didn't mean that what Malachi and Junia had was true love, or that they were meant to be together. Only God knew.

"I'll let you know if Junia says anything," she said.

"And I'll do the same with Malachi."

"*Danki*, Nelson."

"For what?"

"Being you." She yawned.

Yeah, she was tired, and he needed to leave. Mission accomplished, and there was no reason for him to stay. Not a single one.

She smiled.

His heartbeat skipped again. "I've got to *geh*," he said quickly, annoyed with his pulse. Maybe he needed to get his ticker checked.

"Okay, bye—"

He hurried out the door and scrambled down the porch. It wasn't until he ran inside the warehouse that he slowed down. Apparently he wasn't totally done with running away from women. He was also young and healthier than a horse. His quick heart rate had nothing to do with being sick. *I'm still a sucker for a pretty smile.* Eventually Ella's grin would become a common sight to him. Until then he would keep his guard up.

Eighteen

"How did your meeting go today?"

Wendy looked up from the canned chicken noodle soup she'd made for supper several minutes ago. Not exactly a gourmet meal, but it was enough. Her mother had said she wasn't that hungry, and neither was Wendy. "Fine," she said, blowing on her spoon. When she tasted the watery broth, she frowned.

"Kind of a disappointment, isn't it?" Mom crumbled a few crackers into her bowl.

She set down the spoon and started to get up. "I'll make something else."

"Oh no, don't do that." She motioned for her to sit. "I wasn't complaining. Just stating a fact. After having Charity's homemade soups, canned doesn't compare. But I don't mind eating it." She consumed a spoonful. "'Mmm! Mmm! Good!'"

Wendy chuckled and sat back down. "This was my favorite soup as a kid."

"I remember." She touched Wendy's hand. "If your meeting was fine, then what's bothering you? Or am I overstepping my boundaries as a mother to an adult child?"

She hesitated. She was legally obligated not to discuss the Yoders' business with anyone, including her mother, whom she completely trusted. Even if she wasn't bound by lawyer-client privilege, she wouldn't reveal what they had talked about anyway. But the conflict mediation with Barnabas and his daughters wasn't what kept her at her office for the rest of the afternoon. "I'm thinking about closing my practice," she finally said.

Mom dropped the two crackers she'd just picked up. "Really?"

"Yes." She left her spoon in her bowl. Although she'd contemplated it more than once, this was the first time she'd voiced her thoughts out loud. "I don't know who's more surprised—me or you."

"But you love being a lawyer. Ever since you were in junior high you wanted to go to law school. You achieved that dream and more."

Monroe, always present under the table during mealtimes, lay down on top of Wendy's feet. She didn't nudge him to move, enjoying the warmth of his fur through her socks. "I know. And for years, that's all I wanted."

"But things change," Mom said.

She stared at the soup again. In this case, she was changing. She wasn't sure how, why, or what the end result of her metamorphosis would be. She knew only that she didn't want to be a lawyer anymore, although she still wanted to help people. The fulfillment she had from today's meeting with the Yoders proved that, even though she didn't know if they would take her advice and tips or continue on the same path. She couldn't force them, or anyone, to do anything.

But after they left and she started organizing her files—a long overdue task—she looked at her minuscule caseload and balked. In the past she would have spent hours working on a case, determined not only to help her clients but also to come out on the winning side . . . even if it wasn't the right one. Her stomach lurched.

"Wendy."

She lifted her gaze, seeing the concern in her mother's eyes.

"There's something we haven't talked about since you moved in with me, other than you mentioning it when you first left New York. I didn't want to bring it up or pry, and you can tell me to buzz off if you want, but I must ask, does this have anything to do with Parker?"

Parker Williams. At least she didn't flinch at the mention of his name anymore, and when he dumped her almost two years ago, she refused to call him Parker, even in her mind. Cretin, jerk, scumbag, lowlife . . . the negative adjectives were endless. And fitting. "He's not part of my life anymore," she said.

"I know." Mom's voice was gentle. "But whatever happened between the two of you had a strong effect. I could tell, especially after you first moved here."

She nodded. She couldn't deny that when she left New York initially to check on her mother because she'd been worried about her and didn't quite trust Charity at the time, her breakup with Parker was a factor. She'd even admitted to her mother that she needed her because of how hurt she was—and it was the first time since she'd passed the bar that she acknowledged she needed anyone but herself.

"Like I said, if you don't want to talk about this—"

"It's okay." She'd just been an eyewitness to a family willing—some reluctantly and some eagerly—to face their pain and conflict. Maybe it was time for her to do the same. "It's just hard to admit I was such a fool."

Mom shook her head. "I doubt that. You're one of the savviest people I know. I raised you to be." She smiled.

"In the courtroom, sure. But not when it comes to romance." She leaned back, and Monroe moved off her feet. "I spent so much of my life trying to be the best. I worked hard to get the best score on the SAT, to be valedictorian, to ace college and get into law school."

"You worked very hard," Mom said, still smiling. "Your dad and I were proud of you. I still am."

The words were nice to hear, and she never doubted her parents' pride. They weren't shy about expressing their amazement at her achievements, but they never put any pressure on her to be number one. She'd done that all on her own. "But my single-mindedness came at a price. Didn't you and Dad ever worry about me not getting married?"

"'Worried' isn't the right term. But we did wonder. And, full disclosure, we always wanted grandchildren."

"You never told me that," Wendy said.

"I'd seen plenty of my friends put pressure on their kids to marry and have families. I didn't want to do that to you. Your father and I trusted God. If he wanted you to marry and have children, it would happen, regardless of what we said." She adjusted her glasses. "What we did worry about was you working too hard and not enjoying the fruits of your labors."

"You were right to be concerned. I did work too hard, and I started realizing that a few years ago." She remembered the exact day—her fortieth birthday, after she'd celebrated it with legal briefs and law books instead of cake, family, and friends. But it wasn't until two years ago when Parker Williams entered her life that she decided to do something different.

"When Parker first joined the firm, it was hard not to notice him. He was so handsome, smart, and had a brilliant legal mind. When he asked me out on a date, I could hardly believe it. Me, the old maid lawyer who rarely left her office, had caught his eye. If I had more experience dating—any experience, actually—I would have seen the red flags. If I hadn't been so consumed with work, I would have paid attention to the grapevine. I detest gossip, but in this case it was true."

"He was a womanizer?"

"I'm sure he still is." She took a sip of her water. "Mom, he had this way of making you feel like you were special—the only woman he could possibly be with." Her throat caught. "I was so stupid. Turns out there was even a betting pool going on. No one believed I would engage in anything outside of my work."

"Oh, honey." Mom took her hand. "I'm so sorry."

The humiliation she'd felt that day when she discovered he not only didn't think she was special, but he was just trying to win a big pot of money, hit her full force. Tears welled in her eyes. "What I told you about getting passed over for partner several times was true. It was also true that my boss told me I was a workaholic. But I couldn't bring myself to tell you that after I'd fallen for Parker, he broke up with me, and I was the laughingstock of the firm."

"I—" Mom's lips pressed together, her eyes blazing. "How could a top law firm have so many immature employees?"

"They were mostly junior lawyers, some fresh out of law school and clerking for others. Surprisingly, there were a few women who participated too."

"I can't believe this."

"Several of them apologized to me later. And I had plenty of fellow employees who stuck up for me." She managed to smile. "It wasn't all horrible, but it was bad enough that I knew I had to leave for a while. I just didn't expect it to be this long."

Mom squeezed her hand. "I'm glad you told me about this, and I can see why you haven't until now. If I were younger and in better shape—"

"You'd stay right here and enjoy your soup. Or at least try to. I'm glad you have my back, though."

"Always, sweetheart."

She pulled her hand from her mother's. "I'm not excusing Parker or anyone else for what they did, but it was a wake-up call for me. I only knew one way to live—competitively. But living in Marigold, reading my Bible every day, and being closer to the Lord has shown me that's not the way."

"You can still be a lawyer, Wendy. Just don't work so hard, or so much."

"I thought about that. It was one reason I opened up the office in Barton. But I can see I don't want to practice law anymore. I'm burned-out. I don't want to spend my days cooped up in an office or a courtroom. I've had a taste of freedom here in Amish country and I like it, particularly the slow pace and the focus on faith. I've felt a peace I've never experienced. I can see why you and Dad were eager to move here."

Mom's eyes were glassy. "I wish he were still here to see this," she said, her voice thick.

"Me too." She sighed, but it was filled with relief. Revealing the most humiliating and hurtful experience in her life to her mother had been more freeing than she'd anticipated. She probably should have done it sooner. Or maybe this was the exact time she needed to face what happened.

She glanced at their bowls. "Our soup is cold," she said, standing up and taking the bowls. "I'll warm them up."

"How about a sandwich instead?" Mom grinned. "I'm in the mood for PB&J."

She paused. "Oddly enough, so am I." She walked over and kissed her on the cheek. "Thank you, Mom. For having my back and always being so supportive."

"You make it easy, honey. And no matter what you decide to do about your career, I'll always support you." Mom removed her glasses and wiped her eyes with her napkin. She looked up with a wry smile. "Extra jelly?"

Wendy almost laughed. Leave it to her mother to try to wrangle some bonus calories. Considering how diligent she usually was with her diet, what would be the harm? "Yes, but just a little." As she dumped out the soup and made the sandwiches, a thought occurred to her. "Do you think Charity could teach me how to make some Amish dishes?"

"I'm sure she would," Mom said. "She loves to cook."

Wendy nodded and brought the PB&Js to the table. After they ate and her mother went to the living room, Monroe at her heels, she thought about their conversation. At the beginning of supper, she was on the fence about closing her practice. Now she was positive it was the right thing to do. She still had a lot of savings—she'd also been single-minded when it came to having a strong financial portfolio—and she could afford to take the loss on shutting down her business and continuing to explore her current interests. First sewing, now cooking, and in a few months, she would start her new garden. She grinned. *Now this is the way to live.*

·❧·

For the rest of the week, Nelson was in a mental tailspin. He'd been in such a hurry for his new start he hadn't checked with his family to see if they were available to help clear out part of the woods so he could begin building his house. While his father's point that Nelson would have plenty of support was sincere, it turned out everyone had made end-of-year plans. *Daed* had told him to wait, and now he knew why. His parents and brothers had gone south for an overdue three-week vacation, leaving the farm in Owen's hands, with help from Jalon, his cousin Adam, and his other brothers who lived nearby. They were also working on their own home and land improvement projects that were easier to do during the less busy months of the year. That included Malachi. Strange, since he'd expected his nephew to take full advantage of Nelson being less than a baseball throw away from his true love. But when he asked him to help clear out some of the trees behind the warehouse, Malachi declined without saying why.

He wondered if he should mention that to Ella but decided against it. He'd agreed to chaperone them on a date, not get deep into their personal business. If Malachi and Junia were still meeting in secret, they would have to face the consequences. Besides, due to his lack of foresight, he had to work alone for a while until some of his family members could pitch in. He should have listened to his father and not been so impulsive. If he'd had a schedule, he'd be behind instead of ahead, like he initially wanted.

Wednesday and Thursday he worked on felling a few trees, and the hard physical labor not only wore him out but also helped with his stress level. By Friday, though, he knew he had to get his thoughts and lists down on paper, so he went next door to the grocery store. There was a small stationery section in one corner where he could pick up a notebook and a few pens. He'd been in the store so many times he had the layout memorized.

When he walked inside, he was greeted by Ella and her smile. He ignored the jolt to his system and smiled back. If he pretended not to be affected, eventually he wouldn't be. *I hope.*

"Hi, Nelson," she said. "*Wie geht's?*"

He couldn't bring himself to tell her that he was overwhelmed, so instead he said, "*Gut.* Just need some paper and pens." He headed in that direction.

"What kind of paper? Is there a certain type of pen you like to use?" She followed him straight to the stationery section. "If we don't have it here, we can order it for you."

Glancing at her, he said, "Just a notebook and a pen. Nothing fancy." He did have to give her credit for good customer service, something he noticed she always displayed, regardless of her mood. Today she seemed to be in a good one. He hadn't seen her since he'd stopped by her house late Tuesday afternoon. That didn't mean he hadn't thought about her. In between trying to pin down his family, chopping wood, and attempting to come up with a plan, he was keenly aware that when she wasn't upset or cranky and he wasn't annoyed or trying to get away from her, they were able to have a decent conversation. She wasn't his enemy, and he wasn't hers. That made his life a lot easier.

She stood next to him and picked up a plain yellow pad and a pack of twelve ballpoint pens. "Here you *geh*," she said, starting to hand them to him. Then she paused.

"What?" he said, ready to take the objects. They were exactly what he wanted.

She put the pad and pens back. "You should pick out your own," she said.

"Okay." When he grabbed what she had chosen, she put her hand on his arm.

"Are you sure?"

Confused, he turned to her. "*Ya*, Ella. I'm sure I want these."

"You don't have to take them because I said so."

"I'm not." He faced her. "What's this all about?"

She folded her hands in front of her and stared at her feet. "I'm trying not to be so bossy," she said in a low voice.

There wasn't anyone else in the store, so he didn't know why she was whispering. "That's *gut*, but you weren't being bossy. You were helping me."

She looked up at him, frowning. "I can't even tell the difference anymore."

"I tell you what," he said, taking the pad and pens. "I'll let you know if you're being bossy, at least around me."

Her gray eyes brightened a little. Then she smirked. "I think you might enjoy doing that."

He couldn't help but grin . . . because she was right. "I promise not to enjoy it too much."

That made her laugh.

He stilled. She had a great laugh too. Light, but hearty and genuine.

The bell above the door chimed and she turned as a customer walked through. "If you need anything else, let me know."

Nelson nodded and he couldn't resist watching her walk away. She was trying to change an unpleasant quality in herself and that was admirable. He made his way to the counter to check out, stopping to pick up a package of beef jerky for a snack. In the past he'd made his own deer jerky, even before he became a butcher, but he had learned new and improved ways to prepare it when he was training with Samuel. Commercial brands didn't compare, but they weren't bad either.

Ella was still helping the customer and Barnabas came out from the back to ring up Nelson's purchases. "Saw you chopping down some trees the other day," he said as he wrote down the items on a ticket pad. "If you need some help, let me know. Been a while since

I faced a tree, but I could use the exercise." He looked up and leaned forward, glancing at Ella, who was definitely being helpful to her customer as she showed her different brands of laundry detergent. "*Mei dochders* think I'm old and feeble," he said with a wink.

Nelson didn't think Barnabas looked old or feeble. He also couldn't refuse assistance. "I'll take you up on it. Whenever you're free, just come on over. I'll be there." Other than going to Jesse and Charity's for meals, he was solely committed to working on his property.

He paid for his purchases, and when he got back to the warehouse, he sat on the edge of his bed and made several lists of tasks and supplies. Then he turned to a fresh sheet and stared at it. What should he tackle first? Ordering the supplies was a no-brainer, but some of them he couldn't purchase until he finished other tasks first. Why was this so hard for him to figure out?

He shut the notebook and went back outside to work on another tree. At least he knew how to do that, and he was accomplishing something. He'd figure the other stuff out later.

Nineteen

The following week was the first of the year, and along with it came a surprise—a winter thaw. The morning paper forecasted several days of temperatures above sixty degrees. After a month of snowy, cold weather, Ella was glad for the break.

She was also getting a break from fighting with Junia, mostly because her sister was in a sullen mood and had been since their meeting with Wendy. She should be glad Junia wasn't goading her into a fight and testing her resolve to keep her temper in check. But she didn't like that her sister had transformed into a waterlogged dishrag, personality-wise. Junia could be self-absorbed, mercurial, and flighty. She was also creative and, when she wanted to be, a true sweetheart. One thing she'd never been was gloomy.

Ella pulled four loaves of bread out of the oven and set them on top of the stove burners. She'd been baking for the past two days, and she'd made twenty loaves so far—two for her family and the rest to be sold in the store. While she baked, her father and Junia manned the grocery. From what she could tell, her sister was doing her job, and her father hadn't commented on her mood. But she'd caught him casting a few concerned looks Junia's way when she wasn't looking, mostly at mealtime while she was picking at her food.

The delicious scent of hot, yeasty bread filled the kitchen, but Ella couldn't fully enjoy it. Now that she wasn't constantly angry, she'd been thinking about her life in Lancaster. Her mother was on her mind, along with the good times she'd had with Junia. Had they even talked about *Mamm* lately? She couldn't remember. It was getting harder to recall the fun times too.

She briefly wondered if she should talk to Nelson, but she rejected the idea. She assumed he was busy with his renovations. He'd been cutting down trees over the past several days, no doubt preparing to build his house. Good, because he didn't need to spend the entire winter in a cold warehouse. She was surprised when she saw *Daed* out there with him and had almost gone over there to stop her father from doing such hard work. He wasn't a spring chicken. She held back. *I'm not bossy anymore, remember?* But why was Nelson okay with accepting her father's help and not hers?

Now that they were able to speak decently to each other, perhaps Nelson might reconsider. She'd have to make it clear that she wasn't offering her assistance because of an ulterior motive. She genuinely wanted to see him succeed, not because it would benefit her business but because she truly wanted him to realize his dream.

She looked over the loaves and picked the one with the best crust, wrapped it in a clean, dry dish towel and put it in a basket, adding a jar of local honey at the last minute. They purchased the honey to sell in the store from an Amish cottage business in Holmes County, but she always bought a few extra jars to keep at home. After slipping on her coat, she headed over to Nelson's. She didn't hear him working outside, so she went to the front door and knocked. When he didn't

answer, she twisted the knob. The door opened and she went inside—
and was almost knocked off her feet by the smell.

Nelson was on top of a tall ladder, wearing a face mask as he
was rolling on a coat of white paint from a tray on a short platform
attached to the ladder. Three gas heaters were spread throughout
the space, warming the room to a springlike temperature. The back
door was open, probably for ventilation. What was he painting with
that was so noxious?

He set the roller in the tray and came down the ladder, then
stepped back to look at his work. She walked toward him, the sound
of the gas heaters muffling her steps. He was just about to climb up
the ladder again when she tapped him on the shoulder.

He startled, then took off his respirator and frowned. "You
shouldn't be in here, Ella."

"And hello to you too." She started to scowl but realized he wasn't
being a jerk. He was serious. She watched him walk over to his bed
and get another mask out of a package. "Put this on."

"What's that smell?" She drew the mask over her face.

"Oil paint." He moved to the other side of the ladder, underneath
the platform holding the paint. He studied the fresh coat he'd just
applied.

Ella didn't know much about paint, but there was a difference in
the way this stuff smelled compared to what they'd used on the inside
of their house after her family moved in. "Is there a reason you're using
that?" Her voice was as muffled as his, but they could still understand
each other.

He turned to her, and she expected to see the usual annoyance
in his eyes because of her questions. Instead, he calmly answered,
"There were some stains on the walls. The hardware store suggested

using this to cover them up, as long as I wore a mask and kept the place well ventilated."

"Do you need some help?"

"I got it."

"It will *geh* faster with two extra hands." She set the basket on the floor and pushed it away from her with the toe of her shoe.

He paused, as if considering her offer. Then he shook his head. "I'm—"

"You'll let *Daed* help, but you won't let me?" She was surprised at the hurt in her voice, then irritated with herself for blurting out the question. Why did it matter if he turned her down? *But it does.*

"That's different. Cutting down trees is long, hard work." He gestured to the wall. "Painting isn't difficult."

"But there's a lot to paint." She moved closer to him until they were both near the ladder. "I know you think I'm only interested in how you can help *mei* business. But that's not true. Not anymore." She took another step toward him so she could look directly into his eyes so he would know she was telling the truth. Due to his height advantage, she had to lift her head, but they were close enough now that she could meet his gaze straight on. "You believe me, *ya*?"

.⁓෨ঙ⁓.

Nelson gulped. He wasn't even sure what Ella had asked him, his heart was thumping so fast. His pulse had started trotting when he turned around after she tapped him on the shoulder. She'd surprised him, but that wasn't the only reason he was startled. It wasn't even the fact that she'd smiled at him again. Other than the spot of flour on her left cheek, she didn't look any different than when she was helping him at the grocery store. But for a split second, he felt a shock of attraction stronger than he had to any other woman. He'd covered it by handing her a mask, not wanting her to breathe in the fumes while he was trying to get a handle on himself, struggling to be nonchalant.

Now she was so close to him he could see the variegated grays in her irises. He felt lightheaded, and he couldn't blame it on the paint. *What is wrong with me?*

"Nelson?"

He took a quarter of a step back, not wanting to run into the freshly painted wall. What had she asked him? Something about believing her?

"I want to help you reach your dream," she said. "That's all. No other motives."

His heart was galloping now . . . because he did believe her. Despite his vow not to compare her to Miriam and Norene, he did it anyway. When had either of them been interested in his goals? His mind raced with memories—how Miriam had always talked about her problems and only what she wanted, and the way Norene had been an expert at making him believe she was interested in him without really asking his thoughts or opinions. He'd never seen the absolute sincerity from them that he was seeing in Ella's eyes.

"Let me help you, Nelson." Then she smiled.

And his pulse was off to the races. Which was why he spoke one single word. "*Nee.*"

Her smile faded into a confused frown. She opened her mouth, and he was sure she was going to ask him why. His brain scrambled for any explanation other than the real reason—he couldn't be alone with her while his emotions were going haywire. Maybe he had breathed in too many paint fumes. Or he was more stressed out than he thought.

Even if one or both of those things were true, his guard was down, and he was losing the battle to raise it back up.

Ella removed her mask to reveal her lips pressing into a hard line. But it wasn't anger he saw in her eyes. Or irritation. Was it . . . disappointment? "I'm sorry I bothered you." She turned to leave.

He felt like a heel. She was just offering to help him, and he had to be a jerk about it. He reached out to stop her. "Ella—"

She whirled around. Knocked into the ladder. The paint bucket tipped over, dumping oil paint over his head.

.~∾⁓∾~.

Ella gasped in horror as paint covered Nelson's hair and dribbled down the sides of his face. "Oh *nee.*"

He yanked off his shirt, the neckhole getting tangled in the respirator, clearly frustrating him further. She watched, helpless, as he finally removed them both and wiped the paint off his head, making a bigger mess. She had to do something. "Nelson."

"What?!" The hand holding the paint-covered shirt dropped to his side.

"This isn't helping." Without hesitation, she took his other hand and started tugging.

"What are you doing?"

He was angry, and he had a right to be. This was her fault. She shouldn't have been so insistent on helping him. And she shouldn't have backed him up near the ladder. She hadn't realized she was so close until she bumped into it. And now he was paying for her mistake, and she needed to fix it. "I'm taking you to *mei haus.* You can clean up and get a shower there."

He resisted. "It's oil paint. Water won't work."

209

She lifted her chin. She was taking charge, and yes, being bossy. And she'd apologize for it later. He didn't have a shower or even a bathtub to rinse off in—only a large cooler of water, which wouldn't be enough to wash off the paint. "Then we'll try something else."

"Ella . . ." He closed his eyes, and she was 100 percent positive he was counting to ten. When he opened them, he said, "Maybe a shower will work since the paint's still wet. Let me grab another shirt and I'll be over."

"I can get it for you—"

"Ella!"

Oops, she'd gone too far. "Sorry." She scurried toward the door, then glanced over her shoulder. Which was a mistake because she suddenly noticed he was shirtless. Wow. Nelson Bontrager was *built*. She stared at the ground. "I'll meet you in the bathroom. I mean inside. The house. My house." She'd gone from being in control to being unable to speak in coherent sentences. *I have to get out of here.*

She ran across the road and dashed inside, then gathered up some towels and started the shower for him. By the time he arrived, the water was hot and his temper seemingly less so. He walked into the bathroom, and she pulled back the curtain, steam coming from the running faucet. "It's all ready for you."

"*Danki*," he said flatly. He stared at her for a second. "I can do this myself, Ella."

"Oh, right." She left, shutting the door behind her, and said a quick prayer that the hot water would dissolve the paint. Then she threaded her fingers together and stared at the door, wincing inside. What a mess she'd made when all she wanted to do was help. She still didn't understand why he'd told her no, and at this point she needed to let that go. He had his reasons, and other than aiding him in getting the paint out of his hair and off his face, she wasn't going to offer again. She owed him that much.

She went to the kitchen and busied herself with packaging up the bread. She hadn't even told him what was in the basket, and she wasn't sure if he would accept it after what happened.

She was almost done wrapping the loaves in plastic bags secured with twist ties when he came into the kitchen. He was completely dressed, except for being barefoot. He even had nice feet. He'd also gotten almost all the paint off his face. Then she looked at his hair. "Oh *nee*," she said.

"That was *mei* reaction too." He tried to run his hand through the tangled mass of white paint and thick brown hair. His fingers jammed into a glob of paint. He yanked them out and shook his head. "Got any turpentine?"

"You're not going to douse your—" She almost said "gorgeous hair" but caught herself. Where had that come from? She was literally losing her mind today. "You can't wash with turpentine."

"Why not?"

"Because it sounds poisonous. And it smells bad."

"I don't care about the smell. I have to get rid of this." He jabbed his finger toward the paint clumps.

She sprang from the floor, an idea coming to her. "I can cut it out."

"Oh *nee*." He backed away from her. "That's not a *gut* idea."

At that moment, she felt small. Very small and very rueful. "I'm so sorry, Nelson. This is my fault." She looked up at him. "Please forgive me."

.⸙.

There was nothing else Nelson could do but raise the white flag. He was upset about the paint but not with her. He'd made the mistake of putting the pan on the ladder platform. He didn't think about how it could have been easily knocked off, and he probably would have ended up doing it himself. He was also to blame for her running into the ladder. If he had just agreed to let her help him, they would be painting right now instead of standing in her kitchen, talking about cutting his hair. He'd had the water on the hottest setting and used half a bottle of shampoo trying to clean his hair. He smelled nice, but it was a waste.

"Ella." He attempted to run his hand through his hair again, only for it to get stuck. He winced as he yanked his fingers out. "This isn't your fault."

"I knocked over the paint."

"Because I wasn't careful with it." He sighed. "I guess there's no other choice but to get the scissors."

"Okay, I'll be right back."

He plopped down in the chair and looked at several loaves on the table and recognized the packaging. Ella baked the delicious bread they sold at the store? That explained the flour on her face, which was still there when she returned with a huge pair of shears and a light-blue bath towel. His stomach twisted. Maybe this wasn't such a good idea.

"Don't worry," she said, her tone confident. "A few snips and I'll be done."

"Okay." He tried to focus on the bright side. He could have been working with stronger chemicals. It was only hair anyway, and it would grow back.

She set the scissors down, scooped the loaves off the table, and put them on the counter and came back. "I've been cutting *Daed*'s hair for a long time," she said as she moved behind him. "I know what I'm doing."

Her sureness helped his doubt, and he was able to relax a little.

She draped the towel around his neck and stood in front of him, studying his hair. She crossed her arms and leaned her elbow on her hand, tapping her bottom lip. "Hmm."

"What do you mean, 'hmm'?"

"Just trying to figure out the best way to do this and salvage as much hair as I can." At least she wasn't hacking at his hair yet without taking stock of the condition of it, like he most likely would have done.

"Do you always have a plan?"

She moved to stand behind him again. "I try to. Don't you?"

He didn't answer, and soon he heard the snip of the shears.

"Most of the paint is on the top and sides." She fluffed the back of his head. "You have a lot of hair."

"I'm just glad it's not as curly as Jesse's," he said. "When we were younger, his head was always a rat's nest."

"Does anyone else in your family have those curls?"

"Not my siblings, but *mei* niece Hannah does. That's Malachi's sister."

"How old is she?" *Snip, snip.*

"Twelve? Thirteen?" He couldn't remember. It was hard enough keeping up with his siblings, and now that he had several nieces and nephews and one on the way, he couldn't retain all of their ages unless he wrote them down, something he hadn't gotten around to yet.

"I can't imagine growing up with such a big family," she said.

Her calm tone helped him settle down. "Is Junia your only sibling?"

"*Ya.* I have a couple of cousins, but overall our family is small, even the extended ones. I have two aunts who never married." She brushed some hair off his neck and moved to the right side. "They sure did have a lot of opinions about marriage, though."

She mumbled something he thought sounded like, "especially about me," but he wasn't sure. "How's it looking?" he asked, trying to stem his lingering concern that she wasn't going to do a good job.

"It's getting there."

"You sure you're not taking too much off?"

Snip, snip. "I could cut hair in *mei* sleep if I had to."

Her confidence was contagious, and he decided to let her do her work and not question it anymore. He closed his eyes as she silently continued to cut the paint out of his hair. It was kind of nice. And he would have needed a cut in the next couple of weeks anyway. His mother had always cut his hair, and per tradition, she would until he got married, and that wasn't happening anytime soon.

He opened his eyes, and she was standing in front of him, finger combing his bangs. They were almost eye to eye, and she was focused on his hair. Now that he wasn't as upset about the paint catastrophe, the attraction he experienced back at the warehouse came back again. To top it all off, she smelled good too, like fresh laundry and fruit-scented soap. He kind of recognized the second scent. He must have used her shampoo.

She set the shears down and brushed aside his bangs. He barely noticed they felt a little shorter than usual. She was moving closer, examining his hair from all sides. Was she aware that her face was only a few inches from his? He was. And he was aware of everything else, especially how he was feeling right now. How for some bizarre reason—the biggest one being that this was Ella Yoder—he wanted to brush the back of his hand over her cheek, not only to wipe the flour away but to see if her skin was as soft as it looked.

She took another step forward, stubbing her toe against his bare foot and pitching forward. On instinct, his hands shot out and went straight to her waist to steady her. His thoughts were barely registering, but one came to the fore as his hand settled on the waistband of her apron and her surprised gaze locked with his.

Twenty

Ella couldn't breathe, not with both of Nelson's hands resting on the sides of her waist. Was he lightly squeezing too? Hmm, that felt nice. Really nice.

As she righted herself, he dropped his hands fast as lightning and averted his gaze, bringing her out of her stupor. He wasn't touching her because he wanted to. She'd stumbled and he was steadying her. He didn't want her ruining his hair.

Quickly she went back to work, words tumbling out of her mouth. "I cut *mei grossvatter*'s hair once after *Aenti* Tabitha showed me, because *Grossmammi* died when I was ten and *Aenti* Tabitha said I should learn how to cut hair in case I ever got married." All true, except she left out the part where her aunt had said, *"On the out-side chance you ever get married."* She frowned. Even back when Ella thought boys were *ew*, her aunt was predicting her romantic failure.

Nelson definitely wasn't *ew*.

Snip. Oops, she cut off a little too much. Easy to fix, though. *If only I could just shut up now.* It helped that he didn't answer, and as she evened up the other side of his hair, she couldn't resist playing with it a little under the guise of checking the length. It was so soft, thick, and a little damp from his shower. Feeling slightly guilty about enjoying the process, she cleared her throat.

"Something wrong?"

"*Nee*. I'm almost done." She'd gotten most of the paint out, and she could probably stop right now, but she found another spot. And another . . . and then another.

"Sure you're not cutting off too much?"

"Of course not." But when she stepped back and took an overall look, she flinched. In her zeal to remove every bit of paint, she'd given him a short haircut. Very short. Not quite as short as some English men wore, but close. Definitely not the Amish style. Yikes. "Uh . . ."

His hand flew to his head, and he spun around in the chair. "What did you do?"

"There was so much paint—"

He jumped out of the chair and ran to the bathroom with the towel around his neck and leaving a trail of hair in his wake, some tinged with white.

Slowly she placed the scissors on the table and lowered herself onto the chair. She folded her hands in her lap and waited for—

"*Ella!*"

—him to realize how much she'd cut off. She squeezed her eyes shut, grimacing as she heard his bare feet slamming on the wood floor. When he entered, she opened one eye.

"You said you knew how to cut hair!"

The other eye flew open. "I do. I was trying to get out all the paint."

He ran his hand over his head and glared at her.

And they had been getting along so well. She winced. When it came to Nelson, she couldn't do anything right. This time he had every right to be angry. She stood and turned away from him.

"Don't do that," he said.

"Do what?"

"Cry."

"I'm not." But as she spoke, she wiped the back of her hand over her eyes and left the room, wondering if she'd ever have the courage to cut a man's hair again . . . and if Nelson could ever forgive her.

.⁓ঙ৶ৎ.

Nelson ran his hands over his hair again. When he saw his reflection in the mirror, he was shocked. He'd expected a shorter-than-average Amish haircut, not the English cut she'd given him. He was so stunned he didn't even know if she'd gotten all the paint out, and he'd rather have a little paint in his hair than what he'd ended up with. Now he looked like he was still in his rumspringa before he'd joined the church years ago. Everyone in Birch Creek knew he was a member of the church, but he was a stranger in Marigold. He'd have to explain, surely more than once, why he didn't have an Amish cut so people wouldn't think he was unbaptized.

When he walked into the living room, the sight of her by the door holding his things distracted his anger. She didn't look at him as she gave him his coat and set the boots in front of him.

"I'm sorry," she said in a small, un-Ella-like voice. "I won't bother you again." She fled the room.

Should he go after her? He should still be furious with her. It would be easier if he were. He was the one with the weird haircut, not her. But he couldn't stand to see her upset. He never could. He started to head to the kitchen, then stopped. Both their emotions were running high right now, and he wasn't up to getting into another fight—with her or with himself.

He shoved his feet into his boots and didn't bother to put on his coat, choosing to carry it as he crossed the street. He took one last glance at the house before going up his driveway and walking into the warehouse. He had a big mess to clean up. Better to focus on that than his hair.

When he entered the building, he had an unexpected visitor.

Malachi gaped at him. "What happened to you?"

Ella happened. But when he eyed the disaster in front of him, he had to take responsibility. She'd tried to help him. He just wished she hadn't tried so hard. He went to pick up the roller lying in the spilled paint near the ladder and groaned when it didn't move.

"And what happened here?" Malachi appeared beside him.

"An accident." He looked at his nephew. "Haven't seen you in a while. Are you and Jalon finished with the barn addition?"

He shook his head. "Not yet." Then he walked over to Nelson's bed and plopped down on the end, his shoulders sagging.

Nelson pinched the bridge of his nose. He didn't need to face another problem today, but he had a feeling he was about to. "What's wrong?"

"Junia dumped me."

"What? When?"

With an agonized expression, he said, "Two days and three hours ago. I don't know what I did, Nelson. I thought we were fine. I talked to her on the phone, we wrote letters, we even met at—" He waved his hand.

So he and Junia were seeing each other on the sly. He was sure Barnabas didn't know. Or Ella. If she did, she wouldn't have been in a good mood when she arrived earlier today. It also explained why Malachi couldn't spare any time to help him clear trees. He was spending every free moment talking to, and being with, *her.*

"So what happened?"

"I don't know. We were even talking about having another date instead of . . ."

"Sneaking around?"

He hung his head. "*Ya*. Junia didn't want Ella to chaperone us, even though she agreed to it. I didn't know about Barnabas's decision, but when I asked her why we had to keep meeting in private, she finally told me. That's when I insisted we *geh* on a date, with Ella."

"She wouldn't be *yer* only chaperone. I offered to do it too."

He lifted a surprised eyebrow, then sighed. "It doesn't matter now. Nelson, what am I going to do?"

Patting his nephew on the back a couple of times, he said, "I'm sorry, but there's *nix* you can do." He got up and went to pry the roller loose.

"I can't accept that."

He paused, staring at the splattered paint on the floor. He'd said those words to himself more than once after being dumped. "You can't force her to love you."

"But that's just it." He stood and moved in front of him. "I *know* she loves me. Not only has she told me, but I feel it." He put his hand over his heart.

His nephew was coming perilously close to describing his own pain, and that wasn't a path he wanted to travel again. He grabbed Malachi's shoulders. "Listen to me. I know this is hard, but you'll be better off in the end. It's *gut* you know how she truly feels about you before you do something dumb."

Like propose.

"I was going to ask her to marry me."

Too late. He dropped his hands.

"I just don't understand."

"What's to understand?" Nelson heard the bite in his tone, but he couldn't prevent it. "She's probably dating someone else, or decided you don't have the right 'qualities,' whatever that means. Maybe she's already making plans to *geh* back to Lancaster and marry her ex-boyfriend. Or she might be seeing someone right here in Marigold."

He frowned. "What are you talking about? She doesn't have an ex-boyfriend or anyone else."

"That you know about."

Malachi shook his head. "She wouldn't cheat on me."

"You haven't known her that long."

"One month, one day, six—"

"Stop!" Nelson lifted his hand. He didn't want to be mean, but he had to get through to him. "Just . . . stop. She doesn't love you, Malachi. She's been lying to you. Why would you waste your time with someone like her? She doesn't deserve you. Trust me, I know."

"You don't know Junia."

"I know women like her!" That was as much as he was going to admit about his past romantic life. His heart clenched. "They're not worth it, Malachi."

His nephew stared at him. Then he shook his head. "I refuse to believe that. I think something else is wrong."

"Malachi—"

"She's not like other women, and you don't know her like I do. Up until now, we've been able to talk about anything. She reads a lot and is very smart. She draws beautiful pictures too. Best of all, she's also got a *gut* heart, and I trust her. There are things we've only shared with each other."

"Did you tell her about *yer* biological father?"

He nodded. "She didn't judge me or *Mamm*, not even for a second."

That was a mark in her favor. Nelson had to give her that.

"She's also the most beautiful woman I've ever seen. She's everything I've ever wanted in a *frau*."

Except she doesn't want you. Nelson's history was repeating itself with his nephew. But would he have listened if one of his siblings or parents had warned him about Miriam and Norene? Even looking back on the night Norene broke his heart, he recalled Selah's subtle negative reaction when he said he was waiting for her. Would he have listened to her either?

No. He would have done exactly what he did—forge full steam ahead. All he could say was, "I'm sorry. I wished it would have worked out for you two."

"It still can. Junia told me not to contact her ever again, but I need to know why she broke up with me."

"Malachi—"

"And *yer* the only one who can find out."

"*Nee.*" He backed away. "I'm not getting involved. No. Way."

"I'll owe you a huge favor. Whatever you want."

The very last thing in the world he wanted to do was get into the middle of Malachi's relationship problems, particularly since it was dredging up his own past he'd fought so hard to bury. But maybe if Malachi knew the truth behind why Junia had dumped him, he would be able to move on. "I'll talk to Barnabas."

"*Nee.* It has to be Ella. Junia says her father doesn't understand her, or anything else."

"He's got to be aware of a few things."

Malachi lifted his hands. "I'm sure she didn't mean everything, but she's upset with him."

"Why?"

"I don't know. She won't tell me. And she doesn't want me talking to Ella either."

Nelson was losing the battle. "But you want me to talk to her."

He nodded. "Please?"

Good grief, his nephew was stubborn. Rubbing the back of his neck, he relented, knowing that Malachi wouldn't give up. "All right," he said with a heavy sigh, "I'll ask Ella."

Malachi beamed. "*Danki*, Nelson. Can you talk to her now?"

He thought about her last words. *"I won't bother you again."* Not that long ago he would have been happy to hear her say that. He wasn't now, and Malachi was giving him an opportunity to speak to her. Once they talked about Junia, they could discuss what had happened and get back on an even keel again. But it was too soon, for both of them. "I'll see her tomorrow. I've got to clean this up first."

"I'll help." He was looking at Nelson's hair. "It doesn't look bad. Kind of English, though." He picked up the tray, jiggling it a little to break it free from the dried paint, and proceeded to loosen the roller.

Nelson moved to drop his coat on his bed when his foot hit something. He glanced down and saw the basket Ella had brought. Picking it up, he noticed the top of a bread loaf peeking through the dish towel. Was this bread and honey for him? He couldn't be sure since she didn't say anything about it. She might have been on her way to take it to someone else when she stopped by. He set the basket next to his coat and returned to work. He'd take the basket to her tomorrow. *And then we'll talk.*

His spirits were sinking a bit. While he was sure he was doing the right thing for Malachi's sake, he didn't want his nephew to get his heart broken. Unfortunately, it seemed inevitable.

.❧.

"I don't think I've ever had such a well-stocked kitchen," Mom said, peering in the pantry, no doubt looking for something forbidden to eat.

Wendy smiled. The day after they talked about Parker, she visited Charity and asked her for some cooking lessons. Initially she had assumed that Wendy wanted to learn the French cooking Charity seemed obsessed with, but when Wendy pointed out she wanted Amish recipes, Charity understood. *"We'll start with some of Shirley's favorites,"* she'd said as they made a list of recipes and supplies. *"I made some adjustments for her diet."*

That hadn't surprised Wendy. Although she'd been wary of hiring the young Amish woman, she'd turned out to be the perfect caregiver for her mom. And now Wendy had that responsibility, and she took it seriously. But she didn't have to be so strict all the time. "There are still some sugar-free morning glory muffins in the bread box."

"Oh good. Those were delicious."

Wendy pieced together the pattern for an Amish dress she'd asked Eunice to help her with. Her sewing lessons had turned into daylong visits, and for the first time since she could remember, Wendy had a female friendship that wasn't tied to school or work, and those had always been short-lived due to her busy schedule. She was also growing closer to Charity, who was open to answering more of her questions about the Amish faith. It was all so lovely.

Placing a small dish with one morning glory muffin on her walker seat, Mom wheeled over to the table and sat down.

"No butter?"

"I have to watch my figure." She winked. "These don't need butter or jelly. They're perfect on their own." She looked at Wendy's project. "I should have known you would be good at sewing and cooking too."

"I have a lot more to learn." But she smiled at the compliment as she placed three pins in her mouth and matched the fabric edges.

"Maybe next time you can make whoopie pies."

She looked at her mother. "Don't push it. Your blood sugar—"

"Is the bane of my existence." She bit into the muffin.

Despite their frequent discussions about her sweet tooth, Mom was in good health for her age and for being a stroke survivor, not to mention having diabetes. She'd had her latest checkup after Christmas, and although Wendy had expected her numbers to be off due to a few holiday indulgences, she was right on target. "Do you want some coffee with that?"

"Not this late in the afternoon or I'll be up all night. What's for supper?"

"Lentils and rice."

She shuddered. "You know the old saying—'Just say no to lentils.'"

Wendy grinned. Her mother had always been witty, and at times over the years she'd found that annoying. She was more serious like her father. But after living with Mom all this time, she enjoyed her sense of humor. "I love lentils," she said. "One day you might too."

"That's a negative, my favorite daughter."

"I'm your only daughter." Wendy went back to pinning the fabric.

Mom got up, leaned over, and kissed her cheek. "And you're the best." She sat back down. "Have I told you lately how much I love that you're living here? And how happy you seem?"

Pinning the fabric, she said, "Last week. But I don't mind hearing it again."

"You're happy, aren't you?"

"Very much so." Since their talk, she had called the owner of the office building and told her she wasn't renewing her lease in February.

Last Sunday she'd gone to church service with Eunice again, this time visiting her sister's Amish district. In spite of being in a different church, she felt even more at home than she had the first time she went, and she wore her Amish dress the rest of the day. That was part of the reason why she wanted to learn to make her own. She hadn't used her cell phone all week either. It was still plugged in, but she didn't miss it. She was even thinking about buying a stovetop percolator like Eunice and Charity had. But when she showed Mom the picture from Lehman's catalog, she was less than impressed. *"I did my duty with those things,"* she said. *"Give me modern technology any day."*

Mom polished off the rest of the muffin. "What time are you going to E&J's Grocery?"

Wendy glanced at her, confused. "I'm not. Do you need something?"

"No. I just figured since you've gone there almost every day this week, you would be going today." She gave her a sly smile. "How's Barnabas?"

Wendy's cheeks heated and the pin she'd just pushed into the navy blue fabric was crooked. She straightened it, keeping her head down. "He's fine. So are his daughters." At least she thought they were. They weren't at the store at the same time when she stopped by, but Barnabas hadn't mentioned there were any more problems.

She knew she didn't have to visit Yoders' as much as she did. And there were days when she was out for her walks and had tried everything she could to avoid going there, but she couldn't help herself. She thought it was because she wanted to check on the family, but the truth was she wanted to see Barnabas, even if only for a few minutes. She didn't understand it herself, and she felt like a teenager with a crush, except the only crush she ever had when she was a teenager was on education.

Who wouldn't have a crush on him, though? In fact, she thought his eyes were unusually bright and welcoming the last two times she was there. Or was she imagining they were? *More like wishing.*

The doorbell rang, saving Wendy from speaking her thoughts. "To be continued," Mom said, rising from the chair.

"I'll get the door," Wendy offered, already standing.

"Finish your pinning," she said. "Maybe one day you can show me how to work with a pattern. I'm sure it's a pay grade or two above my button-sewing skills." Mom scooted out of the kitchen, Monroe at her heels.

She took several pins out of the quilted red, white, and blue pin cushion Eunice had gifted her on their second lesson and thought about church again. More and more she found herself not only drawn to the simple Amish lifestyle but to their faith. The structure of it appealed to her. The daily practice of living out their obedience to God wasn't just an idea but was intricately woven into the fabric of their existence. She'd never seen or experienced anything like it. And while her mother's church was fine, and the people were incredibly nice, she found herself longing to sing the German hymns in the a cappella Gregorian chant style in the Amish church. She didn't know how to explain the shifts in her thoughts and feelings when she didn't quite understand them herself.

Mom poked her head into the kitchen. "One of the Yoder girls is here."

Wendy's eyes jumped to hers. This was a surprise. Maybe Ella wanted to talk about their progress since the last meeting.

"She had to stop by the powder room for a minute." Mom frowned slightly.

Uh-oh. Wendy gathered up her sewing materials, making sure she didn't lose any pins or tear the pattern. "Is anything wrong?"

"I'm not sure. She said it was important, though." Mom turned around and wheeled her way back to the living room.

Wendy tried not to be pessimistic. Just because her mother was uncertain about Ella's mood didn't mean that the conflict mediation had failed. Even if the Yoder family had made only a little headway in communication, they could count it a success.

She heard footsteps in the kitchen and turned around. But it wasn't Ella standing there. It was Junia . . . tears streaming down her face.

Twenty-One

I've made a horrible mistake!"

Wendy rushed over to Junia, put her arm around her shoulders, and guided her to one of the kitchen chairs. Mom always kept a box of tissues in every room, and there was one in the center of the table. She pushed it toward her. Junia grabbed one, an indelicate sound filling the room as she blew her nose. Wendy waited a few moments so she could gather herself. When she finally did, the words gushed forth.

"I broke up with Malachi and I shouldn't have. I love him, and I miss him so much. I've ruined our relationship, haven't I? This is Ella's fault. And *Daed*'s. He doesn't trust me and she's just jealous. She's always been jealous." Junia blew her nose again. "What am I going to do without Malachi? My life is over!" She flopped forward onto the table and heaved a big breath.

Wendy stared at her. If Junia wasn't Amish, she would have thought the young woman was imitating something she'd seen in the movies or on TV for dramatic effect. But that wasn't the case. She really seemed to think her life was over. Or she was an excellent actress without even realizing it.

Junia sat up and grabbed another tissue. "I'm sorry," she said. "I know my life isn't over. It just feels like it. The one time I'm happy about something, and I ruined it."

Out of habit, Wendy drew on her experience working with unpredictable people and volatile couples . . . then stopped. Junia didn't need a lawyerly response. She needed scripture.

"Where are you going?" Junia asked as Wendy got up from the table.

"To get my Bible." She had recently bought several and started keeping various copies in her room, much like Mom did with tissue boxes. This one was on top of a small shelving unit that housed Mom's Precious Moments figurines. She sat back down and opened it to the table of contents, then found what she was looking for. "'The troubles of my heart have enlarged; bring me out of my distresses!' That's from Psalm 25."

"I'm definitely distressed," Junia said. "But I don't see God bringing me out of it anytime soon." She sighed. "He never has."

"It might seem that way," Wendy said. "Especially when we don't get what we want when we want it and in the time frame of our choosing."

"But I had Malachi."

"Then why did you break up with him?"

"I don't know." She sniffed again.

"There has to be a reason."

Junia turned to her. "Because of Ella. And *Daed*." Tears slipped down her cheeks again.

"They wanted you to end your relationship?"

She shook her head. "They want to control it, like they control everything."

Wendy listened as Junia detailed Barnabas's edict that Ella had to chaperone her and Malachi, and Junia wasn't going to allow that. Then she told Malachi they couldn't meet for a while, but they could continue writing letters and calling. "Malachi was fine with that, although he wasn't happy. I wasn't either. So I started sneaking out to meet him."

"Did you tell him you were going behind your father's back?"

"No. I only thought it would be for a time or two. But then it became more. I knew I was disobeying my father, but I didn't care. Eventually I had to tell Malachi, and he wasn't happy that we were rebelling. He said we had to follow what *Daed* wanted and go on an official date. With Ella. Wendy, she would have to tag along every single time I met with him. I couldn't stand the idea of that."

Part of Wendy wanted to point out how immature Junia's actions were. She also didn't have a complete grasp on why Junia ended her relationship with Malachi. But she had to be patient if she wanted to keep Junia talking. "Is there a reason you don't want her to be your chaperone?"

She sat up straight and tilted her chin. "I don't need one. And even if I did—which I don't—I'd rather be alone than have her always looking over my shoulder. At least I thought that's what I wanted."

So much for conflict mediation being a success. "And that's why you broke up with him? So you wouldn't have to deal with Ella?"

Junia sniffed again. "I know it was dumb. I see that now. But I'm so angry with her and *Daed*. Why don't they trust me?"

Wendy recalled the information she'd gleaned during their last meeting. Junia resented not being consulted about moving to Marigold. Ella called her lazy. Barnabas sat there helplessly. She assumed there had been some passive-aggressive behavior going on with Junia, along with being outright aggressive at some points. While Ella was more open to making some changes, she also obviously harbored a lot of resentment toward her sister and possibly subconsciously harbored some toward her father. *Oh boy. I am out of my depth.*

"I shouldn't have come here," Junia said. "You can't help me."

"That's a big assumption." Wendy faced her. She might not have the professional tools, but she did care about Junia's situation, and the young woman needed to hear some truth. "While I don't know about your family history or your relationship with Malachi, I have seen how you respond to not getting your way. And frankly, it's a big part of the problem."

Junia flinched, but she didn't run out of the room this time.

"You're going to have to make a few decisions," she continued. "Do you want to be with Malachi?"

"More than anything."

Junia was sounding dramatic again, and Wendy had to wonder how many of Junia's feelings were infatuation instead of actual love, but she couldn't make a judgment on that with the present facts. Maybe if she'd had experience with romantic relationships, she could intuit some things. However, that was a can of worms she was going to keep sealed. "Then you need to be honest with him and tell him why you ended the relationship and that you want to reconcile."

"But what if he doesn't want me after I dumped him?" she wailed. "I really hurt his feelings and I feel horrible about that."

"You won't know until you tell him. If the situation were reversed, wouldn't you want to know?"

She pressed her lips together. "Yes."

Junia's answer gave Wendy some hope. "Then you need to offer him the same courtesy. You also need to apologize to your sister and father."

"But—"

"And it should be done during another conflict mediation session."

"It's not going to do any good," Junia said, pouting.

"Did you try any of the exercises I gave you?"

"Um . . . no."

"Then you don't know if it's going to work. This is another choice you have to make. Your family's harmony isn't going to happen if you refuse to participate."

"But what if I do, and it doesn't change anything?"

"Then you still need to be responsible for your own behaviors and choices. And you might have to talk to the bishop about it too. I've learned a lot about your culture since I moved to Marigold. If you and Malachi do get married, you'll be a big part of his family, and he'll be a big part of yours. Do you want him to be surrounded by strife all the time?"

Junia paused, in deep thought. "Maybe I should just move back to Lancaster," she said in a low voice. "It would be easier."

"In some ways, it might, but—"

"I've got to go." Junia popped up from the chair and hurried out of the kitchen.

Wendy sat back in the chair, dread overcoming her. Had she inadvertently made things worse? Barnabas loved his daughters. How would he feel if Junia moved away because of this afternoon's talk? She pressed her fingertips to her forehead. She shouldn't have tried to handle the situation alone. She wasn't a counselor, even though she'd had success at conflict mediation in the past. What she did have in spades was confidence—and pride. And although she genuinely wanted to help Junia, it was also in the back of her mind how grateful Barnabas would be if Wendy had repaired their family relationships. The thought was fleeting, but it had been there.

Her head dropped into her hands. She'd had all the answers for Junia. But she had no idea what to do now.

.ೂಀ.

Later that afternoon, Nelson and Malachi finished cleaning the paint spill and Malachi headed home much more optimistic than he was when he arrived. "You'll tell me what Ella says right away, *ya?*" His expression was full of anticipation.

"*Ya.*"

He grinned. "Okay. *Danki* again. I think I'll get some sleep tonight."

Nelson closed the door and shook his head, recounting the sleepless nights he'd had over Miriam and Norene. He groaned, thinking of all the time he wasted mourning something that wasn't meant to be. While he wasn't impressed with Junia's behavior, he did hope his nephew would get the answer he wanted. If he didn't, hopefully he would handle rejection better than Nelson had.

For the rest of the day, he puttered around the warehouse, restless again. His mind wasn't focused on his task list but on his promise to Malachi. By evening he realized he couldn't wait until tomorrow to talk to Ella. That was only stretching out Malachi's anxiety. He picked up the breadbasket and walked over to the Yoders'.

The store was already closed, so he went to the house and knocked on the door. Right away Ella answered it. Her eyes widened a little as she stood partway behind the door.

"Hi." He gripped the basket handle, unexpectedly tense.

She glanced at the basket. "Is there something wrong with the bread?"

"Was it for me?"

Her stiff expression softened a little. "*Ya.* Unless you don't want it." She started to reach for the basket.

"I definitely want it."

That brought a small smile to her face, although it disappeared quickly. "Is that all you needed?"

He shifted on his feet. "Not totally. Can we, um, talk?"

"Are you still mad at me?" She tugged on her *kapp* string.

Her voice was small again. "*Nee*," he said, telling her the truth. "I'm not mad anymore."

"You should be." She sighed and opened the door wider. "Come on in."

Nelson followed her to the couch. She plopped down on it and leaned forward, her chin resting on her hands as she stared at the fire crackling in the woodstove.

It was nice and warm here, and much cozier than the warehouse. He glanced around the room. No Barnabas or Junia. "Are you alone?"

Ella nodded, not looking at him. "Junia ran away again. *Daed*'s out searching for her . . . again."

Not for the first time, he was questioning Malachi's taste in women. "Why aren't you?"

"I don't care where she is."

Nelson flinched. There was a lot of pain in those six words, although he wondered if Ella was aware. "I don't believe that."

"Believe it."

He went and sat next to her, making sure to place the basket between them. After Malachi left and he was alone with his thoughts, he wasn't just distracted by his nephew's problems or the massive undertaking the warehouse was turning out to be. He remembered how much he enjoyed touching her waist when she had lost her balance, her closeness while she was cutting his hair. And as she stared at the woodstove, it seemed she didn't care whether he was here or not, making him aware that once again he was experiencing unrequited attraction for a woman.

But he wasn't here to focus on his propensity to be attracted to women who weren't interested in him. He was here to help Malachi. "Ella . . ."

She finally turned to him and tilted her head, looking at his hair. "It's not so bad, is it?"

The hope in her tone made him shake his head. "*Nee*. I do look like I'm in the middle of rumspringa, though."

Ella winced. "I'm sorry."

He raised his hand. "You've already apologized, and I'm already over it. Let's move on."

"Okay." She reached to touch her *kapp* string, only to place her hand back in her lap. "Did you cut *yer* hair short back then?"

"During rumspringa? *Nee*. Some of *mei* friends did." He couldn't help but run his hand over the back of his head and down his neck. It felt so weird not having hair back there. He was also concerned he'd get in trouble with the bishop, but according to Jesse's boss, Micah, he was a reasonable man. He'd have to talk to him soon and explain what happened.

"At least all the paint is gone." She angled her body so she faced him, right knee bent and resting on the couch cushions. "I think you look . . . nice. Handsome, even."

"*Yer* just trying to make me feel better." His cheeks heated at the compliment anyway.

She didn't deny his words—only glanced at her lap again.

She doesn't think I'm handsome? He caught himself. It didn't matter what she thought about his looks, or his disappointed reaction. And he needed to get down to business. "Malachi came over today. Did you know Junia broke up with him?"

Her head snapped up. "She did? Why?"

"Malachi wants to know the same thing."

"So that's why *yer* here?"

Nelson nodded. "He's honoring Junia's request not to ask you or your *daed* himself."

She glanced at the fire again. "It's probably a *gut* thing."

"My nephew doesn't seem to think so."

"She's been sneaking out to meet him. Disobeying *Daed*. She said so right before she took off." Ella pressed her lips together.

"I know. She admitted it to Malachi before she ended things."

She did a double take, then stared straight ahead. "*Daed* was furious. Angrier than I've ever seen him. He even yelled at her, and that's when she left. I'm sure she blames me because *Daed* wanted me to chaperone them. And maybe she's right."

He frowned. "Unless you made her break up with Malachi, I don't see how you're to blame for her decision."

"I'm the one who pushed my *daed* and Junia to move here and buy the store. Neither of them wanted to. Well, maybe *Daed*. A little. But I can be persuasive when I want to. She's been upset and unhappy ever since we left Lancaster, until she met Malachi."

"Then breaking up with him makes even less sense."

She sat back against the couch, her chin quivering. "Our business is thriving, but our family is collapsing. Junia and I have been fighting for years, but *nix* like what's happening now. I'd hoped moving here would have given us all a fresh start, away from my overbearing aunts . . . the grief that never seems to completely *geh* away . . ."

He didn't have to ask what they were grieving about. This was the first time she'd mentioned anything about her mother to him, and he watched the sadness appear in her eyes. "I'm sorry, Ella."

"Me too."

Sorry was the only thing he could say. But there was something he could do. He put the basket on the floor, scooted closer to her, and pulled her into his arms.

Twenty-Two

Ella closed her eyes and leaned her cheek against Nelson's broad chest, soothed by the steady beat of his heart. Later she would chastise herself for revealing so many personal things to him, including telling him she thought he was handsome. That had slipped out, and fortunately he didn't react to it. Now all she wanted was to savor the comfort and peace she felt in his arms.

She'd been truthful about his haircut—he was handsomer with Amish hair, but he also made the short style look good. As she snuggled against him, she felt his hand rubbing her upper back in a rhythmic, circular motion. This testy man who had been through the wringer today was somehow managing to give her comfort. Amazing.

The fire crackled in the stove. After a few minutes, he said, "Are you okay?"

She was now, although once she pulled away from his wonderful bear hug, she wouldn't be. She wanted to stay here cocooned in his embrace where all her problems seemed distant. But she couldn't take advantage of his kindness. She moved out of his arms and back onto her previous spot on the couch. "*Ya*," she said, even though she was anything but all right. "I'm okay."

"If Junia is blaming you for her problems with Malachi, she's wrong."

"But—"

"Love can make you do dumb things." He glanced down at the basket near his feet. "Even *ab im kopp* ones."

Ella averted her gaze. "I wouldn't know about that."

"I do."

She wasn't surprised he'd been in love before, especially since she was seeing a different side of him—encouraging, gracious, sympathetic. And cuddly. She couldn't—and wouldn't—forget that. While she'd never seen him with a woman, and he didn't mention he'd had a girl-friend, that didn't mean there wasn't someone in his life.

"Are you . . ." She swallowed, almost afraid to know the answer, even though it shouldn't matter to her. "Still in love?"

"Absolutely not."

The firm way he said that made her take notice. "I've never been in love before," she said.

"Consider yourself lucky." But his reply didn't have the same conviction.

Then she admitted what she'd never dared to say out loud. "I want to get married and have a family. I'm not holding out much hope, though. *Mei aentis* don't believe I'm marriage material—"

"They're wrong about that." His tone was emphatic.

She blinked. "They are?"

The door opened and *Daed* walked inside, distraught. "I can't find her, and the temperature is dropping fast. I don't know what to do." He looked at both Ella and Nelson. If he was surprised at Nelson's presence, he didn't show it. "I shouldn't have yelled at her . . . I shouldn't have gotten so angry . . ."

Ella went to him. "Should we tell the bishop?"

Daed nodded. "We can't avoid it any longer."

Nelson got to his feet. "I'll let Jesse and Micah know. Then I'll head on to Birch Creek."

"You think she might be on her way there?" he asked, his tone hopeful.

"I don't know. It's worth a try, though."

Her father looked at him, so distressed he wasn't even reacting to Nelson's short hair. "*Danki*."

He nodded, and with one last glance at Ella, he left.

She motioned for her father to sit down. "I'll fix you some *kaffee*."

He shook his head, still wearing his coat. "I'm going back out to look for her," he said, moving toward the fire. "I just came over to warm up a bit. Was she wearing her coat?" His voice trembled. "Please, Lord, let her be wearing her coat."

Ella knew she wasn't, unless she had stashed another jacket somewhere. Maybe in Junia and Malachi's hiding place. When she stormed out of the house, she was only wearing a sweater. Although the weather had been mild during the day, once the sun went down it turned frigid again. "They'll find her, *Daed*. She couldn't have gone far. I'll *geh* talk to the bishop—"

"*Nee!*" He turned to her. "I'm making the decisions from now on. Understand?"

She nodded, his outburst jarring but excusable. Still, a lump formed in her throat. He almost never spoke that sharply.

A knock sounded at the door and *Daed* hurried to answer it. Junia wouldn't have knocked at her own house. Dread filled her. This had to be bad news.

When he opened the door, Wendy appeared, bundled in a thick coat and wearing a skirt and stockings. The woman had been a fixture at the store and Ella hadn't known what to make of that. Was she spying on them, to see if they'd taken her advice? Or was she simply a forgetful shopper who should really make a list so she wouldn't have to make so many trips to the store?

"Barnabas." She hurried inside and turned around. "Have you talked to Junia tonight?"

"*Nee*. We haven't seen her since this afternoon."

"She stopped by my house almost two hours ago," she said, worrying her bottom lip.

"Was she okay?"

"No. She was upset. I hoped she'd returned home."

He scrubbed his hand over his face. "Where is she?"

Up until that moment, Ella had refused to give in to worry. She'd overreacted so many times to Junia's antics—she told herself she wouldn't borrow any more trouble. But she couldn't ignore her anxiety anymore. What if something serious had happened to her? What if she—

Ella closed her eyes and silently prayed. Even though she was angry with and resentful of her sister almost all the time now, she didn't know what she'd do without her. *Please, Lord . . . keep her safe.*

.⋐❧.

When Ella left to make coffee, Wendy and Barnabas sat down on the couch. The alarm in his eyes made her heart pinch. "I should have told you earlier that she came to talk to me." Her stomach contorted into knots. "But I wanted to protect her privacy."

"Why did you change your mind?" he asked.

"I'm not sure." She ran her cold palms over her skirt. "I prayed for a long while after she left. For her and you and Ella."

"Thank you."

241

"And then I had this urge to check on all three of you. I'm sorry if I'm intruding too much."

"It's okay." His calm tone was edged with impatience. "What did Junia say?"

She told him about their conversation. Under any other circumstance she wouldn't have revealed what Junia had said. But an inner voice compelled her to be totally honest, and she would deal with the repercussions of divulging the information later.

By the time she finished, he was leaning on his knees, his head hanging. When she started to apologize again, he stopped her. "You did the right thing." He looked at her. "She's an adult, and you respected her privacy."

"There was another reason I decided to come over. I thought—" She paused. She didn't need to tell him this part, but she couldn't keep it to herself. "I thought about what I would want if she were my daughter. And I'd want to know that she was in distress. I'm worried about her, Barnabas. I know she's not my child, or even a friend. But—"

"You're a compassionate woman." He straightened. "You care about people. That's plain as day."

I care about you. The thought came at her fast, and now that it was in her mind, she knew it was true. She cared about Barnabas and his daughters. Oh, what a mess this was. She had no business being involved with the Yoders, and it looked like the conflict mediation was a bust, not to mention her disastrous conversation with Junia. If he wasn't angry at her now, she was sure he would be later.

"I wish I had more to tell you." She started to stand.

"Stay." He put his hand on her arm. "Please. I want you to stay."

She couldn't refuse him, even if she wanted to. She nodded. "What can I do to help?"

He faced her. "I have to tell Bishop Fry that Junia's missing, but I want to try to look for her again. While I'm gone, can you keep Ella company?"

Wendy nodded, ignoring her disappointment that he only wanted her here to help Ella, then irritated with herself that she was feeling that way. "Of course."

"She's not showing it much, but she's upset." His gaze was intense. "It would mean a lot to know that she's not waiting here alone . . ."

They both knew what he was thinking. *In case something bad happened to Junia.*

Ella walked out of the kitchen carrying a small tray with three mugs on it. She placed it on the table. "I'll get the sugar and cream."

"None for me." Barnabas stood up. "I'm continuing the search."

After a pause, Ella said, "Okay. Do you want me to go with you?"

"Stay here. I've asked Wendy to wait with you. Maybe she'll show up while I'm gone—"

The front door opened, and they all turned around. Junia walked in wearing Malachi's coat. He was right beside her.

Wendy's hand went to her chest. *Thank you, God.* Junia was home.

.⁓᪥⁓.

Silence.

Ella shifted on the chair she'd brought from the kitchen. Junia and Malachi were seated on the couch, *Daed* in his chair with Wendy sitting beside him, at her father's request. It did make sense considering Junia had already confided in her, and they might—or more likely, probably would—need her conflict mediation skills. The surprise was how adamant her father was about it. He was also staring at Junia and

Malachi with a resolve she hadn't seen before. He really was making the decisions now.

The tension was oppressive. Junia kept staring at her feet and Malachi's expression was impassive. Wendy kept glancing at *Daed* as if silently deferring to him. They all seemed to be waiting for his signal to talk.

It dawned on Ella that maybe she shouldn't be here. Junia was the one who had to explain herself, and apparently she and Malachi were at least on speaking terms. *Daed* clearly wanted Wendy by his side, and Ella briefly wondered if there was something going on between them that she didn't know about. Which made her the fifth wheel in this dynamic, and she was more than eager to scoot out of here. She stood. "I'll be upstairs—"

Daed pointed to the chair. "Sit, Ella."

She quickly complied. He was speaking English, no doubt out of deference to Wendy.

He turned to Junia. "Where have you been?"

Her chin lifted in her usual defensive stance. But even Ella could tell her heart wasn't in it. "I was just out for a little while."

A muscle jerked in *Daed*'s jaw. "All day is not a little while."

"But—"

"Junia."

Everyone looked at Malachi. His stern tone and expression brooked no argument as he frowned at her. "You need to apologize."

Good luck. But to Ella's amazement, Junia nodded. "I'm sorry, *Daed*. I didn't mean to worry you." She turned to Wendy. "After we talked, I went to the barn."

"What barn?" *Daed* asked.

"The old one in the middle of that field about half a mile from here."

"*My* barn?" Ella clamped her mouth shut. She couldn't even have a ramshackle building to herself.

"Your name wasn't on it," Junia snapped. After Malachi's quick nudge she said, "Sorry, Ella. I shouldn't have said that. But it's where me and Malachi always meet. I kept thinking about what you said, Wendy. That I had a lot of decisions to make." She took Malachi's hand. "I decided to tell the truth. I called Malachi and he picked me up. Then we went back to Birch Creek and talked."

"I'm sorry if we worried you," Malachi said. "I didn't realize until later that she hadn't told you where she was. As soon as I found out, we came straight here."

"I shouldn't have left without telling you, *Daed*. I'm sorry about that too."

"You worried us all," he said, still sounding aggravated. "Including Wendy."

Wendy glanced down. "It's okay, Barnabas."

"*Nee*, it's not. Junia, you can't keep carrying on like this."

"I know." Tears pooled in her eyes, and for once Ella believed they were genuine. "I really am sorry. I never should have disobeyed or worried you. I was so angry, I couldn't think straight. And I was hurt that you didn't trust me." She brushed away the tear running down her cheek. "I see now that I don't deserve your trust. I've been difficult to live with, and I'm making everyone's lives miserable." She turned to Ella. "Especially yours."

Shocked didn't begin to describe how Ella felt hearing her sister's words. Not only was Junia apologizing sincerely, but she was also acknowledging that her bad behavior was on purpose.

Junia turned to Malachi. "I'm so sorry for hurting you."

"You already said that." He patted her hand. "And I forgave you."

She smiled at him, hearts in her eyes. Then she looked at everyone else. "I promise I'll be better. I'll work hard and I won't grumble about it. I want to prove I can be a good daughter, sister"—she leaned closer to Malachi—"and wife."

He tightened his grip on her hand. "Tell them what we discussed."

She looked at *Daed* again. "We decided that you're right. We need a chaperone. We also need to slow things down."

Daed and Ella exchanged stunned looks.

"We promise not to meet alone," Malachi said. "That's what we told my mom and dad. They thought that was an excellent idea."

Daed tapped his fingers against the chair arm. Then he looked at Ella. "Are you still willing to chaperone them?"

While she wasn't ready to trust that her sister's attitude wouldn't turn on a dime, she had truly apologized, something she hadn't done in a long time. The next few weeks and months would be the true test, and she would meet her halfway. "Yes, but on one condition."

Junia's and Malachi's eyebrows both shot up. *Daed* and Wendy looked just as surprised.

Ella turned to Junia, her throat full of sudden emotion. "That you'll accept my apology. I haven't behaved much better. You're right when you said I was pushy and bossy. I'm trying to change that. I can't promise I won't fall into old habits, but I want to be better too."

Junia smiled. "If you hadn't been bossy and pushy, we wouldn't have moved to Marigold. I never would have met Malachi."

"And we do have a successful store. I'm thankful for that," Barnabas added.

But Ella didn't miss how he and Wendy looked at each other. Yes, there was something going on there.

He turned to the couple. "I'm glad you were able to work this out."

"Me too," Wendy said, looking pleased.

"Thank you for helping me," Junia said. "I'm so glad I came to talk to you."

"Malachi, Junia," *Daed* said, his expression serious. "You're making the right decision to take your relationship slow. I know how easy it is to get caught up in the first blush of love. But it's important to take time to get to know each other and make sure you want to spend the rest of your lives together. Better to find that out now than when it's too late."

They both nodded. Malachi released Junia's hand. "I've got to get home."

"Can I walk him to his buggy, *Daed*?"

Daed hesitated, then nodded. "Just don't stay out too long."

"I won't." She jumped up from the couch and left with Malachi.

"I need to be heading home too." Wendy stood, *Daed* joining her.

"And I'll clean up." Ella hurried and picked up the tray, feeling more like a fifth wheel than ever. She dumped out the cold coffee and washed the cups, and she had just finished cleaning out the percolator for tomorrow's brew when her father walked into the kitchen.

"What do you think, Ella?" He stood beside her at the sink.

She stilled. Was he asking her opinion about Junia and Malachi . . . or him and Wendy?

"I guess the proof will be in the pudding." *Daed* leaned against the counter. "One thing I know for sure."

"What's that?" She put the lid on the percolator and set it on the stove.

"Malachi will keep her in line. But he does have his work cut out for him."

Ella smiled. "That he does." She put her arms around him. "I love you, *Daed*."

He returned her hug. "I love you too." Then he stepped back. "I'm sorry I haven't been the father you needed all these years. You and Junia aren't the only ones who need to change. I'll be working on things too."

With Wendy? She almost asked the question out loud. She liked her, and her being here tonight seemed natural, even though she was English and they didn't know much about her. But if her *daed* had feelings for her, that would be a huge problem. He wouldn't leave the church for anything. If Wendy was planning to join, that would be great. But Ella hoped it wouldn't be because she was falling for her father. Joining the Amish wasn't an easy thing to do, and it shouldn't be. Their life and faith were different from the world. It was a lot more than giving up air-conditioning and cars.

She pushed away the thoughts before they muddled her mind too much.

⚬❧⚬

Later that night when Ella had finished her nightly prayers and was tucked into bed, she heard a tap on the door.

"Ella?" Junia said. "Can I come in?"

"Sure."

The room was dark, and she heard rather than saw Junia enter. "Do you remember what we used to do after *Mamm* died?"

Ella pulled back the covers. "Come on in."

Junia scrambled into bed next to her. For a moment neither of them spoke. Finally, she said, "You do believe I'm sorry, don't you?"

"I want to," Ella answered honestly. "But if you really are, then things will have to be different around here. *Daed* and I need help around the house and the store. That means regular hours and none of this running off you've been doing—" She paused, already falling into her worst habit. "I'm being bossy again, aren't I?"

"*Ya*, but I need it right now. And you've got to *let* me do the work. I might not get it done the way you would do it, but it will be done."

"Deal."

"Also," Junia continued, "we both need to mind our tempers."

"I know." Ella frowned. "*Aenti* Cora and *Aenti* Tabitha always bugged me about mine. I should have listened."

"Me too."

"Huh?"

"Oh, they used to get after me all the time for being too hot-tempered."

Ella nearly sat up in bed. "I didn't know that."

"Well, you were busy all the time." Junia chuckled.

"True. Did they ever tell you that you wouldn't get married?"

"Um. *Nee*."

"Oh." *Guess I was the lucky one.*

"While I was at the barn, I thought about going back to Lancaster," Junia said. "I thought it would have been easier than facing what I'd done. How I behaved. But I changed *mei* mind."

"Why?"

"I'd miss you and *Daed* too much. And Malachi, of course. He was really mad at me, Ella. He's always so calm and in a *gut* mood when we're together. I had *nee* idea he could get so angry."

"He's not anymore."

"*Nee*." She giggled. "He sure isn't."

Jealousy tugged on Ella's heart, and she suddenly thought about Nelson again. Or more accurately, thought about being in his arms, and then remembered how nice his hands had felt when they were resting on her waist. Butterflies appeared in her stomach, replacing the jealousy as she recalled everything he'd done for her. Paid for her lunch at Pancho's. Made sure she had a ride home when her anger had gotten in the way of her common sense. Offered her a warm place to cool her temper. Lent her a listening ear. Forgave her for messing up his hair. And gave her his strong shoulder to lean on. *Sigh.*

But there was no use in relishing those times with Nelson Bontrager. He wasn't attracted to her, and he seemed sour on love anyway. Even if he weren't, she was the last person he'd be attracted to. He'd made it clear he didn't like bossy women or want her help with his butcher shop. There was absolutely nothing between them and never would be. A few more minutes passed and her eyes drifted shut.

"Ella?"

Her eyes flew open. "*Ya?*"

"Do you think there's anything going on with *Daed* and Wendy?"

Funny you should mention that. "I don't know. Why did you *geh* talk to her?"

"I couldn't think of anyone else who would understand. I don't mean that as a dig, Ella. It's just . . . She's really nice. And honest. She said some things I didn't want to hear, but I needed to. I think she cares about us, which is strange since we don't really know her that well."

"I think she does too."

"I saw them looking at each other, when they didn't think anyone was looking at them."

"Tonight?" Ella's brow shot up. She had barely noticed, and she wasn't as distressed as Junia. Then again, she wasn't as romantically tuned in either.

"*Nee.* At the store. She kept coming by last week. But maybe I'm just imagining things. Even if they liked each other, there's *nix* they can do about it."

Ella nodded, even though her sister couldn't see the movement. She didn't want her father to get hurt. Her eyes closed again.

"Ella?"

She didn't bother opening them, suddenly remembering her sister's habit of keeping the conversation going until they both nodded off. *"Ya?"*

"Do you ever think about *Mamm*?"

"Ya," she whispered. "All the time."

"I do too. I miss her, Ella. I wish she were here. I'd ask her so many questions about love and relationships."

She felt Junia's hand clasp hers. "Me too, Junia." *Me too.*

Twenty-Three

The next morning, Nelson woke up in a much warmer bedroom. After going to Birch Creek to look for Junia, he'd stopped at Phoebe and Jalon's to tell Malachi she was missing. Turned out she and Malachi were on their way back to Marigold. *"He stopped here so we could meet her."* Phoebe smiled. *"And tell us that they were going to be chaperoned at all times, and they planned to slow things down."*

That was good news, and Phoebe and Jalon were relieved. They also liked Junia. That wasn't surprising. She did make a good first impression. It was the following impressions that were the problem.

It was too late to go back to the warehouse, so he spent the night with Phoebe and Jalon. They'd asked about his haircut, and he explained what happened with Ella. Malachi eventually returned and repeated what Phoebe told him—indeed they were going to obey their parents and not be in such a hurry with their relationship.

The next morning, Nelson helped with the chores and stayed for breakfast. Malachi's younger sister, Hannah, had spent the night with a friend, and right after the meal, Malachi and Jalon left to work on the fence. Nelson cleared the table as Phoebe washed the dishes.

But he was distracted, as he had been since last night when he left the Yoders'. Holding Ella had been impulsive, and he'd told himself he was just comforting her. But that wasn't how he felt with her in his arms. She fit perfectly there, and he'd felt so calm and comfortable, he closed his eyes while she rested her head against his chest. And was very disappointed when she pulled away. He was so confused. He didn't want to feel this way again. Attracted. Connected. Especially not with Ella Yoder. *I don't like her, remember?*

Why couldn't he get his heart on the same page?

"You're quiet." Phoebe handed him a dry dish towel and a freshly washed frying pan.

He shrugged and started drying. "Got a lot on *mei* mind. Building the *haus*, renovating the warehouse, getting *mei* business started." His chest tightened. At the rate he was going, he wouldn't be able to open until April. Or May. His meager savings would dwindle to close to nothing by then.

"Jalon feels bad he can't help you right now, but he and Adam have been wanting to get this new fence put in for a long time." She handed him the pot she'd made oatmeal in. "Once they're done, they'll be free."

Nelson nodded. "He told me." Although Adam was in a wheelchair, he had tremendous upper-body strength and dexterity. He would be a huge help. So would Jalon and Malachi. At this point, anyone would be.

"How are the plans for the shop going?" Phoebe asked.

"What plans?" Nelson muttered, reaching for a wet plate.

Phoebe gaped at him. "You don't have a plan?"

"I do." He grimaced, not liking how defensive he sounded. "I just haven't put it down on paper. Yet."

"Have you talked about it with anyone?"

He paused. He hadn't—not even Barnabas. While they were

chopping down trees, both men were focused on their work, as they should be. During their breaks, Barnabas would talk about the store and about how Ella had done all the groundwork. *"I'd never owned a business before,"* he'd said. *"She taught me a lot of things she learned from studying those books. But I think most of it is natural business sense. She knows what she's doing."*

Due to his reluctance to accept Ella's help, he'd barely listened to what Barnabas said. But he was recalling it now. *"Nee,"* he finally answered.

"Maybe you should. At least you could get some feedback that you're on the right track. I'd offer to listen, but I don't know anything about running a shop." She gestured to the pile. "You're slacking, little *bruder.*"

He smirked at her but picked up the pace, chewing over her words as she finished cleaning up the rest of the kitchen. He had to admit she might be right. Discussing his ideas with a knowledgeable person would be wise, and the most knowledgeable person he knew was . . . Ella.

As he drove home, he realized he'd been foolish all along. He needed guidance, and she was the best person to give it. He would have to set his personal struggles aside and ask her for help—help she'd been offering since they first met.

He was turning into the Yoders' driveway and heading for their barn to put up his horse when the true realization hit—he was being prideful. He'd never asked a woman for help before, and he'd been burned so badly by Miriam and Norene, he didn't trust them. Or his own judgment. It was past time he set all that aside for good and became a serious businessman.

Once the horse was settled in his stall, Nelson went to the store, knowing Ella would be there. But when he walked inside, Junia was at the counter checking out a customer. Instead of her usual put-upon expression, she was genuinely smiling and engaging with the English woman as she bagged her groceries.

"Thank you, Mrs. Carter," she said. "We hope to see you again."

"You sure will." A broad smile appeared on the woman's equally broad face. "Your prices are the best around. So is the customer service."

Junia beamed as Mrs. Carter left. Then she noticed Nelson. "Hi," she said, sounding almost tentative now. "I'm sorry about yesterday. I promise I'm turning over a new leaf."

Nelson nodded. Malachi had insisted she was, and he hoped it was true, for his sake and her family's. "Is Ella here?"

Surprise flashed across her face. "*Nee*. She's at the *haus*. I told her to rest today and I would man the store with *Daed*."

Maybe Junia was serious about making changes. "Okay, I'll head over there." He started to walk away.

"Uh, Nelson?" When he looked at her, she said, "Malachi and I want to see each other this Saturday." A customer walked in and she moved from behind the counter. "Want to join us?"

He blinked. She was actually asking him to chaperone. "What about Ella?"

"Oh, she and my dad will be there. Hi, Mr. Miller," she said to the customer. "How can I help you today?"

Nelson frowned. Seeing Junia genuinely friendly was weird. Good, but weird. He'd tell her later that he would chaperone them, intent on keeping his word. He wasn't sure why he needed to come since both Ella and her father would be there. How many chaperones did one couple need?

He crossed the street and knocked on Ella's front door. After a moment she answered, the same surprise in her eyes he'd seen yesterday when he arrived. Then she smiled. "I'm glad to see you," she said, tugging on his arm. "Come in. I need to talk to you about something."

He entered the warm, cozy living room. A fire blazed in the stove, filling the house with the scent of burning wood. As she shut the door, he said, "That's *gut*. I need to talk to you too."

"All right, but me first." She paused. "Sorry. I'm being—"

"Bossy?"

"*Ya.*"

He chuckled. "That you are." But for some reason, he didn't mind.

Her brow furrowed, then relaxed. "May I please *geh* first?"

Just like Junia's eager friendliness was odd, so was Ella's deference. Odd, but nice. "Sure."

"I owe you a shirt." She pulled a measuring tape from her apron pocket and put it around her neck. "I was just about to *geh* to the warehouse and talk to you about it. I'll just need your measurements."

"You don't owe me anything, Ella."

"But I knocked over the paint—"

"That I was careless with." He shook his head. "I've got plenty of shirts."

"Oh."

He was surprised to see how disappointed she was.

"Well, that's that, then." She slipped the measuring tape off and stuffed it into the pocket of her apron. "Your turn. What did you want to talk to me about?"

·◦≈◦·

Ella placed a stack of books in the middle of the kitchen table next to another tall pile. "That's the last of them."

Nelson's eyes grew round. "I have to read all of these?"

She smiled and sat down next to him. He could have knocked her over with a dandelion when he asked her to help him with his business plan. She was tempted to ask him what made him change his mind, but she didn't want to distract him or have him change it back, so she tugged on his arm again—she had to stop doing that—and sat him down in a chair. Although, come to think of it, he hadn't protested. Or resisted. Or called her bossy. In fact, he'd smiled a little and let her lead.

But none of that was important now. What mattered was developing his business plan, because after quizzing him on what it was, she realized he didn't have one. "*Nee*. Not all of them. But I wanted you to have some choices, instead of me picking out the books I think you need."

"Ah. Okay." He frowned, rubbing his chin.

He was being uncharacteristically uncertain, and she wasn't sure why. Was he already doubting his decision to ask for her help? "Nelson, I promise I won't boss you or try to take over. This is your business. I will respect that."

He turned to her. "I know."

His low, confident tone sent a shiver down her spine. *Oh* nee. Not now. She couldn't be distracted by his tone or looks or the fact that she couldn't stop thinking about his arms around her, even while she was being businesslike. *Get a grip.* She gestured to the books. "Where do you want to start?"

"Um . . ." His confidence seemed to fly away. "I'm not sure. I think I even need help with that."

She tapped her fingers on the spines of the books in front of her, finding the one she needed. "Now, don't be offended by the title." She handed him a yellow-and-black book.

"*Business for Dummies?*" He quirked a brow.

"I'm not saying *yer* a dummy," she blurted. "It's a *gut* book."

He stared at the title. Thumbed through the pages. "This is exactly what I need."

She leaned against the back of the chair. "That's the first one I read when I decided to pursue buying the store." She frowned. "I didn't even confer with *Daed* about it until three months later. I should have talked to him about it up front. But I was worried he would have said *nee*. He never decides anything without thinking long and hard about it. When I presented *mei* case, he didn't have a choice but to agree. In hindsight that wasn't the right thing to do."

"Maybe not, but it turned out well in the end." He set down the book. "I spent the night at my *schwester's* last night. Malachi and Junia had talked to them. Seems like everything is okay."

She nodded. Junia had fallen asleep in her bed, and Ella fell asleep shortly afterward. Sometime during the night her sister got up, since the single bed wasn't made for two. In the morning she helped with breakfast, and Ella was stunned when she offered to work today and give her a day off.

"I think she has changed," Ella said. "At least I hope so."

Nelson nodded. "She even asked me something strange. She wants me to help you chaperone them on Saturday."

"I know. She mentioned it this morning." But she hadn't said anything about asking Nelson. "You don't have to," she said. "*Daed* will be here too."

"I made a promise. To Malachi." He met her gaze. "And you."

Now the butterflies were back. Oh, this was a problem. She shot up from the seat. "Want some *kaffee*? Tea?" *Me?* She tripped over the chair leg at that last thought. What in the world was her mind doing to her?

He reached out and steadied her, pulling away his hand as soon as she regained her balance. "I'm fine. Had a lot of *kaffee* at Phoebe's."

"Okay." But she needed a drink, mostly as a distraction. She grabbed a glass, filled it with water, gulped it down . . . and promptly burped. Loudly. Her cheeks flamed and she couldn't move. Of all the embarrassing things to do.

After a few seconds she looked over her shoulder. He was perusing the dummy book. Maybe he hadn't heard her . . . but he'd have to be deaf not to. There was nothing else she could do but acknowledge it. "Excuse me," she said, sliding onto the seat. When she finally looked at him, he was smiling. Then he winked and went back to reading the book.

She was tempted to melt into her seat. More shivers and butter-flies appeared, along with a soft warmth throughout her body. She picked another book, *Business Plans 101*, and handed it to him. "When you're finished with the first one"—she couldn't bring herself to call it the dummy book out loud—"I recommend starting on this next. You can also *geh* through all of them while *yer* here and choose the ones you want."

He took it from her. "This one's fine too. I'll read them this week. Anything else I should do?"

"Once *yer* finished reading them both, you can follow the busi-ness plan guidelines and write *yers* down."

He nodded. After a brief pause, he said, "Would you, uh, mind looking it over when I'm done?"

She smiled. "Of course not. And whenever you want to read any of these," she said, gesturing to the two piles, "just let me know."

"I will." He got up. "*Danki*, Ella. I'm feeling better about this already."

That made her grin. She still wasn't pleased that he'd turned down her offer to make him a shirt, but this was even better. "I'm here anytime you need me."

He was looking at her again, an inexplicable expression crossing his features. Then he scooped up the books. "Got a lot of reading to do," he mumbled as he started to leave the kitchen.

She wanted to tell him to stay, that they could read the books together, even though that was normally an individual activity. He didn't need her to read to him, and no doubt he would think she'd lost her mind at the suggestion. And she must have, because more than anything she didn't want him to leave. But there was no other reason for him to stay.

When he reached the doorway, he turned to her. "See you Saturday."

And once he was out of her sight, she collapsed onto the table, her head resting on her folded arms. Even though he was only coming for Malachi and Junia's sakes, she couldn't stop the thought wafting through her head. *I can't wait.*

·✦·

"I'm stunned."

Wendy looked at her mother as she sat down at the two-seater table in front of the picture window at Pancho's. "About what?"

"This is our second Taco Tuesday in two months." She grinned and unwrapped the brown cloth napkin holding her silverware and put it on her lap. "That never happens. I'm not only stunned, I'm positively giddy." She smiled. "Thank you."

Wendy nodded, returning her smile but also mentally rebuking herself for not treating her mother more often. She'd been so obsessed with doing everything perfect when it came to taking care of her, especially following a strict diet. But seeing how happy Mom was to get out and eat tacos—something so simple—she recognized she should have been doing it all along.

"I really enjoyed meeting Eunice," Mom said as a busboy set a basket of chips and salsa in front of them. She reached for a chip. "I can see why you two are friends."

Before lunch, Wendy had taken Mom to Eunice's shop, and the women chatted as Wendy looked for fabric to make another dress, even though she wasn't finished with the first one. As she usually did when she went to the fabric shop, she stopped at the display of white *kapps*. It seemed odd to wear an Amish dress without the *kapp*, even though she was only wearing it on the Sundays she went to church with Eunice. Wearing a *kapp* might be considered offensive since she wasn't Amish, but she was drawn to them nevertheless, and reluctantly moved on from the display.

She stared blankly at the menu in front of her. Mom's order was a no-brainer, but Wendy wasn't all that hungry. Even during her shopping, she was thinking about last night's events. Before she went to bed, she said a prayer of thanksgiving that Junia had returned home and to her senses, along with an extra thank-you that she hadn't made the situation worse, as she'd feared.

"All right, young lady." Mom lightly snapped the plastic-coated menu shut. "Something's bothering you."

The words and pictures of Mexican dishes came into focus. She quickly decided on a single taco with guacamole salad on the side and closed her menu. "Nothing's bothering—" She nipped the lie in the bud. Her mother knew her better than anyone, and she was right. Despite last night's happy ending, something was on her mind. "I'm not bothered, per se. But I've been thinking about a few things today."

"Such as?" Mom refolded her brown napkin in her lap.

261

Where to begin? Her thoughts about Barnabas and her fascination with the Amish faith were blending together and confusing her. Her mother was looking at her expectantly, so she decided to bring up the safer subject. "Did you and *Daed* ever think about joining the Amish?"

"Heavens, no. We liked our conveniences too much. We also enjoyed our church. I still do." She took a sip of water. "I admire the Amish commitment to simplicity and their faith, and how they band together as a community. Your father did as well. But we never had a single thought of joining them. I think you know more about the Amish than I do . . . Oh."

Wendy could see that her mother understood. "Yeah. *Oh*."

The waitress appeared and they put in their order. On a lark, Wendy added sopapillas for dessert.

"Sopapillas?" Mom raised a brow after the waitress left. "There really is something going on with you, isn't there?" She leaned forward. "Do you want to become Amish?"

"I . . . I don't know."

Mom sat back. "Is this because of Barnabas?"

She stilled. She hadn't talked about Barnabas with her mother, and the only time Mom had seen him other than at the store was when he came over that day and asked for her help. "Why do you ask?"

"You went over there last night."

She could kick herself for telling her mom where she was going when she left the house. But she didn't want to keep anything from her either. "I had to take care of some . . . business."

Mom tapped her chin, not saying anything for a long moment. Wendy picked up a chip and broke it into pieces but didn't eat a nibble. Finally, Mom said, "All right. I won't ask about him anymore. Let's get back to joining the Amish."

Wendy let out a silent breath of relief. She had to admit to herself that if she were Amish, it would be easier to explore whether there was anything between her and Barnabas. But the possibility of romance was probably the worst reason to join a church, especially one so entwined with daily life as the Amish church was. "I guess I have been thinking about it. A little."

Mom's eyes lit up as a platter of four tacos was placed in front of her. They paused to pray, then she continued talking. "Wendy, I want to be clear about one important thing. I don't want to influence you one way or another, whatever you decide for your future. I don't expect you to live with me forever or forsake living the life you want because you feel obligated to me. I can get another caregiver."

"Mom," she said, touching her hand. "I don't feel obligated. I'm honored to take care of you."

"Oh, honey." Her bottom lip trembled. "I'm touched to hear you say that. And I've told you many times how much I love having you with me. I just want you to know that I'll be okay, whatever you decide." She smiled. "God's got my back. He always has."

She nodded. Wendy could see how the Lord had her back too, and how he had brought her to Marigold, even though she had been so sure she'd spend the rest of her life living in New York as a lawyer. They started eating, and she regained her appetite.

After demolishing her third taco, Mom said, "Can I ask you a question?"

"Of course." She scooped up the last bite of guacamole salad.

"What is drawing you to the Amish faith?"

She set down her fork. "I'm still working all that out. But what I can say is that lately I've been closer to God than I've ever been, and when I'm in an Amish service, that closeness grows. I do like the simpler life too, and the dress feels comfortable. I don't miss the busyness of worldly living. Eunice's church, and her sister's, have been so welcoming. Most of all, I'm at peace." She usually was, although Barnabas and his daughters had interrupted some of that, but she wouldn't have had it any other way. "I want to strip away all the things that have hindered my relationship with God. Everything the Amish do is connected to him, from their work to their lifestyle to their worship." Unexpectedly, tears filled her eyes. "I long for that kind of relationship with him. I need it."

Mom didn't move, as if she were processing everything Wendy had said. Wendy was processing it too, because the jumbled thoughts in her head sounded so clear when she spoke them aloud, and they were all true.

"They have a lot of rules," Mom said, her expression serious.

"The *Ordnung*. I know. And from what Charity, Eunice, and Priscilla shared with me, I'm fine with them."

"You'll be giving up a lot."

Wendy smiled, everything coming into place. "Compared to what I would be gaining, it means nothing."

Mom smiled. "Sounds like you're close to making up your mind, then."

She was closer, for sure. She needed to do some more research and tell Charity, Eunice, and Priscilla her thoughts. That would be easier now that she had already discussed some of them with her mother.

They finished their tacos, and the sopapillas were so good Wendy wondered why she'd never ordered them before, except for an irrational fear of carbs and sugar. Not that she would go off the deep end and overindulge all the time, but she was relaxing her stance on her own diet too.

As Wendy drove them back to their house, the doggie bag of the one extra taco Mom had ordered was placed firmly on her lap, and a bag of fabric and notions sat in the back seat. She was eager to get back to sewing. They were both quiet in the car until right before they reached their house. They were both almost to the door, Monroe's excited barks coming from inside, when a buggy pulled into the driveway. They turned around. Barnabas was in the driver's seat. *He's still wearing my scarf.*

"Hmm." Her mother grinned.

"Mom—"

"I didn't say a word." She opened the door as Barnabas got out of the buggy. "I'll be inside, minding my own business."

Wendy almost chuckled. She knew her mother would be peeking through the front window curtains as soon as she walked into the living room. She waited to make sure Mom navigated her walker over the small step leading into the house, then shut the door and met him halfway down the driveway. She stopped in front of him, immediately noticing a change from last night. The lines of tension she'd seen on his face recently had disappeared, and his eyes were warm. Her heart skipped in her chest, even faster than it normally did when she was around him. "Hi, Barnabas."

"Hi, Wendy."

"What brings you by?" She was sure he was here to thank her for last night. He was the kind of man who would go out of his way to do that. *A wonderful man.*

"I was wondering . . ." He gestured to his buggy. "Would you like to go for a ride?"

Twenty-Four

That afternoon, after Nelson went back to the warehouse and started reading *Business for Dummies*, Malachi surprised him by showing up and offering to help him hack the brush and a few short trees in the woods behind the building. They mostly worked in silence. They weren't felling larger trees, but the job needed concentration. Two hours later they were sitting on a log having a much-needed drink of water.

"Looks like you've got enough cleared to haul off." Malachi removed his navy blue beanie, his sweaty blond hair mashed against his head.

Nelson hadn't worn a hat. Or a coat—just a pullover sweater he'd shoved on before work. The short thaw had changed into a typical January freeze, but with the physical activity he didn't feel the cold. "I'm close," he said. "I figure when *Daed* and the rest of the family get back from Pinecraft there'll be more than enough to fill a wagon." He turned to his nephew. "I appreciate the help."

He smirked. "I had some extra time on *mei* hands." Then he turned serious. "I'm seeing Junia Saturday night at her *haus*. Would you like to—"

"Tag along?"

He grinned. "*Ya*."

"Junia beat you to it." He told Malachi about his encounter with her at the store.

"So what do you say?"

"I gave *mei* word to your *mamm* that I would watch out for you." And to Ella, but he wasn't going to mention that.

Malachi grinned. "*Gut.* Junia will be—" He suddenly guzzled down the rest of the water.

"Junia will be what?"

He jumped from the log. "Better get back to work."

Nelson followed him. "What about Junia?"

But Malachi ignored him, grabbing his machete and attacking the brush again.

With a shrug, Nelson joined him, not wanting to waste a minute of his nephew's assistance. Soon he was immersed in his task, and it was almost two hours later when Malachi had to quit working and go back home. "See you on Saturday," he said, getting into his buggy.

"You're not stopping by the store?" Nelson asked. He was sure that Malachi would take the opportunity to see Junia. In fact, that might have been the real reason he was helping Nelson. "Junia's working today."

He shook his head. "I'm going straight home. Like I said, we're serious about slowing down."

Huh. Seemed like his nephew had his head on straight after all.

After Malachi left, Nelson worked a little longer, then headed over to Jesse and Charity's. He decided to walk instead of drive. He was leaving well before suppertime, and he had his coat to keep him warm if he needed it and a flashlight to guide him home in the dark. Before he left, he glanced at Ella's house. Once he'd started talking to her about the business, his trepidation about asking for her help went away. Her confidence and knowledge were rubbing off on him. For the first time, he truly believed he could create and run a business. He should have allowed her to help to begin with.

He continued toward his brother's when a buggy appeared in the distance, and when it neared, he waved to the driver. Soon it was close enough for him to see who it was. Barnabas, who had a smile on his face. He started to wave again, then saw the passenger in the seat—Wendy Pearson, Jesse's neighbor. She gave him a little wave too.

The buggy passed and Nelson almost did a double take. That was an unusual sight. Then he shrugged. Barnabas's business was his own. Nelson whistled as he kept walking, wondering what delectable food Charity was preparing tonight, feeling more relaxed than he'd been in a long, long time.

.⚬⟨⟩⚬.

Giddy. Wendy's mother had used the word earlier that day, and it was perfect for how she felt as Barnabas drove past Nelson, whose surprised expression almost made her laugh. She was still a little astonished herself that she was riding in his buggy. When he asked her, she didn't hesitate—just got her coat and climbed right in, ignoring her mother's questioning expression.

"You warm enough?" he asked, giving her a glance.

She nodded, the buggy blanket he'd placed over her lap tucked around her. From the moment he'd tapped the reins on the back of the horse's flanks and they drove off, she'd been delighted and surprised at the different sounds she was hearing—the rolling of the wheels, the jangle of the reins, the creaking of the buggy itself. But the sound she loved the most was the *clip-clop* of the horse's hooves on the asphalt road. The rhythm was soothing. There was something to be said for having a calm, steady presence next to her too, even though he hadn't said much since they left her house.

"This is nice," she finally said.

"Glad you like it." A long stretch of silence occurred before he spoke again. "You did say you wanted to ride in a buggy someday."

He remembered that? She'd almost forgotten, even though it was true. "Thanks for making that happen for me."

"I also wanted to tell you how much I appreciate what you did for Junia."

"I wished I'd come over sooner," she said, still feeling a little guilty she had waited so long.

"You did exactly the right thing."

She glanced at him, seeing his Adam's apple bob up and down in his throat. "You don't have to thank me, Barnabas. I'm glad everything is working out."

"For now, and hopefully for the future. Only my daughters can determine that. But I learned something from you. Not just that day in the office but also during the other times we've talked. For too long I pawned off responsibility for my girls. After my wife died, I had a few rough years." He paused. "A decade of them. My sisters took over my family after that, and while I needed them to step in, they aren't the easiest women to get along with. They were particularly hard on Ella, and it was obvious they favored Junia, although they weren't all that easy on her either. I think they pitted the two of them against each other, then grounded them for fighting."

She could only imagine how hard this was for him to admit.

"I don't want to blame my sisters for all our problems, and they were there for us when we needed them. But when my grief started to clear, they were in control of things. The girls were arguing a lot at that time, although less than they do now. Every time I tried to step in, either Tabitha or Cora—sometimes both—would cut me off, telling me they had everything under control." He looked at her. "Neither of them ever married, and I wonder sometimes if they saw my daughters as the children they never had. Both Junia and Ella have some of their traits. The stubbornness. Thinking that they're always right."

"It sounds like a difficult situation."

"It was. When Ella talked to me about moving to Marigold, and I agreed to it, Tabitha and Cora were so upset they refused to speak to me. I don't know if the girls are in contact with them either."

"Did you move to get away from your sisters?"

"At the time I didn't think so." He nickered to the horse, and it slowed its steps. "Now I can see that was part of it. I'm embarrassed to say I took off instead of confronting them and standing my ground, because it was the easier thing to do. When I saw what Junia did, how she took responsibility for her words and actions, I was—" He faced straight ahead. "We're not supposed to be prideful . . . but at that moment, I was proud of my daughter."

Wendy knew all about the Amish emphasis on humility and avoiding pride. But she didn't blame him for feeling that way about Junia. She was proud of her too.

"I'm going back to Lancaster," he said, turning the buggy down her road.

Her breath caught. "You are?"

"For a few days. Maybe a week. Business is slow during the first of the year, and the girls can handle it themselves now that Junia is committing to the job." He coughed into his hand. "I don't want to be more of a bother to you, but I have a favor to ask."

"You're never a bother, Barnabas."

He looked at her, and his smile warmed her more than the buggy blanket. "Would you mind checking in on them a few times while I'm gone? Their truce is still fresh. I plan to talk to Nelson about it too, but I don't want to put the responsibility all on him. The girls respond well to you. Maybe you can teach them some more conflict mediation if the need arises.

"I have to clear the air with my sisters. For their sakes, but mainly my own. I appreciate everything they did for me. I don't know how Ella and Junia—or I—would have made it without them. But things are different now." He smiled. "I'm different, in no small part thanks to you."

Wendy didn't know what to say. He did seem like a changed man, although with all the same good qualities. He had a confidence that she hadn't sensed before. Not a blustery one, like she'd seen in many of the men she worked with in Manhattan. Just a man who'd figured out something very important and was acting on it. "I'm so glad, Barnabas. And of course I'll keep a watch out for them, if they'll let me."

"They will. I'll see to it." He smiled. "What do you think about your first buggy ride?"

There was something natural about sitting in the buggy, and she was experiencing the same feelings she'd had when she changed her style of dress, started sewing, and began living a simpler life. The silence that had dotted their conversation had given her time to notice the scenery and to marvel at all God had created. She'd even talked to God during those moments, feeling the closeness that she was experiencing more and more lately.

Yet all she said was, "I like it."

He nodded, and she stared at his profile for a moment. There was also something more she liked than just riding in the buggy. It was the man sitting next to her. Once again, he needed her help, and she was happy to give it to him. If friendship was all they had between them, she would accept that . . . and be content. It was better than not having Barnabas Yoder in her life at all.

·⸱⊱✦⊰·

"You think that's enough food?" Junia teased.

Ella looked over the plates of snacks and treats covering the counters and nodded to Junia. "Nelson's coming over, remember?"

She grinned. "He does have a big appetite. I'm going to see if they're here." She dashed out of the kitchen.

Chuckling, Ella unwrapped a plate of potato chip cookies, one of her favorites. She hoped the men would like them too. Sometimes she dipped half of them in melted chocolate, but she remembered Nelson didn't like chocolate, so she refrained. She also sent a batch with her father yesterday before he caught the bus to Lancaster. Both she and Junia had been shocked when he said he was going back to see *Aenti* Tabitha and *Aenti* Cora. "There's some personal business the three of us need to sort out," he said. Then he asked, "Have either of you two talked to them since we moved?"

Ella shook her head. So did Junia.

He frowned. "They sure are stubborn. *Maed*, you don't know how sorry I am for not being there when you needed me. I was so broken up over your *mamm* . . . but that's not an excuse."

"It's not your fault we had so many problems," Ella said, not wanting him to blame himself.

"Ella's right. It was ours." Junia kissed him on the cheek. "We're to blame."

He hugged them tight. "I'll be back in a few days, or maybe next week. Depends on how things *geh*. Stay out of trouble, *ya*?"

Both Ella and Junia nodded, and he finished the conversation by telling them that Wendy would check in from time to time. "Nelson too. I talked to him about it yesterday."

Although Ella wanted to protest, mostly because they didn't need two people to make sure she and Junia were behaving like adults, she held her tongue. Not enough time had passed for either of them to be trusted. They both had a lot to prove. Hopefully by the time *Daed* returned, he would have settled things with his sisters, and maybe they would all be on speaking terms again.

With nothing left to do in the kitchen, Ella went to the living room where Junia was peeking out the front window. She hadn't said much about her date this week, although she had mentioned Nelson would be coming. Ella didn't bother to tell her she already knew that. Now that the time was here, she was grateful he'd agreed to come over. If he hadn't, she would be a third wheel. An awkward one too.

"They're late." Junia stepped from the window, worrying her hands.

Ella glanced at the clock. "Three minutes late. Don't fret, they'll be here." For some reason she felt a little self-conscious and started smoothing the front of her plum-colored dress. It was an older one but still nice. Junia said they were planning on playing cards all night, so she didn't bother putting on one of her best ones. Tonight wasn't anything special anyway. Just some cards with her sister's boyfriend and his uncle. A plain ol' Saturday night.

Junia glanced at Ella's moving hands. "Don't fret, Ella."

She rolled her eyes, putting her hands behind her back. "I'm not fretting, because I don't have a reason to. It's only Nelson."

"Only Nelson." Junia grinned. "Right."

Her sister had been acting like this all day—like she had something up her sleeve. Teasing, giving her knowing looks, saying weird things.

But maybe that was how she dealt with her growing anticipation for Malachi. She hadn't seen him for over a week—the longest they'd been separated since they first met.

Three raps on the door and Junia threw it open. "Hi, Malachi." She ducked her head and looked at him through her lashes.

He stared at her. "It's been nine days—"

"Seven hours," she said. "And—"

"Fifteen minutes." He was grinning so hard Ella thought he'd permanently break his smile.

Behind him was Nelson, shaking his head and chuckling. Junia and Malachi went straight to the kitchen as he walked in. "Should we *geh* after them?"

Ella looked in the direction they went. "*Nee.* It's been nine days, seven hours, and twenty minutes—"

"Fifteen." He lifted his index finger. "But who's counting."

They both laughed . . . and it felt good. Easy too. She would have offered to take his coat, but he wasn't wearing one, of course. "How's the reading going?" She walked over to the couch and sat down.

"I'm almost finished with the business plan book." He sat down next to her but kept plenty of space between them.

She tried not to be disappointed. "Great."

"Then it's on to the written plan. I jotted down some notes, so I'm a third of the way there." He leaned back. "*Danki* again for loaning the books to me."

"Happy to do it."

Nelson tilted his head. "You are, aren't you? You really do like to help people. That's why you're so *gut* with your customers."

Ella hadn't thought about it, but now that he mentioned it, he was right. "It's just *gut* business," she said, resisting the prideful urge to bask in his compliment. She needed to switch the subject. "By the way, you don't have to check on me and Junia while *mei daed* is away. We'll be fine."

He didn't reply right away. Then he met her gaze. "What if I want to?"

"Are you two going to hang out here or are you going to play cards with us?" Junia said as she entered the room. "Ella made a ton of food just for you, Nelson."

"I made it for everyone else too." She shot a look at Junia, who was grinning. What was up with her tonight? It was almost as if she were plotting something—what that might be was anyone's guess.

"Don't want to miss out on that." Nelson got to his feet and headed for the kitchen.

Ella followed, and soon they were munching on corn chips, mixed nuts, and potato chip cookies.

Nelson particularly liked those. "Never had a cookie with potato chips in it. Seems unnatural." He downed another one. "But *appeditlich*."

For the next several hours, they played different card games— Dutch Blitz, rummy, and Crazy Eights. Malachi and Nelson were particularly competitive, but it was Junia who ended up winning the most hands. When it was time to go, she said, "Is it okay if we spend a little more time in the living room?" She gave Ella a pleading look. "Alone?"

Malachi held up his hands. "We'll behave ourselves. Promise."

Ella exchanged a look with Nelson, who nodded. "Jesse's expecting you back in an hour," he said, glancing at the clock, which read nine thirty.

"I understand."

When they were gone, Ella started clearing the table. "Is the whole family chaperoning now?"

Nelson helped her. "Unofficially. Considering recent events, it's not a *gut* idea for him to break curfew."

She nodded, and they both cleaned up the kitchen, much like the first time they'd had dinner together. He put the cards into the box and Ella covered the half-empty bowl of mixed nuts with aluminum foil. When he picked up the glasses and put them in the sink, she said, "I'll wash those later."

"Won't take any time to do them now." He turned on the water and let it run.

She walked over to him, feeling a little cheeky. "This is *mei* kitchen, by the way."

"Oh, that's plain as day to anyone with eyes and ears." He put the stopper in the sink.

"If I say I'll wash something later," she said, moving closer to him. "Then that's what I'm gonna do." She reached over and turned off the tap.

He turned it back on.

She turned it off.

He grinned and turned it on again. But when she reached out to turn it off, he grabbed her hand . . . and didn't let go.

276

Twenty-Five

Tonight was a surprise. Nelson hadn't expected to have as much fun as he did. He and Malachi of course went after each other while they played cards, as they always had growing up together. But it was good-natured, and the Yoder sisters went right along with it. The other nice thing was that the lovey-dovey couple had kept their ardor down to a negligible simmer, which made the atmosphere much more comfortable. And now he couldn't resist teasing Ella a little bit, he was in such a good mood. He knew this was her domain, knew she'd get a little fussed up if he took over the dishes. And she had.

What he didn't expect was how his heart was galloping in his chest. Or maybe he knew all along what he was doing, and it was time to raise the white flag where his feelings for Ella were concerned. They had been dancing around each other long enough.

Still holding her hand, he drew her closer, a mix of fear and attraction coursing through him. He'd been down this road before. Difference was, he'd never felt this way with Miriam or Norene, like his heart was going to explode in his chest and he wouldn't be able to breathe if he wasn't holding her hand right now. This woman who had exasperated him, fussed at him, and bossed him around was also the most giving, loyal person he'd ever known. There was no guile to Ella Yoder, and she was more than willing to admit when she was wrong or made a mistake. Better yet, she was willing to correct it. Willing to change.

He needed to make some changes himself. Starting right here . . . right now. He leaned down.

"Nelson?"

He smiled.

She smiled back, but there was uncertainty in her eyes. "Are you going to kiss me? Because if you are, I have to warn you I've never been kissed, but I get the impression that you've done some kissing yourself and I don't want you to be disappoint—"

He covered her mouth with his, partly because she was talking too much but mostly because he wanted to, more than anything. When they parted, he whispered, "Whoa."

Her eyes widened. "Is that a *gut whoa*, or a bad *whoa*?"

He tightened his grasp on her hand. "*Gut.* Definitely *gut.*"

"Ahem."

Nelson jumped and stepped away from Ella, but not too far, and he was still holding her hand as Junia and Malachi zipped into the room. His nephew was giving him the smirk to end all smirks.

"Excuse me," Junia said, wedging her arm between them and separating them. "Who needs a chaperone now?"

"You were right, Junia," Malachi said with a laugh. "There *is* something going on between them."

"*Nee*, there isn't," Ella said, looking at Nelson, who was now several feet from her since Junia had pushed him away, but only because he let her. *This time.*

He grinned at her. Then walked over to Malachi. There would be time for them to talk later about what happened, and their kiss was the perfect end to a wonderful evening. "*Gute nacht*, ladies."

"Bye!" Junia called out brightly.

As he and Malachi left the Yoders' and headed for Jesse's, Nelson started to whistle.

"You're not going to tell me what just happened back there?"

"Nope."

"Really?"

He turned to his disappointed nephew and shook his head, intent on keeping the sweet memory of Ella's kiss to himself.

·❧·

"You've got to tell me everything," Junia said, dragging Ella out of the kitchen and to the living room. "Every detail. Is that the first time you kissed him?"

Still in a daze, Ella couldn't respond. Only Nelson Bontrager could make her speechless. She could still feel the touch of his lips, soft and gentle, on hers. That's what kissing was? No wonder everyone made a big deal about it.

"You're not being fair." Junia crossed her arms over her chest. "I would have told you all about me and Malachi if you'd wanted to know."

Ella highly doubted that. "I don't, by the way. These things are supposed to be private."

"Oh, all right." She smiled. "But I knew it. I told Malachi a month ago that you and Nelson liked each other."

That was news to her, although she'd known for a while that she liked him. From his kiss, she now knew he reciprocated. Which didn't make all that much sense to her. She jumped up from the couch and started to pace, nibbling on her thumbnail.

"What?" Junia asked.

"I'm confused. It wasn't that long ago that we didn't like each other."

"And now you're kissing." Junia sighed. "That's how love works."

"Huh?"

"There's a fine line between love and hate."

"That's harsh. I never hated Nelson." She wasn't supposed to hate anyone, or even speak the word. Nevertheless, she'd thought it a few times over the years, usually about Junia. It was so nice that they weren't at odds with each other anymore.

"That's just a saying. Of course you didn't hate him." She gave her another knowing look, except Ella had no idea what it meant. "And now you like each other. Honestly, I didn't think I'd have to explain this to you."

"But why? And when? He was so mad at me last week about the paint and his hair. And then before that, he was tired of me bossing him around."

"Nelson seems like he can handle himself."

Boy, can he. And now that she thought about it, she really liked that aspect of him. The way he could take charge. Sure, he was a little uncertain about his business, but that was normal since it was something new. Otherwise, he was always in control. Like tonight, when he kissed her—

"Ella."

"What?" She turned to Junia. How could her sister interrupt her while she was reliving the best part of the night?

"Sit." She patted the seat next to her.

Apparently it was a night for firsts. Junia was telling her what to do. Ella sat.

"I don't have that much experience with dating," Junia said.

"You don't?"

She frowned. "*Nee*. Believe it or not, Malachi is the first boy I ever kissed."

"That's a surprise."

"Good grief, Ella. What kind of woman do you think I am?"

"Never mind. Continue."

"Malachi is a good man. So is Nelson. They wouldn't be kissing us if they didn't like us. Trust me, Nelson likes you. I think he has since the first time you two met."

"That's impossible. We couldn't stand each other . . . Oh." She thought about the fine line between like and . . . *dislike*. She preferred that term. "I can't believe Nelson felt the same way about me that I do about him. Why didn't he say anything?"

"Who knows? Don't question it, Ella. Just enjoy."

Yet Ella couldn't just enjoy this, not when she was still so bewildered and still unsure about Nelson's feelings. He never said he liked her, although his kiss showed that he did. But what if he was regretting it? What if right this minute he was wishing he'd never kissed her?

Junia yawned. "I'm going to bed. Remember, I'm opening the store tomorrow."

"Sure." She stared at the woodstove, which was now filled for the night. Either Junia or Malachi must have taken care of that.

"See you in the morning."

"*Ya*." She sank down on the couch. "See you." She heard Junia's footsteps on the stairs, but she couldn't stop looking at the flames in the stove as dread slowly came over her. His kiss seemed too sudden to be the real thing, and she suspected Junia was making up the like versus dislike thing. *Mamm, how I wish you were here to explain all this.*

She hurried up to her room, shut the door, and turned on the battery-powered lamp on her nightstand. She took out her diary and sat on the edge of the bed. Pencil in hand, she started writing.

Dear Diary,

Nelson Bontrager kissed me tonight . . . and I don't know what to do.

·⟡·

The next morning, after the best night's sleep he'd had in ages, Nelson got up and dressed for the day, still thinking about Ella. And the more he thought about her, the more he was sure of his feelings. Strange, because he'd spent so much time fighting being around her and then fighting how he felt. But one kiss and one look in Ella's eyes after that kiss and he knew beyond any doubt that she was the woman for him. Finally, he understood what Malachi had been saying all this time. How he was so sure about his feelings for Junia. Because he felt the same way about Ella.

He cut off three huge pieces of Ella's bread—she was an excellent cook, which was a bonus for him!—and slathered honey on one of them. As he chewed, he tried to switch his focus to work. He'd set today as the deadline to finish reading *Business Plans 101* and start in earnest writing his. The faster he finished that, the sooner he could see Ella . . . and they could talk about what happened last night. He wished he could do that this morning, but they both had work to do. After the store closed, he would go see her. Maybe he would have his plan done by then too, and she could read over it. He took another bite of bread, imagining her tucked in the crook of his arm, reading his chicken scratch. He smiled. *Perfect.*

Once he polished off the rest of the bread, he reached for the book but stopped when he heard the *clomp*ing of horse hooves outside. He got up and opened the door. His jaw hit the floor. Norene Yoder, now Norene Miller, was scrambling out of her buggy and walking toward him.

"Can I come in?" She glanced at her feet, then looked at him again. "Please?"

He crossed his arms. "Why are you here?"

"I need to talk to you." She took a step forward.

Nelson stepped back. "About what?"

Her face took on that pinched, offended look she used to have when she didn't get her way. Then she sighed. "I'll only take a few minutes of your time. I promise."

He hesitated, then opened the door. "I've got stuff to do, so make it quick."

"You don't have to be so rude."

"Seriously?" He spun around. "Have you forgotten what you did to me?"

"*Nee.*" She pressed her lips together and looked at her feet again. "That's why I'm here. To apologize."

"Consider it accepted. Now *geh.*"

"Nelson, don't be like this." She moved closer to him. "I know I was wrong for cheating on you with Ben. I see that now." Her eyes filled. "I think . . . I think he's cheating on me."

Nelson stilled as tears rolled down her cheeks. "Ben wouldn't . . ." Would he? He'd always assumed Ben was a nice, affable guy who wouldn't hurt a bee or a fly, and had been an innocent party to Norene's deception. But maybe he'd known all along that she and Nelson were seeing each other. "What makes you think that?"

"He's been distant. I cook and clean and do the wash, and take care of the house, and he doesn't seem to notice or acknowledge what I do. He used to be so . . . attentive."

Was she seriously coming here and complaining about her marriage? Even if Ben had known he was part of Norene's cheating, Nelson was starting to feel sorry for him and grateful for himself. "That's your problem, not mine."

"Maybe if he saw me with you, he would get a little jealous." She moved closer to him. "He would act the way he used to."

"I thought you were here to apologize, not ask me to deceive your husband."

She was inches away from him now. "Nelson," she purred, looking up at him the way she used to when she tried to manipulate him. "It's only a teeny-weeny favor. And I really am sorry I hurt you. I didn't think it was such a big deal, but I can see now that it was. You truly loved me, didn't you?" Before he could move, she threw her arms around his neck and kissed him.

He pushed her back . . . and saw Ella standing behind her.

.⋘⋙.

The knot of dread that had been forming in her stomach since she woke up this morning disappeared when she saw Nelson kissing another woman, replaced with a sharp, deep pain, as if she'd been punched in the gut. Here he was kissing someone else, hours after he'd kissed her—sweetly, tenderly, as if it meant something to him.

Obviously it didn't. And that was the reason she came over here, to find out if the kiss was real or an impulse he was regretting.

That didn't matter anymore. Not after what she'd seen.

She turned on her heel, suddenly feeling numb.

"Ella," he called, coming up behind her.

She didn't stop walking. Didn't look at him. Couldn't say anything past the hard lump in her throat.

"Ella!" He jumped in front of her, bending down and gripping her shoulders. Not hard, just enough to force her to stop. When she tried to shrug him off, he held firm. "That's not what it looked like."

"It looked like a kiss," she squeaked. She sounded like a frightened mouse. Where was her strong, bossy voice when she needed it?

"It was—"

"Let me *geh*." She tried to shove off his hand.

"Not until you listen to me."

"Nelson!"

They both looked to see the woman standing in the doorway, and Ella's heart sank past her knees. Junia was pretty, but she was shredded wheat compared to this woman. As for Ella . . . she'd never stand a chance against someone so beautiful.

"We haven't finished," she said, giving Ella an annoyed look.

"Oh yes we have." Nelson let go of Ella's shoulders, turning to face the woman. "You need to—"

Ella took the opportunity to escape. She ran down the road, not knowing where she was headed until she found herself staring at the old barn in front of her. She walked inside, although the boards on the walls were so sparse, she was technically still outside. She didn't care. She sat down on an old apple crate, too dead inside to think. Or cry. All she could see was Nelson kissing someone else.

"Ella."

She heard his voice but didn't look up, not even when he walked in and crouched down in front of her.

"Ella . . . please . . . look at me."

"Leave me alone."

"Not until I explain what happened back there."

She shifted away from him. "I don't care. *Geh* on back to her."

"Ella—"

"I said leave!" She faced him, throwing the full brunt of her anger at him. "I won't let you make a fool out of me ever again. Don't talk to me, don't look at me." She lifted her chin. "You don't exist to me anymore."

.⁓⊶⊷⁓.

Nelson slowly got up, still blinded by her words and the fury behind them. He'd seen Ella cross. Angry. Even furious. But the rage coming from her eyes and words hit him square in the chest.

After she took off, he yelled at Norene to leave. She did, but in a huff, as if he and Ella had inconvenienced her. The woman was truly off her rocker. But there was nothing he could do about it, and she was Ben's problem now. Nelson had a bigger problem of his own. He had to calm down Ella. He'd chased after her until he saw her going into the barn. He stopped before going inside, needing to catch his breath so he could tell her that he hadn't kissed Norene—she kissed him.

But she wasn't even giving him the chance.

He turned from her, his own anger building. This is exactly what he wanted to avoid—another heartbreak. Although the situation wasn't the same as it had been with Miriam and Norene. Ella was rejecting him. And her rejection was so paralyzingly painful, he could hardly draw breath. Had he fallen that hard for her?

Yes. He had.

He tried to turn his feelings to stone, the way he did after seeing Norene and Ben together. But they wouldn't. Instead, they were so raw all he could do was walk away. Three times he'd been burned, and this one was the worst. By far.

Fine. If this was how she wanted things to be, he would make it happen. She didn't exist for him either. He'd been able to avoid her before and he'd do it again. This time he had far more motivation.

Without another word, he walked out of the barn and out of her life. For good.

Twenty-Six

Ella's whole body trembled as she watched Nelson leave. What had she done? She'd promised herself, her family, and God that she would control her temper. And the one time she desperately needed to the most, she'd unleashed it on Nelson. *I told him he didn't exist to me.* That was the worst thing she'd ever said to anyone. And she said it to a man she cared deeply about.

She rose from the crate and paced, shivering with each step, even though for once she was wearing a coat. How could she have been so awful to him? Yes, seeing him in another woman's arms was horrible, but she should have at least listened to him like he begged her to. But no, she let her emotions and rage take over.

She tried to tell herself it didn't matter. She wasn't in the wrong here—he had kissed someone else. But she couldn't stop seeing the urgent pleading in his eyes when he was in front of her or hearing the anguish in his voice. She halted, covering her face with her hands. *Lord, what have I done?* She fell to her knees and started to cry.

Suddenly she felt a strong arm around her shoulders. A gentle tug into thick, warm arms. She leaned against Nelson's chest, inhaling the soothing scent of his sweater as she wiped her face with the back of her cold hand.

Minutes passed as they sat on the barn floor cradled in each other's embrace, and neither one of them said a word. She nestled against him, marveling at her own behavior. She should be running away from him. But she couldn't. Not until he told her the truth about what happened.

"You came back," she whispered.

"Yeah. Surprised myself with that one."

"Why?" She lifted her head. "I said awful things to you."

"Did you mean them?"

Ella hesitated, but only for a second. "*Nee.*" She gazed into his eyes. "Why were you kissing that woman?"

He stared straight ahead, and the dread reappeared. She had a bad feeling he was about to let her down in the gentlest way possible. "She's *mei* ex-girlfriend."

"Oh." She leaned against him again, relishing their closeness as she feared it would be the last time she would be in his arms. "Are . . . are . . ." She couldn't even ask the question.

"Are we getting back together? Absolutely—"

She shut her eyes, bracing herself.

"—not."

She opened her eyes and lifted her head. "Then why were you kissing her?"

"She was kissing me. And your timing couldn't have been worse, by the way."

She scooted out of his arms and moved to sit in front of him. "This is *mei* fault?"

"*Nee, nee.*" He took her hand. "This is completely her fault."

Ella listened as he told her how Norene wanted him to make her husband jealous. "That doesn't make any sense."

"I know. I wouldn't do it even if it did." He thrust his hand through his short hair. "Last year I wanted to marry Norene. I was all prepared to ask her, but then I saw her kissing Ben. He's her husband now."

She frowned. "She was cheating on you with Ben, and now she wants to cheat on Ben with you. She's got a problem."

"More than one. She was using her usual trick on me to get me to comply—kissing me. She used to do that all the time when we were dating. If I said anything she didn't want to hear, she'd kiss me so I would shut up. And it would work."

Ella didn't like the jealousy winding through her at that moment. Then she sat up. "Wait. I was talking when you kissed me last night."

"That's different."

"How?"

He threaded his fingers through hers. "That kiss was genuine. Norene's never were."

Well, she had her answer now. He had meant to kiss her. "Do you regret it?"

"*Nee.*" A soft smile played on his lips, then disappeared. "Do you?"

She shook her head. "That's why it hurt so much to see you and Norene—"

He held up his hand. "Let's not speak about that again, okay? I want to put it out of my mind."

Ella did too.

"I need to come clean about a couple of things," he said, sitting cross-legged in front of her. "When I met you, I did everything I could to avoid you."

"You had a reason to," she said, cringing at the memory of their first meeting. "I was pretty rude. And blunt."

"True, but that wasn't the main reason. Norene isn't the only woman I wanted to propose to. Before her, I thought I was in love with Miriam. Come to find out that the whole time we were dating, she was corresponding with her ex in Michigan. She dumped me to go back to him. Last I heard, they were married too."

"Oh, Nelson, I'm so sorry."

"Then when Norene cheated on me, I told myself I was done with women."

That one statement explained a lot of things. His annoyance and standoffishness, for starters. Her heart ached for the pain he'd endured.

"But you wore me down. I'm sure you didn't even know it. I didn't fully realize it until last night."

"I don't understand."

"I'm not sure I do either. All I know is, you're the one for me. That's why I came back, Ella. I couldn't leave, and I would do whatever was necessary to convince you that what happened with Norene wasn't my doing. And if it meant getting my heart broken over and over until you forgave me . . . then I was willing to accept that too."

If her heart wasn't already a puddle of mush, it would have been now. To know he would go through more emotional pain just for her . . . She put her hands on his knees and leaned forward. "You won't ever have to. You're already forgiven."

His shoulders relaxed, his smile back in place. "There's one other thing I wanted to tell you," he said, also leaning forward.

"What's that?"

"Your *aentis*? The ones who said you weren't marriage material?"

"Yeah." She scowled. "Why are you bringing that up?"

"Because"—he cradled her face—"I want you to listen carefully and understand what I'm saying. You, Ella Yoder, are one hundred and fifty thousand percent—"

"That's not a real number—"

"Shhh." He put his finger over her lips. "You are definitely marriage material. You're smart, giving, and loyal."

His words should make her feel good, and they did. Sort of, even though he sounded like he was describing a Labrador retriever. She glanced at her lap.

He tilted her chin until they were looking directly at each other. "The first day I met you, I thought you were cute. Bossy, but cute."

Her pulse quickened. "And now?"

"You're the most beautiful woman I know. Inside and out." He closed the distance between them and kissed her.

Before she knew it, she was in his arms again. When they stopped kissing, she realized she was in his lap. "Uh-oh," she said.

He blew out a long breath and set her back on the barn floor. "You know what this means."

Nodding, she had to smile. "We're gonna need a chaperone."

.ૹ.

Wendy pulled into Yoders' parking lot, taking notice of the renovations to Nelson's future butcher shop and the almost completed little white house behind it. It had been over a month since she'd last set foot in the grocery store, and three weeks since Barnabas had returned from Lancaster. He'd stopped by her house to thank her for watching over Ella and Junia, even though he didn't have to. He'd already found out that Ella and Nelson were together, and he seemed happy about that.

Then she had to tell him the hardest thing she'd ever told anyone. *"I can't see you anymore."*

He looked shocked, as she suspected he would. She'd planned to explain her reasons to him if he asked. He didn't, and when she shut the door and his buggy left the driveway, she wasn't sure if she was ever going to see him again.

As she brought her car to a stop in one of the parking spaces in front of the store and shut off the engine, her nerves crashed together. She hadn't seen Junia and Ella either. She was thankful for that, because she didn't want to hurt them the way she feared she'd hurt Barnabas. But it had to be done. Just like what she had to do today.

She got out of the car. The mid-February air was crisp, cutting through her black stockings, and snow crunched underneath her black tennis shoes. She huddled into her plain coat that covered her plain dress and headed for the entrance, stopping right outside to take a deep breath. She could finally explain herself to the Yoders. She just hoped they would forgive her.

She entered the store and saw it was empty. Junia was behind the counter, writing in her spiral notebook. When she lifted her head, she was smiling. Then it disappeared.

Wendy rubbed the back of her knuckles as she approached her. Junia's expression was shuttered, although she feigned a smile. "Hi, Wendy. Can I help you?"

"Is your father here?"

The fake smile slipped from her face. "Why do you want to know?"

She had to admire her loyalty to Barnabas. If Ella was here, she would be the same way. "Can I talk to him for a minute?"

Junia paused, then nodded. "I'll ask." She walked to the back of the store, only to come right back again. "He's in the office."

"Thank you," she said, aware that Junia was watching her as she walked away. Barnabas was blessed to have two wonderful daughters. She glanced at the garden section, now filled with tools and seeds, before knocking on the door.

"Come in," he said.

Her heart warmed at the voice she hadn't heard in so long and had dearly missed. She walked inside, her heart heaving as she saw something she'd never seen on his face—emptiness.

"What can I do for you?" His tone was curt.

"I—" She'd planned how to tell him for over a week now, but now the words escaped her. "I . . ."

His hard expression turned concerned. He got up from the chair. "Is something wrong, Wendy?"

"No." Her mouth quivered. "I just came back from a meeting."

"What meeting?"

"With Bishop Fry."

He frowned, his brow arching in confusion.

"I told him . . ." Her heart warmed, the joy she'd felt after talking to the bishop filling her up. She hadn't said anything to anyone yet, not even her mother. "I'm joining the church, Barnabas. I want to become Amish."

He didn't move—not a single inch or muscle. Just stared at her for a long moment, as if he was in shock. Then he finally spoke. "He answered," Barnabas whispered. "He answered me."

"Who?"

He grabbed a tissue out of the box on his desk and dabbed his eyes, then looked at her again. "Tell me everything."

They both sat down, him in his desk chair and her in the opposite one. "First, I'm sorry that I pushed you and your family away. I had to be sure about this decision for myself. I didn't need any . . ."

"Distractions? Influences?"

"Yes." She almost said *ya*, as she'd been taking *Deitsch* lessons from Charity. But she wouldn't officially speak the language until she was baptized. "I've been thinking about this for a long time. I believe God's been leading me to this decision, even when I was working in New York. I was never happy there, although I did my best to pretend I was. I played the game of the career woman living a successful life in the most exciting city in the world.

"But that's all it was—a game. Until I moved to Marigold and found out there was another way to live. One where I could become closer with God, closer with my mom, and have a real community that wasn't just the Uber driver, the doorman, and the guys who dropped off my takeout."

Barnabas frowned, looking a little confused. "Doorman?"

"Never mind," she said, managing a smile. "I didn't renew my office lease, and I purchased the plot of land next to Mom, the one in between us and Jesse and Charity. I hope to start building my little house soon, without electricity and to the Amish standard. I talked with Micah and Jesse, and they said they would help." Her throat grew thick. "He said everyone would help."

He smiled. "When is your baptism?"

"We didn't set a date. I still need to go through the instruction." She leaned forward. "I'm so happy, Barnabas. Never in my life did I ever think I'd go without my phone for five minutes, much less gladly give up my worldly lifestyle to serve God and others. I wanted you to be the first to know."

Barnabas got up from his chair and closed the office door. Then he knelt beside her. "I didn't think this would happen," he murmured.

"I had so much doubt." He glanced at the ceiling. "I should have known better than to doubt him."

"I don't understand."

"I've been praying for you to join the church, Wendy. I'll have to admit it was for selfish reasons, though. And when you said we couldn't see each other, I was sure it would never happen. Just know this—whatever happens between us, you joining our community is what truly matters. I don't ever want you to feel you have to push me or my family away. We'll always be here for you."

Her pulse quickened. "Us?"

He took her hand. "Wendy, will you—"

The door burst open. "*Daed*, why is this closed? . . . Oh."

Wendy, her hand still in Barnabas's, turned to see Ella standing there.

Ella's gaze jumped from hers, to her father's, then back again. "Um, is this what I think it is?"

"*Nee.*" He got to his feet, his knees creaking a bit, then let out a little laugh. "It's not what it looks like."

Wendy's spirits fell. For a minute she thought he was going to . . . certainly not propose, but maybe—

"Because it looked like you were proposing to Wendy." Ella frowned a little. "Which would be strange, considering she's English."

"I wasn't proposing," he said, looking at Wendy again with a smile. "But I was going to ask her out on a date."

"What?" both women exclaimed.

He turned to Ella. "Out," he said, shoving her out the door.

"But, *Daed*—"

"I'll explain later." He shut the door on her, then looked at Wendy again. "That didn't work out the way I planned."

She stood up and went to him. "Most plans never do. And I'm

happy to go out with you, Barnabas. After we ask the bishop what's proper."

"Of course." He took her hand again. "You changed my life, Wendy. And now, God willing—"

"I might be a part of it."

He chuckled. "We sound like Junia and Malachi."

"And Nelson and Ella." She smiled.

"Who's going to be our first set of chaperones?" he said, moving closer to her.

"How about all four?"

He took her in his arms. "This might not be proper," he said, leaning his cheek against her hair. "But we'll keep it between us."

She closed her eyes and smiled. *For now.*

Epilogue

NOVEMBER

Dear Diary,

Today was such an exciting day! The past several months have been too, which is why I haven't written anything recently. Exciting, hectic, and so full of love. First, Daed and Wendy got married three weeks ago. No one was surprised about that, just like they weren't surprised when she joined the church. And even though she had already started building her house, they barely had the frame up before she put a stop to it, knowing she and Daed would be together. The wedding was wonderful, and Daed is so happy. I'm tearing up just writing about it.

Two weeks later, Junia and Malachi were married. What a feast! I'm still marveling at how big their family is, and it keeps getting bigger. Charity and Katharine had their babies, and three of the other brothers are expecting with their wives. And there's still Perry, Mose, Mahlon, and Elam to get married, although Perry is the only one who is of marriageable age. Junia and Malachi moved into our house, and he's working with Nelson at his butcher shop.

Oh, the butcher shop! Nelson finished it in April, and he's had customers out the door ever since, particularly since his reputation as an excellent butcher started picking up steam. I remember when he smoked his first ham in the smoker he bought—so yummy! He really is gifted when it comes to butchery and creating his own meats. I had no idea. Well, maybe a little. He did allow me to do a lot of taste testing.

And about me and Nelson

"Hey!" Ella's pencil dragged across the diary page as Nelson came up behind her and scooped her up in his arms. "I was finishing my entry."

He rolled his eyes and sat down on their bed, snuggling her in his lap. "I think it can wait, don't you?"

"But I was just getting to the best part." She laid her head on his shoulder, her fingers combing through the back of his hair. It had grown out a few months ago, and she'd cut it for him twice, being extremely careful both times. "About how our wedding was the most wonderful one—"

"That's a little prideful." Nelson leaned his chin against her forehead.

"*Ya. Yer* right. Oh, I need to mention how, before we got married, you proposed at our secret place." Junia and Malachi were more than happy to give it up once they heard it was originally Ella's. Then it became hers and Nelson's, until the barn fell over the next day. Thank goodness no one was there. "And how you were so sneaky about your proposal. And nervous."

"Me, nervous?" Then he nodded. "I was petrified."

She sat up. "You never told me that before. What were you afraid of?" When he looked away, she put her arms around him. "My answer would always have been yes."

He kissed her, taking her breath away. "So where will we *geh* to escape our chaperones?" He grinned. "Not that we need them, thank goodness."

She glanced at the diary sitting open on the small desk across from their bed. They'd gotten married two days ago, and while everyone celebrated with as much enthusiasm as they had with the other couples, Ella was tired of festivities. They even talked about having a double wedding with Junia and Malachi to save some time, trouble, and expense, but Junia wasn't having it. She still had a bit of her selfish side.

Now that the wedding was over, all she wanted to do was settle down with Nelson, run the grocery store and butcher shop—they were now combined—and when God willed it, have a family.

"I don't think this is the best part," he said, intruding on her thoughts.

She lifted her head from his shoulder. "What do you mean?"

He ran his hand over her cheek, something he did often in private, and she loved it. Then he leaned over and kissed her again, cuddling her close. "The best is yet to come, Ella Bontrager. Trust me."

She did. Because deep in her heart . . . she believed it.

Acknowledgments

Writing a book isn't just a solitary endeavor, and I want to give a big thank you to my editors Becky Monds and Karli Jackson for their valuable insight and help in bringing *The Proposal Plot* to fruition. I also want to give special thanks to my daughter, Zoie Fuller, who provided her paint expertise and only gave me a slightly weird look when I asked her what kind of paint Ella could spill on Nelson's head. It helps to have a kid who works in a paint store. ☺ As always, my biggest appreciation is to you, dear Reader, for going on another journey with me. I hope you enjoyed Nelson and Ella's story as much as I enjoyed writing it.

Discussion Questions

1. Ella is a go-getter, but she's impulsive and often leaps before she thinks. Are you an impulsive person, or do you like to take your time when considering decisions?

2. After being romantically rejected twice, Nelson starts to doubt himself. Have you ever doubted yourself after being disappointed? How did you regain your confidence?

3. Nelson's father tells him he shouldn't be afraid to walk out in faith. Think of a time when you needed to trust your faith. Was it difficult? Why or why not?

4. Wendy is shocked that she's so dependent on her cell phone/technology. Are there times when you find yourself dependent on your phone or computer? What do you do to unplug?

5. Throughout the story, Wendy is drawn to many aspects of Amish culture. What do you appreciate about the Amish and their way of life?

6. Ella and Junia's relationship devolves to the point they can't talk without fighting. How important is good communication in relationships? Discuss a time when communication was a struggle for you and how you overcame it.

7. As Ella and Junia's relationship deteriorates, Ella thinks God isn't listening or answering her prayers. Discuss a time when you felt God was far away and your prayers weren't answered. Looking back, are you able to see how God had answered your prayers?

8. Wendy thinks about Galatians 1:10: "For do I now persuade men, or God? or do I seek to please men? for if I yet pleased men, I should not the be the servant of Christ." What does this verse mean to you?

9. Ella struggles with keeping her temper in check. What advice would you give to someone who has anger issues?

10. Nelson refused to ask Ella for help for several reasons. Was there ever a time when you struggled to ask for help when you needed it?

About the Author

With over two million copies sold, Kathleen Fuller is the *USA TODAY* bestselling author of several best-selling novels, including the Hearts of Middlefield novels, the Middlefield Family novels, the Amish of Birch Creek series, and the Amish Letters series as well as a middle-grade Amish series, the Mysteries of Middlefield.

.~⊱❧~.

Visit her online at KathleenFuller.com
Facebook: @WriterKathleenFuller
Instagram: @kf_booksandhooks